DRAGON PEARL

YOON HA LEE

THORNDIKE PRESS

A part of Gale, a Cengage Company

 GALE
A Cengage Company

Farmington Hills, Mich • San Francisco • New York • Waterville, Maine
Meriden, Conn • Mason, Ohio • Chicago

Recommended for Middle Readers.
Copyright © 2019 by Yoon Ha Lee.
Introduction copyright © 2019 by Rick Riordan.
Illustrations © 2019 by Vivienne To.
Thorndike Press, a part of Gale, a Cengage Company.

ALL RIGHTS RESERVED
Thorndike Press® Large Print The Literacy Bridge.
The text of this Large Print edition is unabridged.
Other aspects of the book may vary from the original edition.
Set in 16 pt. Plantin.

LIBRARY OF CONGRESS CIP DATA ON FILE.
CATALOGUING IN PUBLICATION FOR THIS BOOK
IS AVAILABLE FROM THE LIBRARY OF CONGRESS

ISBN-13: 978-1-4328-6098-1 (hardcover)

Published in 2019 by arrangement with Disney-Hyperion, an imprint of Disney Book Group.

Printed in Mexico
1 2 3 4 5 6 7 23 22 21 20 19

This one is for
Arabelle Sophie Betzwieser,
my favorite Dragon

A THOUSAND
DANGEROUS WORLDS

Min is just your average teenage fox spirit, living with her family on the dusty backwater planet of Jinju.

Oh, sure, like all foxes, she can shape-shift into whatever she wants: human, animal, even a dining room table. And yes, she has the power to Charm — to manipulate human emotions and make people see things that aren't there. But that's not very exciting when you're stuck in a small dome house, sleeping every night in a crowded common room with your snoring cousins, spending every day fixing condensers in the hydroponics unit. Min yearns to join the Space Forces like her older brother Jun did — to see the Thousand Worlds and have marvelous adventures!

It's not like her mom will let her use magic anyway. Unlike other supernaturals, such as dragons, who can control weather, and goblins, who can conjure things out of thin air, fox spirits have a bad reputation. According to the old lore, foxes used to change shape to trick and prey on humans. Min's family wouldn't even consider doing such a thing, but due to lasting prejudice, they have to hide their true nature.

One day, an investigator from the government pays a visit to Min's mom. He brings horrible news: Jun has disappeared. Worse, Jun is suspected of treason — of abandoning his post to search for a fabled relic that has the power to transform worlds: the Dragon Pearl.

Min knows that Jun would never desert the Space Forces. Something must have happened to him. He needs help! Unfortunately, nobody seems interested in what Min thinks, especially after she knocks the investigator unconscious for insulting her brother's honor. Her family decides to ship her off to the boondocks to keep her out of further trouble, but

Min has other ideas. She runs away from home, intent on following Jun to the stars. One young fox spirit, alone against the galaxies, will risk everything to find her brother and discover the mystery of the long-lost Dragon Pearl.

Buckle up, fellow foxes. Get ready for epic space battles. Prepare yourselves for magic and lasers, ghosts and dragons, interstellar pirates and warlike tigers. The Thousand Worlds hold all sorts of danger, but there are also priceless magical treasures to be discovered. And if Min succeeds, she might not only save her brother — she might save her entire planet.

Dragon Pearl will be like nothing you've ever read: a zesty mix of Korean folklore, magic, and science fiction that will leave you *longing* for more adventures in the Thousand Worlds!

Rick Riordan

DRAGON PEARL

ONE

I almost missed the stranger's visit that morning.

I liked to sleep in, though I didn't get to do it often. Waking up meant waking early. Even on the days I had lessons, my mom and aunties loaded me down with chores to do first. Scrubbing the hydroponics units next to our dome house. Scrounging breakfast from our few sad vegetables and making sure they were seasoned well enough to satisfy my four aunties. Ensuring that the air filters weren't clogged with the dust that got into everything.

I had a pretty dismal life on Jinju. I was counting the days until I turned fifteen. Just two more years left before I could take the entrance exams for the Thousand Worlds Space Forces and follow my brother, Jun, into the service. That was all that kept me going.

The day the stranger came, though — that day was different.

I was curled under my threadbare blanket, stubbornly clinging to sleep even though light had begun to steal in through the windows. Then my oldest cousin Bora's snoring got too loud to ignore. I often wished I had a room of my own, instead of sharing one with three cousins. Especially since Bora snored like a dragon. I kicked her in the side. She grunted but didn't stir.

We all slept on the same shabby quilt, handed down from my ancestors, some of the planet's first settlers. The embroidery had once depicted magpies and flowers, good-luck symbols. Most of the threads had come loose over the years, rendering the pictures illegible. When I was younger, I'd asked my mom why she didn't use Charm to restore it. She'd given me a stern look, then explained that she'd have to redo it every day as the magic wore off — objects weren't as susceptible to Charm as people were. I'd shut up fast, because I didn't want her to add that chore to my daily roster. Fortunately, my mom disapproved of Charm in general, so it hadn't gone any further.

All my life I'd been cautioned not to show off the fox magic that was our heritage. We lived disguised as humans and rarely used our abilities to shapeshift or Charm people. Mom insisted that we behave as proper, civilized gumiho so we wouldn't get in trouble with our fellow steaders, planet-bound residents of Jinju. In the old days, foxes had played tricks like changing into beautiful humans to lure lonely travelers close so they could suck out their lives. But our family didn't do that.

The lasting prejudice against us annoyed me. Other supernaturals, like dragons and goblins and shamans, could wield their magic openly, and were even praised for it. Dragons used their weather magic for agriculture and the time-consuming work of terraforming planets. Goblins, with their invisibility caps, could act as secret agents; their ability to summon food with their magical wands came in handy, too. Shamans were essential for communicating with the ancestors and spirits, of course. We foxes, though — we had never overcome our bad reputation. At least most people thought we were extinct nowadays.

I didn't see what the big deal was about using our powers around the house. We rarely had company — few travelers came to the world of Jinju. According to legend, about two hundred years ago, a shaman was supposed to have finished terraforming our planet with the Dragon Pearl, a mystical orb with the ability to create life. But on the way here, both she and the Pearl had disappeared. I didn't know if anything in that story was true or not. All I knew was that Jinju had remained poor and neglected by the Dragon Council for generations.

As I reluctantly let go of sleep that morning, I heard the voice of a stranger in the other room. At first I thought one of the adults was watching a holo show

16

— maybe galactic news from the Pearled Halls — and had the volume turned up too high. We were always getting reports about raids from the Jeweled Worlds and the Space Forces' heroic efforts to defend us from the marauders, even if Jinju was too far from the border to suffer such attacks. But the sound from our holo unit always came out staticky. No static accompanied this voice.

It didn't belong to any of the neighbors, either. I knew everyone who lived within an hour's scooter ride. And it wasn't just the unfamiliarity of the voice, deep and smooth, that made me sit up and take notice. No one in our community spoke that formally.

Were we in trouble with the authorities? Had someone discovered that fox spirits weren't a myth after all? The stranger's voice triggered my old childhood fears of our getting caught.

"You must be misinformed." That was Mom talking. She sounded tense.

Now I really started to worry.

". . . no mistake," the voice was saying.

No mistake what? I had to find out more.

I slipped out from under the blanket, freezing in place when Bora grunted and flopped over. I bet starship engines made less racket. But if the stranger had heard Bora's obnoxious noises, he gave no sign of it.

I risked a touch of Charm to make myself plainer, drabber, harder to see. Foxes can smell each other's magic — one of my aunties described the sensation as being like a sneeze that won't come out — but my mom might be distracted enough not to notice.

"How is this possible?" I heard Mom ask.

My hackles rose. She was clearly distressed, and I'd never known her to show weakness in front of strangers.

I tiptoed out of the bedroom and poked my head around the corner. There stood Mom, small but straight-backed. And then came the second surprise. I bit down on a sneeze.

Mom was using Charm. Not a lot — just enough to cover the patches in her trousers and the wrinkles in her worn shirt, and to restore their color to a richer green. We hadn't expected visitors, especially anybody important. She wouldn't have had time to dress up in the fine clothes she saved for special occasions. It figured she'd made an exception for herself to use fox magic, despite the fact that she chastised me whenever I experimented with it.

The stranger loomed over her. I didn't smell any Charm on him, but he could have been some other kind of supernatural, like a tiger or a goblin, in disguise. It was often hard to tell. I sniffed more closely, hoping to catch a whiff of emotion. Was he angry? Frustrated? Did he detect Mom's magic at all? But he held himself under such tight control that I couldn't get a bead on him.

His clothes, finely tailored in a burnished-bronze-colored fabric, were all real. What caught my eye was the badge on the breast of his coat. It marked him as an official investigator of the Thousand Worlds, the league to which Jinju belonged. There weren't literally a thousand planets in the league, but it encompassed many star systems, all answering to the same government. I'd never been off-world myself, although I'd often dreamed of it. This man might have visited dozens of worlds for his job, even the government seat at the Pearled Halls, and I envied him for it.

More to the point, what was an investigator doing here? I could only think of one thing: Something had happened to my brother, Jun. My heart thumped so loudly I was sure he and Mom would hear it.

"Your son vanished under mysterious circumstances," the investigator said. "He is under suspicion of desertion."

I gasped involuntarily. Jun? Deserting?

"That's impossible!" Mom said vehemently. "My son worked very hard to get into the Space Forces!" I didn't need my nose to tell me how freaked-out she was.

I remembered the way Jun's face had lit up when he'd gotten the letter admitting him to the Academy. It had meant everything to him — he would never run off! I bit the side of my mouth to keep from blurting that out.

The investigator's eyes narrowed. "That may be, but people change, especially when they are presented with certain . . .

opportunities."

"Opportunities . . . ?" Mom swallowed and then asked in a small voice, "What do you mean?"

"According to his captain's report, your son left to go in search of the Dragon Pearl."

I wasn't sure which stunned me more: the idea of Jun leaving the Space Forces, or the fact that the Dragon Pearl might actually exist.

"The Pearl? How . . . ?" my mother asked incredulously. "No one knows where it —"

"The Dragon Council has made strides in locating it," the investigator said, rudely cutting her off. "And they would pay handsomely to have it back in their possession. If he found it, your son could have found the temptation irresistible. . . ."

No. I knew my brother wouldn't risk his career by trying to cash in an artifact, even one as renowned as the Dragon Pearl.

Mom's shoulders slumped. I wanted to tell her not to believe the investigator so readily. There had to be some other explanation.

"Jun is not here," she said, drawing herself up again, "and we have not heard from him, either. I'm afraid we can't help you."

The man was not put off. "There *is* one matter you can assist us with," he said. "Your son's last report before he left — it included a message addressed to Min. I believe that's your daughter?"

A shock went through me when he said my name.

"I have been sent here to show it to her. It may offer clues to Jun's location — or the Pearl's. Perhaps he wrote it in a code language only she would understand."

"Again, I think you have the wrong impression of my son," Mom said haughtily. "He is an honorable soldier, not a traitor."

"So you say. But I am not leaving these premises until I have shown Min the message. Are you not curious to see his last communication?"

That did the trick.

"Min!" Mom called.

TWO

I ducked back around the corner before she could spot me, waited a couple moments, then walked out to greet them both. My nose tickled again, and I stifled a sneeze. "Yes, Mom?" I asked, pretending I hadn't been eavesdropping on their conversation.

Mom briefly explained the situation to me. "This man has a message from Jun," she said. "He'd like you to tell him if you see anything unusual in it." I could hear the skepticism in her voice.

I nodded sullenly at the investigator, resenting the fact that he had accused Jun of deserting. Still, there was a silver lining: The man seemed unaware that we were foxes.

"Please, let me see the message," I said, remembering to speak formally.

The investigator looked down at me. If I'd been in fox shape, my ears would have flattened against my skull. His expression wasn't condescending, as I would have expected. Instead, I could sense him measuring me. And now I could smell some suspicion coming off him. Did he think I was hiding something?

He drew a data-slate out of a pocket, tapped on it, and showed me a message marked with Jun's seal — nothing fancy, just his name done in simple calligraphy.

I scowled at the fact that they'd been snooping into my brother's private correspondence, but there was nothing I could do about it now.

Hello Min,

Don't tell Bora, but there are even more chores on a battle cruiser than there are at home. I can't wait until my first leave. I have so many things to tell you. I've made lots of friends. Together we've been exploring a new world, just like Dad. My friends help with the chores sometimes, too. Did I mention the chores?

Love,
Jun

I blinked rapidly. I wasn't going to cry, not in front of this stranger. I handed the slate to Mom so she could read it, too. Jun's letters to us had been few and far between. The Thousand Worlds lacked faster-than-light communication technology, so all interstellar messages had to be delivered by courier. I couldn't bear the idea that this might be the last we ever heard from my brother. The investigator had to be wrong.

Still, the message's contents gave me hope. There *was* a hidden meaning in there, all right. Jun had never complained about chores the whole time we were growing up. He was trying to tell me that something was wrong. Who were the "friends"? Were they really friends, or troublemakers he'd fallen in with? Why

25

hadn't he included any of their names?

The most worrying clue was his mention of Dad. For one thing, our dad had died seven years ago, when I was six. And for another, he had never been an explorer. According to Mom, he'd been a skilled technician. What was Jun trying to imply?

How much of this did I want to reveal to the investigator, though? I didn't trust the man. After all, I didn't know anything about him or his motives. On the other hand, I couldn't thwart him too obviously. That might get my family in trouble, and if he decided to investigate us further, our secret — that we were fox spirits — might be exposed.

I'd hesitated too long. "Min," the investigator said in a disturbingly quiet voice, "can you tell me anything about this?"

"He's just complaining," I said, doing my best not to sound grudging — or concerned.

His gaze captured mine. "That's not the whole story, is it?"

I wasn't going to rat Jun out to some

stranger. "I don't know what you mean."

I smelled an extra whiff of worry from Mom. She wanted me to do something in response, but what?

"Many powerful people are interested in the Dragon Pearl," the investigator said, as if I couldn't have guessed that. "If it has resurfaced, it is imperative that it be recovered by the Space Forces and not some unscrupulous person."

I understood why that was important. According to legend, the Pearl could transform an entire planet in a day. Dragons controlled terraforming magic, but they were not nearly that fast and efficient — it took years for teams of trained workers to make a world fully lush and hospitable. As a citizen of Jinju, I was especially aware of that fact. Jun was, too.

With a sinking feeling, I remembered why Jun had wanted to go into the Space Forces. *I want to learn how to help Jinju, to make life better for everyone here,* he had told me more than once.

He wouldn't have stolen the Pearl for *our* benefit, would he? Surely not.

"I don't know anything," I said quickly.

The investigator looked dubious.

Fortunately, Mom intervened. "I assure you, my son would never desert, and my daughter is telling the truth."

I was grateful to her for supporting us and shutting him down.

Then she surprised me by adding, "Perhaps you would like some refreshments before heading to your next stop?"

I suppressed a groan. I didn't want this man here any longer than necessary. Not even Charm could disguise the modesty of our dome house. I tried to remember how well I'd wiped down the lacquered dining table that we brought out for special occasions. All our other furniture was scratched, banged-up plastic. Great-Grandmother had brought the red-black table and its accompanying red silk cushions when she immigrated to Jinju. Mom was going to make me drag it all out for this horrible man who thought Jun had done something wrong.

The man cocked his eyebrows at Mom. I bristled. I bet he doubted we had anything good to offer him. The thing

28

was, we didn't. But Mom had invited him, which made him a guest, which meant I had to treat him politely.

"I'll stay for a meal," he said, as if he were doing *us* a favor. "We can discuss matters further."

"Min," Mom said with a sigh, "get the table ready. You know the one."

"Yes, Mom," I said. She meant the nice table. I had a better idea, though. Especially since I was dying to know what else the investigator had to say about Jun.

On the way to the dining area that adjoined the kitchen, I passed the common room, where my four aunties were still huddled in bed. "Privilege of age," they always said about their sleeping late. Of course when I tried lazing about, I got cuffed on the side of the head. Not hard, but it still infuriated me.

Once I reached the kitchen, I grabbed settings out of cupboards and drawers and laid them out on the counter: chopsticks, spoons, and bowls for rice, soup, and the small side dishes called banchan, like mung bean sprouts and gimchi, spicy pickled cabbage. I grabbed real rice, imported from off-world and saved for special occasions because it required too much water to grow, instead of the crumbly altered grains we produced locally. After hesitating, I added some of the fancier foods and drinks we saved for festival days, like honey cookies and cinnamon-ginger punch. As I worked, I tried to listen in as Mom and the stranger talked in the hallway, but their voices were too low.

"I'm just about done, Mom!" I called out so she'd know to bring the guest in.

Then I concentrated hard, thinking about rectangles, right angles, and straight lines. About the smooth, polished red-black surface of that lacquered table. If I was going to imitate a table, I had to appear better than the real thing.

Charm swirled and eddied around me. My shape wavered, then condensed into that of the knee-high table. I couldn't put out the table settings now — Mom would have to take care of that. In the meantime, while I could only observe the room as a blur through the reflections on my surface, I could listen pretty well.

Most foxes only used shape-shifting to pass as humans in ordinary society. My true form, which I hadn't taken since I was a small child, was that of a red fox. I had one single tail instead of the nine that the oldest and most powerful fox spirits did. Even Great-Grandmother, before she'd passed several years ago, had only had three tails in her fox shape. When the aunties had told us stories about magic and supernatural creatures, and taught us lore about our powers, they had cautioned us to avoid shifting into inanimate objects. It was too easy to become dazed and forget how to change back into a living creature, they'd warned. I'd experimented with it on the sly, though, and was confident I could pull it off.

I heard footsteps. Mom's I would have recognized anywhere. She had a soft way of walking. The investigator also stepped quietly — too quietly, almost like a predator. Like a fox.

"Where did your daughter go off to?" the investigator asked.

A flicker told me that Mom was looking at the countertop where I'd left the settings out. "Pardon her flightiness," she said with a trace of annoyance. "She's been like that a lot lately."

Is that so? I thought.

Mom began transferring the dishes onto my surface. I endured the weird sensation of being a piece of furniture. Even as a table, I had a keen sense of smell — a side effect of being a fox. The rich aroma of cinnamon-ginger punch would have made my mouth water if I'd been in human form. It didn't always work in my favor, though. The cabbage pickles were starting to go sour. I bet the investigator would be able to tell.

Clunk, clunk, clunk went the dishes as they landed on my surface. Mom wasn't slamming them down, but they sounded loud. Then she put the silk cushions on the floor for the courier and her to sit on.

I had a sudden urge to sneeze, which felt very peculiar as a table. It wasn't my own Charm causing it —

Mom?

I concentrated to get a better picture of what Mom was up to. I was right — she was using more Charm! And this time she wasn't doing it to fancy up her clothes. Rather, her Charm was focused on the investigator, who still hadn't given his name. She was trying to get him to lower his guard, by using the kind of magic she had always told me honorable foxes never resorted to. The prickling sensation intensified, although it wasn't directed at me.

I quivered with outrage. Some of the platters on my surface clanked. The investigator froze in the middle of reaching for his chopsticks. "What was that?" he asked.

"Maybe there was a tremor," Mom said after a brief pause. "We get those from time to time." I could smell her suppressed anger, even if she was hiding it from the investigator. She was onto me. I was going to be lectured later, I just knew it.

Surely the investigator wouldn't fall for her excuse? This region was old and quiet, no volcanoes or anything. But I resolved to tamp down my reactions.

"You must have traveled a great distance to reach us here in the outer rim," Mom said. "I'm sorry I can't be more helpful in the matter about my son. Serving in the Space Forces was his dream, you know. I can't imagine that he'd turn his back on it."

His voice was curt. "Your daughter's hiding something, Ms. Kim. If you don't help me determine what it is, then I will be forced to open a general investigation into your family. In my experience, everyone has dirty laundry. Even in a place like Jinju."

He didn't get any further. I wasn't going to let him get away with threatening my mom! Especially since our family did, in fact, have a secret we couldn't afford to reveal. My senses jumbled as I resumed human shape. I shook the dishes off my back. But I hadn't reckoned on getting burned by hot soup as it splashed out of upturned bowls. I yelped. My flailing caused more of the dishes to crash on the floor and break. I was going to have kitchen cleanup duty for the rest of my life.

"Min!" my mom shouted. She attempted to grab my arm and yank me out of there.

I dodged her, flung a shard at the man, and scooted backward. I didn't want to get too close, because he was a lot bigger and it would've been easy for him to overpower me. On the other hand, I wasn't going to run away and leave my mom alone with him.

Mom made another grab for me. "This is *not* the way," she said in a taut voice. "Let me handle it."

It was too late. The investigator and I locked gazes. "Foxes," he hissed. His eyes had gone hard and intense, like a predator's. Even with the gimchi dumped over his head and dripping down the bridge of his nose, he looked threatening. I could smell the anger rising off him. "So *that's* why they needed the cadet."

Before I could react, he lunged for me and snatched me up by the throat. I scrabbled for air, my fingernails lengthening into claws, and tore desperately at his fingers.

"Please," Mom said, low and fast. "I'll make her tell you anything you need to know. Just let her go."

"You're in no position to bargain, Ms. Kim," he said. "Do you realize how bad it will look that one of your kind joined the Space Forces only to go rogue? Or how paranoid the local population will become when they realize that anyone they know could be a fox in disguise? I have no choice but to inform the authorities about your presence here." He reached into his coat, and his fingers closed around something that gleamed.

I panicked, thinking he was going to draw a blaster. I turned into the densest, heaviest block of metal I could manage. Gravity yanked me straight down onto the man's foot. Mom sneezed in response to my shape-shifting magic. The investigator didn't scream or even grunt, just remained silent. That scared me most of all.

Making rapid changes exhausted me, but what choice did I have? The world swam around me as I took human shape again. My clothes tugged awkwardly at my elbows and knees. I'd gotten the garments' measurements wrong.

Gray-faced, the man bent over to examine his foot. Before he stood upright again, I snatched up a saucepan and brought it crashing down against his head. He fell without a sound.

THREE

All my aunties had woken up by now. Mom had to explain the situation to them while the oldest one complained about having her sleep interrupted. Still, even she had to admit that we were in trouble.

Mom and the two strongest aunties dragged the unconscious investigator into the parlor. I looked away, feeling a little guilty about all the trouble I'd caused, though the sound of his head *thunk-thunk-thunk*ing across the threshold gave me a moment of vindictive pleasure. They laid him on a quilt as if they were going to nurse him back to health. The quilt would have to get washed afterward. I could guess who'd be stuck with *that* task.

Mom took me aside while the others fussed over the investigator. Her fury gave off a bitter, acrid smell. "I've told you time and again that using our powers will get us into trouble," she said. "And to make matters worse, you had to attack the man. I could have gotten rid of him and he'd have been none the wiser."

I bit my tongue to keep from pointing out that she'd been using fox powers herself. I just stared at the floor and muttered, "Yes, Mom."

"Go clean up the mess in the dining room," she said after a searching pause. "I'll deal with you later."

I recognized that grim tone and didn't argue. Instead, I headed back into the dining room, seething, and retrieved a threadbare rag. We used to borrow a robot housekeeper from the neighbors, but it had broken down a year ago. I missed that housekeeper almost as much as I missed my brother, whatever trouble he had gotten into.

While I knelt and scrubbed, Mom and the aunties held council in the parlor. "We can't simply kill the man. Even if we were the ones being threatened, we'd wind up taking the blame," said the one I disliked the most, Auntie Kim Areum. Bora's mom. For once I agreed with her, though.

"We can't throw Min to the authorities, either," Mom snapped back.

Good to know, I thought.

As I was trying to eavesdrop on the rest of the conversation, Bora and her younger brother clomped into the dining room, tracking dark pickled leaves all over the floor. "Hey," Bora said in a hushed voice, "did you throw a tantrum with our *food*? And why's there a dead guy in our parlor?"

"He's unconscious, not dead," I said.

"How do you know?"

"Look," I said, not wanting to get into it with her, "I have to clean this up." I stabbed my finger toward the corner.

"Could you stand over there?"

Manshik obediently trudged to the corner. Unlike his sister, he wasn't so bad. He was the only boy out of all my cousins. Most foxes choose to be female, like Mom and all my aunties, because it is traditional. Manshik had insisted on being male, though, because he wanted to be like Jun, and no one in the family hassled him about it.

"Seriously," Bora said, planting herself in my way when I attempted to mop up some spilled cinnamon-ginger punch, "what's going on?"

She was going to be in my face until I gave in, so I explained.

"I can't believe you were going to serve the investigator that nasty stuff," Bora said, wrinkling her nose at some dark pickled leaves, as if that were the most important thing that had happened. "We're the only family in the county that will touch it."

"Food is food," I said. How could I get Bora to go away? Mom and the aunties were discussing my fate, as well as that of the investigator, and I couldn't hear them while Bora was nattering at me. I scrubbed harder. Maybe if I ignored her long enough, she'd get bored and scoot.

". . . call the local magistrate," Auntie Areum was saying. "Surely they'll understand that —"

"Hey." Bora kicked at a bowl to get my attention. Its contents scattered, making a greasy mess of the section of floor I'd just scrubbed. "Min, stop spacing out."

I lost my patience and flung the dirty rag at her face. She shrieked as though I'd scalded her.

Manshik ran forward and tugged on her arm. He always hated it when people fought. I scowled at him and he blanched.

Mom appeared at the doorway. "What in the name of heaven — ?" She stared at the rag on Bora's face, then strode forward and plucked it off. *"Min,"* she said.

"Bora got in the way when I —"

"I'm not interested," Mom said. "Min, this situation is serious. I need you to do what you're told for once, with no loopholes or clever tricks."

I kept my hands loose at my sides, even though I wanted to ball them into fists, and I put on my meekest expression. "I'm sorry, Mom. I'll get back to work."

"We're going to have an *even longer* discussion after we've figured out how to protect the family," she said, frowning severely at me. "Starting with your inability to follow directions. Bora, Manshik, why don't you get to work in the hydroponics dome."

My cousins knew better than to argue with Mom when she was in this mood. They bowed and scurried off.

"Seonmi," another one of the aunties called to my mom, "come back here and let the children sort things out among themselves. We have matters to settle."

Auntie Areum added, "Your daughter's been a handful ever since —"

The oldest auntie shushed her, but I knew how that sentence would have ended. *Ever since Jun left.* My mouth tasted sour. Still, I kept quiet. The last thing I needed was to draw the adults' attention once more.

Mom handed me the rag. I pasted a smile on my face, then made a show of scrubbing. Now I felt angry about the quantity of food I'd splattered over the floor while fighting the courier. Aside from the dark pickled leaves, I'd picked out the good stuff, because Mom would have wanted to impress a guest. We never had much of it on hand, and it had gone to waste.

At least with Bora and her brother gone, I could concentrate on eavesdropping.

"We can't drug him into forgetfulness," the oldest auntie was saying in a whiny tone. "They'd consider that an even worse offense than using Charm. Such terrible luck, having an investigator show up at our house . . ."

"What?" Auntie Areum asked. "You expect our local hospital to be able to detect subtle poisons?"

"I'm more concerned about what Jun's gotten tangled up in," Mom said. Her voice dropped to a whisper. "The investigator seemed to think that Jun's being a fox is significant. He said, 'That's why they needed the cadet,' as if the fleet had recruited Jun specifically because of his powers. It wasn't just normal distrust of our kind."

"Too bad we can't just keep the investigator Charmed here," Auntie Areum said.

I almost dropped a bowl I'd been putting into the sink as I imagined the stern investigator meekly following Auntie Areum around and smiling at everything she said, maybe even doing some of the chores normally assigned to me. Too bad indeed!

"No, someone would notice his absence and come looking for him," Mom said.

While I wrung out the rag and freshened it up with clean water, Mom and the aunties squabbled over the appropriateness of bribery. Predictably, Mom opposed it, while the oldest auntie and Auntie Areum argued that it would save trouble down the line. They let it slip that they'd stashed some jades — interstellar chits more valuable than our planetary currency — in the rickety old storeroom cabinet. I should have guessed it had a false bottom for hiding things.

While they discussed which local officials would be the most helpful if we bribed them, my mind puzzled over the investigator. There was no way — especially now — I'd be able to get more information out of him about my brother's disappearance. Just what had Jun been trying to signal with that letter?

I stopped cleaning for a few minutes and listened intently. The adults gave no sign that they'd noticed the lull in my action. With any luck, they'd gotten caught up in their own concerns and wouldn't notice if I slipped away.

I crept outside and peeked through one of the windows in the hydroponics dome. Bora had herded her brother and our other cousins inside. Good. I'd have a few minutes' peace for thinking.

At any other time, I would have enjoyed gardening with them amid the luminous green columns of our crops. Outside of domes like this, plants struggled to grow on dusty Jinju. Only purple-tinged shrubs and low trees thrived. Right now, though, I couldn't relax into the familiar work. Mom was mad at me, not without cause, and I had to figure out how to get myself — and the rest of us — out of this fix.

First, I needed to get the spilled food out of my hair. Our home had a single sonic shower for all of us. Usually I had to wait my turn, but now, with everyone else otherwise occupied, the stall was free. The shower frequently made a grating buzzing noise no matter how often I had tinkered with it. Luckily, it wasn't too loud this time. No need for Mom to know I wasn't still doing chores.

I'd just finished changing into a fresh tunic and pair of pants, when Bora pounded on the bathroom door. "Are you done yet? I need to wash my hands!"

Be nice to her, I reminded myself. She could probably smell my annoyance, just as I could smell hers. It was hard to lie to a fellow fox. I tucked a stray strand of hair behind my ear, then stepped out of the bathroom.

Bora wrinkled her nose. "Took you long enough to clean yourself up."

"We're not all as talented as you are," I said dryly.

Bora scoffed. "You're just jealous you can't make your hair presentable without magicking it up."

Pointedly, I turned my back on her. "Don't you have somewhere to be?" I asked. I headed to the laundry room to drop off my soiled clothes. If only I'd

46

been born half a month earlier, I would be the older one and wouldn't have to put up with her attitude.

She followed me. "Too bad Jun messed things up for the rest of us."

"There has to be more to the story," I shot back. "The investigator probably left out details to see if he could catch us in a lie."

She ignored my response, as usual. "And you're just as bad as Jun! What were you thinking, attacking a guest?"

"I thought he was going for his gun! You would have done the same thing."

Ordinarily Bora would have needled me further about my rashness, but she still had my brother on her mind. "All Jun's big talk about rising through the ranks and finding allies who would help him make Jinju a better place, and what does he do? He runs off and disgraces the whole family."

Bora and I had never gotten along, but she and Jun had often spent time together. For the first time, I wondered if she missed him as much as I did, despite all the gibes.

"I'm sure it's just a misunderstanding," I said.

It had to be. Jun and I used to sneak outside late at night and stare up into the sky with its jewel-spill of stars and moons. As we lay there, he would talk about how much he wanted to serve on a Space Forces battle cruiser and visit every one of the Thousand Worlds. Also, unlike me, he was obedient — he always played by the rules.

"The investigator seems convinced that Jun went after the Dragon Pearl," I went on, thinking aloud. "But Jun is no renegade. He'd make a terrible smuggler or pirate."

The corners of Bora's mouth turned up in a suddenly sly expression. "I'll make you a bet."

Footsteps approached. By mutual silent agreement, we slipped into the next room and hid behind the door, waiting for them to pass us by.

After they had gone, Bora whispered, "If Jun comes back within a year, I'll do all your chores for the next six months."

Yeah, like *that* would ever happen.

She'd weasel her way out of the agreement. Nevertheless, I couldn't resist a bet, especially since I knew — *knew* — my brother was being falsely accused. The satisfaction of proving her wrong would be enough for me.

"And if he doesn't?" I asked, also whispering.

"You'll do mine."

I held my hand out. She laid hers atop it, palm to palm. "Done," I said.

She tossed her head. "Get ready to clean the toilet often, Min." Then she glided out of the room, not bothering to shut the door behind her.

Ha. Cleaning the toilet, while gross, wasn't hard. Dealing with the hydroponics ecofilters, on the other hand, was a different matter. If they failed, we'd all starve. Or worse, we'd have to eat nasty outdated ration bars until a real ecotechnician could fix the system. The job always fell to me because I was the only one in the family who could coax the filters to behave. Mom said I'd picked up the knack from my technician father. When I was very small, he had encouraged me to work alongside him, and I'd enjoyed it. I was proud of my skill with machines, but on the occasions I caught Mom watching me use Dad's tools, her expression was sad.

Even if I won Bora's bet, I'd still end up having to do all the maintenance work. I certainly couldn't rely on her to keep the ecofilters running. She'd probably had that in mind when she proposed the bet.

From down the hall, a snatch of conversation drifted to me, distracting me from my thoughts.

". . . send Min to Jaebi Village." It was my oldest auntie, sounding very firm. ". . . still have some friends there. The authorities can't arrest her if they can't find her, and Jaebi is so remote, nobody goes there if they can help it."

No way was I going to let myself be shipped off to some family friends I'd never heard of! I shuddered just thinking about it. But it was clear I couldn't stay home after what I'd done, either.

That, plus Bora's sniping about Jun, made up my mind: I would go after my brother. Someone had to track him down, and I was the best person for the job. I'd avoid being exiled to somewhere horrible and isolated. Best of all, once I disappeared, my family could blame me for assaulting the investigator and using fox magic, and they could escape punishment. I was sure my wily aunties would figure out a way to convince the local authorities to keep the family's true identity a secret.

I slipped over to the closet where we kids stored our personal items. As second oldest, I had the second-highest shelf to myself. It contained all my meager belongings: faded clothes, folded to my mom's painstaking standards; my breathing masks, along with some extra filters; an outdated data-slate that I had to share whenever someone asked; and a patched-up backpack, which Auntie Areum had been about to throw out until I begged for it.

And one more thing: a brush-and-ink portrait of Mom, Dad, Jun, and me as a baby, done on pale silk, which was marred only by a blotch in the lower left corner. I'd tried to remove the stain, but I couldn't do much without risking damage to the work. If it weren't for this portrait, which Jun had left with me, I wouldn't remember Dad's face at all.

Jun and I had inherited Dad's quizzical eyes and his narrow chin. I had Mom's smile, which I seldom saw on her anymore. In the portrait, she was smiling faintly, as though trying not to laugh at something one of us had just said.

All four of us were wearing festival clothes. I could imagine the bright colors and embroidery, the latter cunningly hinted at by stylized dabs of ink. I hadn't owned any garments that fine since my father's death.

I rolled up the silk and tucked it into a scroll case made of battered green plastic. The portrait deserved better. I used to imagine purchasing a replacement case carved from imported mist-ivory or sable-wood, but our money had to be saved for more important things. The plastic case did the job.

Then I retrieved the backpack and stuffed my possessions into it. While I could outfit myself with the help of shape-shifting magic, maintaining the illusion required effort and a good memory for details. I'd save that for times when I had no other choice. The masks and filters went into a pouch on the front, while I nestled the scroll case among some folded pants.

I shouldered the backpack and crept toward the storage room. This would be the tricky part. The adults were still talking loudly enough for me to hear them, though it was hard to discern the words from here. That didn't mean they wouldn't hear me rummaging through the cabinet. I'd have to be quiet.

"Min?" said a small voice from behind me.

I'd been so focused on the adults, I hadn't heard Manshik pad around the corner with a basket full of laundry. I decided to go on the offensive before he asked what I was doing with my backpack. I gestured for him to follow me into a side room. "Weren't you supposed to do that earlier this morning?" I demanded in a hushed voice.

That may or may not have been true. I knew Manshik, though, and he was young enough to get flustered easily.

No such luck today. "You're not going

somewhere, are you?" he asked, frowning.

"Of course not," I lied. "Since you had the basket, I decided to use my backpack to take my dirty clothes to the laundry room."

He held the basket out helpfully. Heaven save me from cooperative younger cousins. I performed my best smile and emptied some of my clothes into the basket, deliberately rumpling them in the process.

"Thanks," I said, keeping the sarcasm out of my voice with an effort. "I have to check the air filters, okay? If anyone asks, I'm going to be busy for a while."

Manshik pulled a face. "Your mom seems mad —"

"She can come get me when she's ready to yell at me. Just go ahead and deal with the laundry." As he trotted off, I eyed my mostly emptied backpack and sighed.

At least no one interrupted me when I went to the cabinet. I carefully slid open the false bottom and was amazed by the size of the cache inside. We could have been living a little less frugally all these years!

But right then, I was thankful for my aunties' thriftiness. As much as I hated to steal from them, I needed some jades. Fox magic wasn't any good for conjuring money — fake currency and other valuables disappeared soon after they left our hands. And I had to be prepared for a long trip.

Then I hesitated. If my family ended up having to bribe authorities in order to stay out of trouble, who knew how many chits they would need. I ended up only taking a couple of fistfuls.

My backpack felt heavier and heavier with each tiptoe I took toward the back door. I'd never even flown before, and here I was preparing to journey to the stars. What other choice did I have? I had no intention of going to jail or being shuttled off to the boonies. More important, Jun needed me.

Once I stepped outside, I didn't look back.

FOUR

Like everyone over the age of ten, I knew how to drive a hover-scooter. Technically you couldn't get a license until you were sixteen, but out where we lived, no one cared about such things. In the city of Hongok, where I was headed, I couldn't count on the patrols being lax. I took a moment to shift into a slightly older version of myself. The extra two inches of height was nice, if dizzying, even though it meant my clothes no longer fit as well.

That wasn't going to be enough of a

change to disguise me, though, if Mom decided to report me lost. I concentrated and summoned my magic to make small adjustments, not large ones: a flatter nose, glossier hair, smoother skin. I wanted to look prosperous enough to fit in with the other city dwellers, but not so wealthy that I'd attract thieves. The magic determined that I should be wearing emerald rings on one hand, sparkling brightly even in Jinju's ruddy light.

There was also additional weight at my hip: Charm had supplied me with a pouch. I opened it up and found a slightly shimmering but official-looking license corresponding to my new guise. Fox magic was handy that way, if sometimes unpredictable — once you envisioned what you needed, it covered all the details. I hadn't practiced Charm enough to have complete control over it yet, and I was dismayed to see that my alias was Kim Bora, the name of my most annoying cousin. The rest of the ID looked good, though, so I decided not to mess with it.

Once I reached the spaceport in Hongok, I hoped to book passage on a ship before any of the authorities caught up with me. After that, I'd have to get to a hub large enough that I could Charm information out of a sufficiently high-ranking Space Forces officer. Jun had never let any hints drop about the location of his battle cruiser, for security reasons. At least I knew the name of the ship he'd been assigned to: the *Pale Lightning.* Somehow I had to reach it so I could find out what had happened to him. All without being arrested and sent back home.

The enormity of the task before me was overwhelming. But I refused to allow myself to get discouraged. I'd just have to take it one step at a time.

First, get to the spaceport. The city was several hours away, and I should have worn better protective gear for the ride. I had on my mask, which always smelled faintly metallic no matter how fresh its filters were, and a helmet. The crisp air chilled me as I sped along the road. I wished I'd been able to grab a jacket on the way out of the house.

It was still early, and Jinju's reddish sun glared through the morning mist, tinting the low clouds the colors of fire. I passed domes of varying sizes, which protected their inhabitants from the dust and the fickle weather. Some glistened like jewels in the blossoming light, while others had cracks patched with ugly but functional globs of sealant. When I was younger, I'd helped a neighbor with that kind of repair job, because I'd earned a reputation for being handy. Of course, I'd almost fallen off the roof, but I'd done good work. The last time I'd checked it, the repair was holding up beautifully. With any luck, I wouldn't have to do anything like that where I was going.

For a moment I allowed myself to imagine what it would be like to breathe clean, sweet air without having to wear a mask every time I went outside. In the holos, fully terraformed worlds were lush and verdant, with trees rustling in the wind and flowers that flourished without having to be coddled in the protected gardens of wealthy people. If the Dragon Pearl truly had resurfaced, it could make that dream a reality.

I only passed a few other travelers. Most dome dwellers didn't visit the city often — there were too many things to deal with at home. But as I drew closer to Hongok, other scooters and larger vehicles zoomed past me. Just the sight of the dust they kicked up made me want to cough, even though my mask filter was doing its job.

In the outskirts of the city, the domes were larger, like overambitious mushroom caps. The largest buildings weren't domes at all, but spires spearing up into the sky. They dated back to Jinju's early days, before the terraforming project had faltered. The oldest families dwelled in the spires, even though not all of them had held on to their wealth over the years.

The city's name, Hongok, meant *ruby*. Maybe it had looked like a gem once — in the dreams of its founders, if nowhere else. I'd seen views of it from orbit on the news services: a glitter-mass of silver and gold rising from the darker ruddy plateau on which the city had been built, the needle-flash of starships arcing to and from the spaceport. Down here, though, I could see that the spires had discolored patches, and there were cracks and potholes in the streets. The scooter hovered a few centimeters above the surface, but it had a tendency to wobble when passing over the larger fissures. If Jinju had been terraformed properly, we'd be prosperous enough to afford better construction and maintenance.

I wished I could skirt Hongok's boundaries to approach the spaceport, but the city was so sprawling I was sure I'd get lost. I would just have to go straight through and pretend I had legitimate business.

I slowed down as the West Gate loomed before me. It was flanked by two statues of four-legged, lion-maned haetae, or guardian spirits. *Wish me luck,* I thought in their direction. I knew security would be tight due to Thousand Worlds regulations over spaceport access. I could see why people from other areas had to protect themselves against raiders and pirates from the Jeweled Worlds, but in Jinju, which had so little of value, the additional precautions were just a nuisance. I'd have to rely on Charm to deal with the guards if they got suspicious.

I spotted a pair of red-uniformed officers at the West Gate. They were busy chatting with a woman in the flashy robes I associated with traders. After they finished dealing with her, they looked me over.

"You there!" called one of the guards, a squat man with a mustache that drooped like a plant that hadn't been watered for a week.

I braked too suddenly and lurched forward, catching myself against the scooter's handlebars. I pulled off my helmet and cast my eyes down the way I'd seen Bora do when she was talking her way out of trouble. "Sir?" I asked.

"Identification," the officer said in a bored voice. "Come forward slowly, and no sudden moves."

"Here you go," I said, drawing the license out from its pouch. I admired it surreptitiously. Even the holographic seal in the center, depicting Jinju's pearl-and-carp symbol, looked convincing.

"Kim Bora," the guard read from the ID.

I grimaced at the reminder of the bet I'd made with her, and what was at stake: Jun.

The guard caught my expression and scowled at me. "You have some problem, miss?"

"Sorry," I said. "I just remembered that I forgot to put some food back in the fridge. The entire kitchen is going to reek of rancid gimchi by the time I get back." I wrinkled my nose, which wasn't an act. I could smell it just thinking about it. Was I never going to escape the stuff?

"Oh, leave her alone," the guard's cohort said. I liked her immediately. "Remember the last time you had us over and there was a bowl covered with mold in the middle of your — ?"

"You're fine," the first officer muttered to me. "Go on through."

I smiled brightly at him and accelerated. As I passed, I heard the second guard saying, "You need to get a new robot to replace the one you broke. . . ."

Funny, I'd never thought of guards as going home and having chores like the rest of us. Or having broken-down robots, too, for that matter.

Would life be any easier off-world? I was looking forward to getting away from

Jinju for the first time, though I wished I were leaving under better circumstances. Had my family realized by now that I had disappeared? I regretted making Mom worry, especially because Jun had gone missing, too. I probably should have left a note, but I didn't really want her to know my plans — she might have tried to track me down. Anyway, it was too late now.

After I'd left the West Gate behind, I stopped next to a directory. It resembled a thick rectangular column, each face with a screen you could use to search for shops or addresses. A pair of giggling kids, not much older than six or seven, were entertaining themselves by getting one side to project holographic images of various landmarks and making them virtually collide. At the moment, a temple had the city's oldest spire protruding through its bell.

I did my best to ignore the kids while I asked the directory the fastest route to the spaceport. Even from here I could spot the high spire and the gleaming flash of starships flitting in and out, but Hongok's streets were a tangled mess, and I didn't want to waste time going in circles. A map popped up with the route highlighted. It would take me through the Market District. I'd always loved its bright colors and mixture of smells and gossip, although Mom thought poorly of most merchants. (Then again, Mom disapproved of practically everything.) In any case, I'd have to take care not to attract the attention of the guards there. They had a reputation for demanding bribes from out-of-towners, and I couldn't afford to waste my precious supply of jades before I got off-planet.

I oriented myself and sped away, but not before the kids had "rammed" my scooter with a hologram of the spire image. Distracted by the sight, I swerved and almost left my designated lane before straightening out. *Concentrate,* I reminded myself. *Don't get into any trouble.*

Traffic crowded the streets: speeders, which seated up to six; personal scooters like mine; and the occasional pedestrian. On a wealthier world, teams of dragon weather engineers would control the climate. In Hongok, everyone was obliged to wear masks and endure whatever the weather brought.

At the edge of the Market District, faded neon signs advertised bars and restaurants. Groups of old people gathered around outdoor tables marked with nineteen-by-nineteen grids for playing baduk. A dancer spun and leaped to the beat of an improvised drum. I longed to linger, maybe even watch a match of baduk. At home we had a cheap old set we hardly ever took out anymore.

Instead, I parked my scooter in a designated area in walking distance of the spaceport. The vehicle itself was dented and its paint job could have used retouching, but Mom had insisted on buying the best biometric lock we could afford. It was programmed to recognize the way the adults, Bora, and I drove, and it would seize up if anyone else attempted to make off with the scooter. No one was allowed to park here overnight, so the authorities would use its tracker to identify the owner and levy a fine when I failed to return tonight. Sorry, Mom.

The Market District enfolded me. People shoved past without apologizing, or spoke rapidly in loud voices. Whenever

I spotted the guards with their distinctive blue armbands, I slipped sideways into the crowd.

Just when I was congratulating myself on having evaded a swaggering knot of guards, another group of officers pelted from a side alley and ran into me. I yelped.

"Watch yourself, citizen!" said one of the guards, her brows lowering as if I'd caused the collision.

It was too late to duck away and lose myself amid a chattering group of tourists in out-of-season robes. "Excuse me," I said, reining in my impatience. "I wasn't paying attention to where I was going."

"Obviously not." She looked me up and down, as though my clothes were broadcasting criminal intentions. Only then did I realize that she was only a few years older than me, scarcely an adult.

Three other guards had taken notice. "Hey, Eunhee, what's keeping you?" one of them called out. "That girl giving you trouble?"

The officer who had spoken had the

flushed skin of someone who had been drinking too much cheap wine, and he reeked of the stuff. The last thing I wanted was a confrontation with drunken guards.

But in short order, the rest of them surrounded me.

FIVE

"Haven't seen you here before," the tall-est guard said, regarding me sourly. The guard had a scar slashing across their face and an empty left eye socket, not even a cybernetic replacement. Like all the guards, they wore a badge with their family name on it. This particular badge also had a small symbol next to the name that let me know they should be addressed neutrally, as neither female nor male.

"No, Officer," I said in my most respectful tone. "I live out in one of the steadings." Giving even this much detail made me wince, but I couldn't get away with saying nothing.

"Pretty well dressed for a steader," Eunhee said. Her gaze settled on my hands.

My fingers twitched. The emerald rings that Charm had provided me were nicer than any jewelry my family owned. The rings wouldn't last long once they were off my hands, but what choice did I have? Especially since I wanted to hang on to my money, which had the virtue of being real.

I slipped the largest ring off my finger and toyed with it, saying, "I'm afraid I'm going to get lost in here." If I couldn't escape the guards, maybe I could wrangle something out of them. Why not a personal escort? They might be useful for fending off thieves.

Eunhee's eyes brightened with greed. "Something could be arranged."

The tallest guard shook their head but didn't do anything to interrupt the transaction. "Where are you headed, anyway?"

I thought quickly. I should be here to buy something. What wouldn't cost too much but would prove handy once I got into space? To my mortification, my stomach rumbled before I could come up with an answer.

Eunhee laughed, then plucked the ring out of my grasp. A tickling sensation fizzed through my bones. The ring flickered like a malfunctioning hologram as Eunhee slipped it on her little finger. Had she noticed? No, she grinned down at it with a covetous smile. I knew the ring would quietly evaporate into a flutter of spent magic once I was safely out of sight, and I didn't feel the least bit sorry for her.

"You're clearly in need of a feeding," the tallest guard said with a trace of malice. "We'll show you a good place to fill your belly, and in return you can treat us to a few drinks?"

I bobbed a bow. "Of course!" I said. I was outnumbered, after all.

The four guards chivvied me along, joking about this merchant or that tourist, or recounting favorite bribes. Remembering the time someone had bought them off with prawns — real prawns, not vatgrown flavored protein — made them smack their lips. I couldn't help resenting the things they took for granted.

My heart sank when we stopped in front of a lavish garden with arches covered in artfully arranged vines. Pink flowers drooped from the vines in curling sprays, and their fragrance dizzied me. I couldn't imagine how much effort the gardeners must have put into maintaining the flowers outside of a hydroponics unit.

Eunhee shoved me forward into a courtyard full of bamboo tables and chairs. A few other customers were there, enjoying a midafternoon snack. "Go on," she said, smirking. She pulled out a chair for me at the closest empty table. "This spot looks good. We'll let you order first."

I seated myself demurely and stared at the chopsticks in front of me. The guards dragged over more chairs. A graceful young man emerged from one of the archways, bearing a tray with cups of fragrant jasmine tea.

The cups were the first clue that I needed to get out of there fast. I recognized good celadon when I saw it. The porcelain's translucent blue-green sheen was unmistakable. This place was definitely out of my budget range.

Still, I didn't want to seem too eager to escape, especially when the officers were already suspicious. Besides, even if they were corrupt, they might have some information to offer me.

I smiled at Eunhee. "Any exciting news from off-world?" I asked. There was a rivalry between planet-bound security and the Space Forces. The guards might be all too willing to gossip.

"I haven't heard anything special," Eunhee said.

The tallest guard frowned. "An investigator came through recently. And not just any investigator, either. He came in on a special courier vessel. Even its port of origin was classified. Whatever he's involved with, it's big. He was tightmouthed, though. Probably thinks he's too important to deal with people like us."

I felt a jolt of fear go through me, and I tried not to show it. The investigator's special status implied that Jun was in serious trouble. More than ever, I wished we could have coaxed further information from the man. But the saucepan had brought an end to that, and I'd left it to my family to clean up the mess.

Eunhee interrupted my thoughts. "Well, a hotshot investigator isn't going to linger in a dump like Hongok, so who cares about him?" She stared at my rings. "Those are the biggest emeralds I've ever seen." She reached for my hand.

I wanted to nip her. The one-eyed guard might have revealed more if she'd let them keep talking.

I pulled off the rings and cast them on the table, where they spilled in a tumble of facets brighter than cat eyes. "What could be important enough to bring an investigator here, anyway?" I asked Eunhee, though her attention was clearly elsewhere now. "I thought all the action was on" — I picked a random planet I'd heard about on the news a couple days ago — "Maesil."

"Oh, that's old news," Eunhee said dismissively as she tried on another ring.

A third guard, a man with orange highlights in his spiky hair, joined in. "The *real* action is in the Ghost Sector. According to a drunk spacer who was spilling secrets last night, a lot of ships — even Space Forces battle cruisers — are gathering there, despite its reputation."

The Ghost Sector had earned its name from what had happened to a planet within it, the Fourth Colony, whose entire population had perished when they'd angered disease spirits a few centuries ago. The planet had remained uninhabited ever since, and it was thought to bring bad luck to anyone who tried to land there. Then what was drawing all the ships? I wondered, but I didn't dare ask my question aloud.

"I guess even Space Forces Command can't keep a lid on that much activity," the one-eyed guard said with a snort.

"Maybe they're doing a sweep of the pirates," ventured the fourth guard. " 'Bout time, if you ask me."

"I've heard rumors that the tiger captain — you know, Hwan? — is involved," said Spiky Hair. "I've never trusted supernaturals in positions of power."

"I've never trusted supernaturals *anywhere*," said the fourth guard, and they all laughed.

Uh-oh. That was my cue to leave, before they figured out what I was. "Uh, I need to wash my hands before we eat," I said, standing up.

The one-eyed guard nodded. "Eunhee, go with her."

Eunhee looked longingly at the rings I'd left on the table but got up as ordered. We asked the server to show the way, and he led us through the arches and into the restaurant proper. Eunhee walked closer to me than I found comfortable, which was undoubtedly the point. If I'd been an ordinary human, she would have been able to grab me easily.

We passed a doorway to a private dining room that stood empty. I made the most of the opportunity and snaked out my foot. Eunhee tripped and fell forward, knocking down the server.

While they were untangling themselves, I dashed into the private room, out of their line of sight. Quickly, I changed myself into the most innocuous thing I could think of: an extra chair.

"Where did she go?" I heard Eunhee demand.

The server wasn't having any of it. "If

you have some notion of sneaking your *associate* in to rob this establishment," he said in a loud voice, "I assure you that I am not fooled."

"What's all the ruckus about?" The manager had emerged from the back.

"Your employee is falsely accusing me of being a thief," Eunhee said. "I could write him up for that. And there could be consequences for your restaurant."

By the time they'd taken the argument to the manager's office, I was only too glad to shift into the form of a server, complete with a uniform and tray, and glide back out the way I'd come.

It wasn't until I was several blocks away from the restaurant, when I paused to catch my breath and change into my sixteen-year-old disguise, that it occurred to me — I'd left my backpack behind.

SIX

I'd lost the jades! And, even more precious, the only portrait I had of my family. I couldn't conjure up replacements — they wouldn't last. I considered venturing back to retrieve my backpack, but with the restaurant staff on alert and four city guards angry that I'd cheated them of their "emeralds," that wouldn't be a good idea.

How was I going to book passage without real, permanent money? My bad luck today had shown me that magic wouldn't

78

solve every problem. But now it was literally all I had at my disposal.

I decided to keep going toward the spaceport and hope for the best. I thought furiously as I hurried through the streets. From what the guards had said, it sounded like something fishy was going on in the Ghost Sector. I wondered if Jun's battle cruiser was there. If I could somehow find a Space Forces officer, I might be able to trick them into giving me classified info.

For most of the way, my view had been obscured by Hongok's spires. I rounded a corner onto the road that led to the spaceport proper and my breath caught in wonder. A dazzle of lights flashed from the landing area, like a necklace of captive stars. A control tower rose from the main building, piercing the sky. It wasn't as tall as the spires I had passed, but it was better maintained, shining red-gold in the sunlight.

By now it was late afternoon. I hadn't made as good time as I'd hoped when I set out, and I didn't want to be wandering around after dark. There were some hostels near the spaceport, but I couldn't stay at one of those even if I'd had the money. I wanted to get off-planet tonight, in case anyone was searching for me.

My heart hammered as I approached the entrance to the main building, which was flanked by two glass booths. Inside each one was a guard wearing a badge that displayed a red star and a stylized dagger, representing airport security. I slowed, not wanting to appear too eager. I'd learned from the news that on a planet like Jinju there were always people desperate enough to try to stow away on a ship and seek a better life on a richer world. The guards were there to prevent that from happening. They were looking out for both the ships' interests and the would-be refugees', since some captains weren't above mistreating unauthorized passengers.

Unlike other runaways, though, I had the advantage of fox powers. As I joined the line to get in, which was only a few people long, I exerted just a touch of Charm, hoping it would get me past security. I didn't want to wear myself out using it too often, but this particular hurdle — making it into the spaceport —

was a critical one.

The person in front of me was clearly a spacer. The sleeve of their suit was covered with tiny enamel pins, one for each of the worlds they had visited. Jun and I used to make a game of memorizing the different pins. I'd never been able to remember more than just a few of the most famous worlds. Now I spotted some I knew, though, like Madang, fabled for its gardens. And Cheongok, mostly ocean with scattered archipelagos, where the descendants of dragons sent their children to learn the art of weather-craft. The spacer had even visited Jaebo, known for its staggering wealth, where the rulers of the Thousand Worlds governed from the Pearled Halls.

Jun had always wanted to visit every one of those worlds. When we were younger, he'd been glued to the holo shows that showed glimpses of life elsewhere. I'd sit by him, enthralled by the stories he spun about traveling together as we squinted at the staticky images. If only I had enough jades to book a tour and see them all myself! It wouldn't be the same without my brother, though.

I looked away from the pins, reminding myself of my goal: getting to Jun's ship. I double-checked my Charm, just in case. The license, when I fished it out, still listed me as Kim Bora, so I'd have to get used to answering to her name.

"Come forward, citizen, and present your identification," the security inspector snapped from her booth.

I flushed. While I'd been woolgathering, my turn had come. I approached and showed her my medallion.

The inspector scowled at the ID. I started to sweat. But she waved me through the doorway scanner. I heard a faint hum. "Nothing amiss," the inspector said. "Please continue."

Dizzy with relief, I emerged into the brightly lit foyer and paused to get my bearings. The spaceport was busier than I'd expected. Jinju wasn't exactly a popular destination. Spacers only stopped here to resupply on the way to more interesting places.

People paid me little attention as they bustled back and forth. Eateries promised the best food in the outer rim, which I doubted, but the smell of vegetable fritters made my mouth water. I hadn't had anything to eat all day. It was tempting to grab a bite, but I knew I shouldn't delay.

Elsewhere, shops hawked sad-looking souvenirs, such as pieces of cloth embroidered in the local style. When I looked at them up close, I could see the stitching was crooked. I wasn't great at fancy needlework, mostly because it wasn't something I had time for, but I did do a lot of mending.

I headed for one of the digital information kiosks along the wall. Below one of the display screens, someone had scratched graffiti with a knife. It said, in unsteady letters, DON'T PLAY DICE AT NARI'S. What looked suspiciously like a blotch of dried blood underscored the word *dice.* Well, that advice was easy enough for me to follow. I wasn't good at playing dice, and Charm didn't make me any better at it, as I'd discovered as a child.

Too bad I couldn't simply look up the last known location of my brother's battle cruiser. That kind of information wouldn't be available on a public kiosk. I could, however, check a galactic map to see if anyone docked here was headed toward the Ghost Sector. If a lot of Space Forces ships were in that area, maybe the *Pale Lightning* was among them. The closer I could get to the battle cruiser, the more clues about Jun's disappearance I could gather. At least that's what I hoped.

I hated the idea of my brother being anywhere near the cursed Fourth Colony. I thought back to his message: *Together we've been exploring a new world, just like Dad.* Was that why he had mentioned Dad, because he had somehow gotten involved with ghosts? I shivered at the thought.

I asked the kiosk for a list of commercial transports that had room for a passenger and might be willing to leave tonight. Just my luck, only one starship was headed anywhere near the Ghost Sector in the next several days: the *Red Azalea.* It listed its next major stop as a big space hub, Gingko Station, at the edge of the sector. That would work. Once there, I might be able to find out more about the *Pale Lightning*'s current location.

I checked the *Red Azalea*'s safety record and reputation. It was a freighter, not a luxury cruiser, but that wasn't such a bad thing — it would be easier for me to keep a low profile on a freighter. The kiosk indicated that the captain — Captain Hye — was willing to take on "working passengers" and that she could be found at . . . oh. Nari's. Apparently Captain Hye liked to gamble during her downtime.

Fine. I pulled up a directory of the spaceport and memorized the directions to Nari's gambling parlor, as well as the *Red Azalea*'s current berth. Then I took a deep breath to steady myself and headed for the stairs to the upper level.

Even if I hadn't consulted a map first, finding Nari's would've been easy. As I approached, I heard the clattering of dice and the sounds of shouts and laughter, as well as the faint strains of sinuous music. A surprisingly tasteful statue of a three-tailed fox stood next to the open doorway, one paw upraised as if in greeting. In the lore, fox shifters gained tails as they aged — up to nine, anyway — as a reflection of their power. I once asked Mom why I only had the one tail, and she told me not to be so literal. The statue gave me pause, though. Most people thought foxes were bad luck, so why would a gambling parlor put one up on display?

I stepped over the threshold to find a tall, broad man lurking in the dim light of the foyer. A bouncer, I assumed. As he looked me over, a diminutive woman came up to greet me. She wore a sleeveless dress of fine silk, and I could just make out an elaborate tattoo of a fox and a pine tree covering most of her upper left arm. "Welcome to Nari's," she said, smiling as if I were a particularly delicious snack.

I was taken aback for a moment, because normally I wouldn't have been allowed anywhere near a gambling parlor. Then I remembered that I looked sixteen in my current disguise.

I embarrassed myself by sneezing all over her. I wasn't even able to cover my mouth in time. Normally I didn't sneeze in reaction to my own magic, which meant —

The woman's smile froze. "You're . . ."

I stared at her, silently begging her not to say it out loud. If I wasn't mistaken, she was a fox, too — one I didn't know. Which made sense, since my mother never would've let me near anyone involved with gambling.

"My name is Kim Bora," I said rapidly. "I'm just here to talk to one of your, um, guests."

"I see," the woman said, her eyes narrowing. "Come with me. Quickly, now."

I followed, somewhat reluctantly, but I needed to find Captain Hye.

The woman led me past tables of gamers rolling dice in cups, and others where people were playing with flower cards that had distinctive red backs. In another room, an audience watched in intent silence as a pair of opponents played janggi. The player with the grumpier face moved a cannon to capture a piece. I couldn't tell who was winning. I wouldn't have minded lingering, but the woman shooed me into a cramped back office. My palms began to sweat. Maybe this hadn't been the brightest idea. What did she want with me?

To calm my nerves, I surveyed the room. Despite its small size, it was crammed with luxuries. One wall displayed a painting of a starship shooting over an ice planet's horizon, with highlights picked out in luminous gold and silver. The desk was made of real wood, with grain so deep and lustrous I could have lost myself tracing it with my eyes. A small shelf unit even contained books, the old-fashioned kind, heavy with the sooty smell of ink and aging paper. I thought of the rickety dome dwelling I had left behind and wished I could live surrounded by such wealth.

"You have the look of Areum and her sisters," the woman said without inviting me to sit. She didn't sit, either.

Oh no. She knew my family.

And she wasn't done. "But your magic smells most like Seonmi's."

This was a wrinkle I hadn't considered. I'd never realized that someone would recognize the scent of my family's magic. "I'm sorry, I don't know what you're talking about," I said, looking the woman squarely in the eye.

She snorted. "Don't play games with

me. You're that daughter of Seonmi's, aren't you?"

A pit opened at the bottom of my stomach. She'd figured out who I was. Was she going to turn me in? Maybe my best move was to run —

The woman shook her head. "You don't have to worry about *me*," she said with an odd bitterness. "I'm the cousin they never talk about — Nari."

"I have no idea who you are," I said with perfect honesty. Still, I couldn't resist sniffing the air. She did smell a little like my aunts, now that I was paying attention. There wasn't much physical resemblance — she had an exaggerated prettiness that I'd never seen in Mom or my aunties — but with a fox, that didn't mean much. Why hadn't Mom ever told me about her?

"Your mother and aunts and I all grew up together," the woman said. She pointed toward a chair. "Sit, sit."

Now I did. "I'm sorry about whatever happened," I said, wondering what could have gone so wrong.

"Well, you didn't come here to discuss

old history, I'm sure," Nari said. "So, Min — did I get that right?"

I started. I hadn't told her my name. She couldn't be completely out of touch with my family if she knew it.

"You must be . . . how old beneath that Charm of yours?" She sniffed the air, and I wondered what my scent revealed to her. "Not old enough to follow Jun into the Space Forces, or you'd be gone already."

So she knew about my brother, too. Perhaps Mom still talked to her once in a while, even if they were estranged? I could only imagine that she'd kept Nari a secret from me to protect me from a "bad influence."

Nari smiled at me, her teeth glinting. I was forcibly reminded that we were both foxes, and foxes were predators. "I've been keeping track," she said, "in case I can ever repay your mother the favor I owe."

That sounded promising. "Favor?" I asked before I could stop myself.

She gestured toward the doorway and the cards, the dice, the excited chatter of gamblers. "She and I started this business together. After she met your father, though, Seonmi wanted to leave it behind and start a family. She gave me full ownership and wished me well." Now she sounded resigned rather than bitter.

My eyes prickled, and I blinked away sudden tears. I had asked my aunties about my parents' past on a few occasions, but they'd always looked so sad that I hadn't had the heart to persist. And after trying in vain a few times, I'd learned not to ask Mom herself. Never had I imagined, though, that my mother's background had involved a gambling parlor. I couldn't envision her in a place like this.

"The rest of the family disapproved of our business, of course," Nari went on. "They didn't care how profitable it was. In fact, they considered the money tainted. They cut all ties to me and it took so long to forgive Seonmi that they never really got to know your father before he . . ." She trailed off. "Well, you know how that story ended, and you have the look of someone in a hurry."

I ground my teeth in frustration. My

older relatives, including the ones I had been living with all these years, had once turned their backs on my parents? I was tempted to keep Nari talking so I could learn more, but she wasn't wrong about my being in a hurry.

"Thank you for telling me the truth, Aunt Nari," I said, trying out the name. "It was very . . . eye-opening. But right now I'm looking for the captain of the *Red Azalea*."

Nari's expression softened. "Your mother brought you up to be polite, I see." She smiled. "So, you seek Captain Hye. I have a better idea, though."

I wasn't interested in hearing it. I had to keep sight of my mission. "I don't mean to be rude, but I really do need to talk to the captain. Please." I said *please* in the same tone I used when I needed to convince Mom I wasn't up to any tricks.

"Hear me out first," Nari said. "What's your rush, anyway?"

I didn't want to give her any details. It would be too dangerous to tell her what I had done to the investigator. Then again, I had to come up with a plausible reason for running away. So I landed somewhere in between. "Mom thinks I'm a troublemaker," I said. "She's threatening to send me to the middle of nowhere until I straighten out. I'd rather go and see the rest of the galaxy. I have to leave before my family catches up to me."

Nari's eyes glinted cunningly. "Stay here and work for me instead. I can keep you hidden from our relatives. You're a bit young, but your Charm will compensate. Whatever your family's told you about foxes having to lie low, if I know them, they've exaggerated the risk. You can serve refreshments and use your magic to make people comfortable. There'd be profit in it for both of us. Once you've saved enough, you can move on — but maybe by then you'll have changed your mind about getting off Jinju in such a hurry." She winked at me then.

I wavered. I didn't plan to hang around. On the other hand, if she *thought* I did, maybe she would advance me some pay. I was still worried about not having any money for passage.

"The stories I could tell you about the

wild days your mother and I had as kits!" Nari went on, sensing my weakness. "Of course, if you're really in a hurry, I won't have time. . . ."

If I was honest with myself, I was dying of curiosity. I couldn't imagine my mom as having been anything like Nari, ever. I supposed I could safely afford to spend a few hours at the gambling parlor. At the very least, I could earn some tips.

"I'll think it over," I said, knowing better than to agree to anything too quickly. "Let me try it out tonight and see how it goes." I could ask one of the patrons or a bouncer to point Captain Hye out to me when Nari wasn't looking.

She smiled, her teeth gleaming white and sharp, like fangs. "Excellent," she said. "You'll fit right in here."

DON'T PLAY DICE AT NARI'S, the graffiti had said. I wondered what had happened to the person who'd left that warning. *I'm a fox, too,* I told myself, *and ready for anything Nari can throw at me.*

But what if I was wrong?

SEVEN

Before Nari let me out of her office, she explained my duties. Mostly she wanted me to wander around serving "refreshments" — her code word for the various kinds of wine on offer — while using my Charm to encourage customers to relax. People got tense when they were gambling, she told me, especially when they were losing. "Don't try to influence the games — that's against the rules," she said. "Just make sure they're having a good time. And don't let them hassle you. I'll have the bouncers keep an eye out for trouble."

Then she directed me to conjure an outfit more appropriate for a gambling parlor, to replace my traveling clothes.

"Something like what you're wearing, but not as fancy?" I asked, eyeing the brocade dragon-and-phoenix design that patterned her silk dress.

Nari laughed as if I'd said something particularly amusing. "Oh, my dear. Fancier, if you can manage it."

Though I knew my mother would be horrified if she saw me serving drinks in her former gambling parlor, I had to admit I was happy about having the chance to use magic without limits or lectures. I took a moment to imagine a costume, then concentrated on making it materialize. Charm spun me a gray silk blouse stiff with embroidery and studded with small golden pearls that winked in the light like captive moons. Having the time to focus properly helped me magic up a perfectly tailored pair of slacks and slippers to match. Gold jewelry with more pearls glittered at my throat, ears, and wrists, and a gold hairpin held my hair up in an elaborate chiffon.

"Not bad," Nari said, as if I were another pretty trinket decorating her office. "You're definitely Seonmi's daughter, maybe even more powerful than she was. One of these days I'll tell you about the tricks she played. She was better at making crowds dozy than I was."

My mom, powerful with Charm? And using her magic against groups of people? The thought unsettled me. To say nothing of the idea of my mom, who always wore plain clothes around the house, in an elaborate dress like Nari's. I couldn't picture it at all.

Nari brought me a mirror so I could check my appearance. I already knew I looked good, though. Maybe even good enough to impress the customers.

"Come," Nari purred. She took my arm and guided me out onto the floor. "Your shift will end in four hours. Can't push you too hard on your first day, after all."

First and last *day,* I thought, wondering how I was going to convince her to advance me some money later tonight. She *had* said she owed Mom a favor. . . .

"Yong!" she called. One of the bouncers, who had been looming over a table of card players, made his way over to us. He was even larger than the man I'd met at the door. His vest was made of the same brocade as Nari's dress. That, plus the tattoo that covered half his face in a lace-like pattern, made him look a bit like a floor lamp. But I noticed a slight lump under his vest, indicating a hidden weapon. I bet people didn't underestimate him twice.

"Yong, this is a new greeter," Nari said to the man. "Her name is Min. Show her around while I see to business, will you?" With that, she whisked off.

"Pleased to meet you," I said to Yong, smiling up at him and wishing I'd chosen to be taller. "My name is actually Bora," I added, flashing him my ID. No reason he needed to remember the name Min.

Yong grunted in response. He gave me a wordless tour of the gambling parlor's various rooms. The entire place had been done up in red for good fortune, with gold-tone ornaments hanging from the walls. Any less restraint and the effect would have been tacky. Lively music played from hidden speakers, and I found it catchy.

My eyes went round when he took me past the private room in back for what looked like very intense card games. The gamblers casually tossed around handfuls of chits worth sums that could have kept my entire family fed and clothed for a year.

For that matter, Nari seemed to be doing pretty well herself as the owner of this establishment. What a different life Mom could have had. Did she ever regret her decision? I wondered.

"Is Captain Hye somewhere in here?" I asked Yong. "Nari mentioned her. . . ." I hoped this was vague enough not to raise Yong's suspicions. I was wary of using Charm on him. If he worked for Nari, he had to know about fox magic.

"Nari's warned you about her, huh?" Yong said, sounding weary. "She's at the high-stakes table."

"In that room we just passed?" I asked casually.

He nodded. "Woman with the red shirt and the scar on her chin. Her luck's decidedly unpredictable. The way things look right now, she might even gamble her ship away."

I suppressed a huff of alarm. I couldn't let that happen if I was going to get off-planet tonight! Why couldn't I have picked a captain who didn't have a gambling habit? Still, maybe Captain Hye's bad luck could be turned into an opportunity for me. I just had to get in there and talk her into leaving. But how?

At this hour, more people were coming to Nari's to try their luck at various games, so I had to attend to my duties. I smiled at chattering gamblers while I shuttled to and from the bar with drinks. Yong and the other bouncers, dressed in identical uniforms, watched from their stations, their expressions professionally forbidding. One woman in a fancy fur coat raised a fuss when she lost everything at dice. Yong escorted her out as she jabbered that she just needed one more throw. I stifled a pang of unease. My use of Charm was encouraging people to stay longer and lose more money.

As the minutes wore on, I got better at determining which people had a real gambling habit and which had come to keep their friends company or enjoy a fun night out. I couldn't always tell by how well or poorly dressed they were. But the gamblers had a haunted look in their eyes, and they stank of desperation.

I was starting to get an idea of why Mom had chosen to leave the gambling parlor behind. She wouldn't approve of me being here, either, and especially the way I was using Charm. In the past, I'd only wielded it in small ways, not on whole groups of people like this. It took more effort than I was used to.

"You there!" a gambler called out, a man with a red face and a beard that had seen better days. "Another cup of cheongju, if you would!"

I smiled coolly at him. "I'll be right back." *Cheongju is rice wine,* I reminded myself. I'd never had it, but my mom and aunties sometimes indulged on New Year's Day, or offered a cup to the ancestors.

Nari kept the wine in a dizzyingly crowded bar in the back, next to the tiny kitchen that dispensed snacks for favored guests. No one had told me the name of the wizened female bartender. She scowled at me every time I appeared to retrieve a drink for one of the customers.

Inspiration struck. "Cheongju, please," I said, "and a gukhwaju as well, for Captain Hye." Gukhwaju was chrysanthemum wine. I picked it at random, mainly because it came in a fancy bottle, so I figured it was the good stuff.

The wizened woman's scowl deepened. "Hye's luck has changed, eh? Well, that won't last, but it's her funeral."

The way she said this aroused my curiosity. "What do you mean?"

She laughed sourly. "I'm surprised you haven't figured it out already. The boss magicks up the wine. It makes people's luck go sour. The authorities come in regularly to ensure that the *games* aren't rigged, but they fail to detect what she does to the *refreshments*. Gamblers always like to drink when they think they're winning big, so the wine ensures that they end up losing anything they might have won. That way the parlor always comes out ahead."

I tried to suppress the sick feeling in my stomach. Maybe my mom wasn't right about everything, but the fact that she'd parted ways with Nari should have set off alarm bells in my head. No wonder she frowned on the use of Charm. I'd have to get out of there as quickly as possible. I didn't want to be complicit in my aunt's deceit one minute longer than necessary.

I waited impatiently while the bartender poured the two drinks and set them down. "Thanks!" I said, snatching up the tray as soon as she was done.

It took all my self-control not to run. I'd draw attention to myself if I tripped and spilled the drinks. The red-faced man had finished up the current round of dice and was now cheering on a friend. "Here you go," I said, and produced the cheongju with a flourish.

He tipped without looking at me. I almost choked when I saw the large denomination of currency he'd laid in my hand. I stammered my thanks and made my way toward the high-stakes room, not looking left or right. If no one made eye contact with me, then hopefully I could avoid having to serve any more drinks before I reached my target. Behind me I heard a couple of people calling out, but I ignored them and walked faster. I snuck a glance toward Nari, who was chatting with a man dressed in extremely expensive clothes. I hoped the conversation would keep her distracted for a while.

My luck held. A woman looked up as I entered the back room, but she didn't summon me over. Gamblers were playing at two of the high-stakes tables. One of the games I recognized as a flower cards variant; the other I hadn't seen before.

I spotted Captain Hye straight off. She was the only one in a red shirt, and she had a spacer's pallor. She frowned at her hand of cards, and sweat stains showed at her back. I had to get her out of there.

"Captain Hye," I said in my sweetest voice, "here's that gukhwaju you ordered." I exerted just a bit of Charm, not only in the captain's direction but also toward the other players around the table, to convince them it was likely she had asked for a drink while they were distracted.

Captain Hye looked puzzled. Then her eyes turned calculating and she reached out greedily for the cup. I watched as she took a big gulp. I hoped I could get her out of here before her luck worsened.

The captain drew a card, frowned again, and sighed deeply. Apparently she was having trouble making sets, which is how one scored points. She completed her turn and leaned back, shaking her head.

I glanced around for an excuse to linger and spotted some empty glasses to collect. As I passed Hye, I whispered in her ear, "I was wondering if I might have a word with you."

She blanched. "I'm not ready to go yet," she snapped. "Just one more game."

Her companions laughed. "They're onto you, eh?" one of them said with a smirk.

"Shut up," the captain hissed.

I cursed silently. Sure, the wine had given me a great excuse to seek her out, but it was also interfering with her playing, and she was too preoccupied to talk to me. I should have served her a glass of water instead. I didn't know how long the effect of the magic wine would last, either.

Hye's agitation, and her friend's comment, told me that she was already deeply in debt to the house. That gave me an idea, although I felt bad about taking advantage of her. But it would get me off Jinju and her away from Nari, so we'd both win, right?

"I have an offer for you," I said into her ear as I glanced at the doorway. Yong was approaching. He must have noticed that I was chatting for too long instead of serving drinks. I had to make this quick. "A colleague of Nari's needs passage off-planet. If you do that for her, Nari will cancel your debt. Just don't let on to your friends."

For a moment, Captain Hye looked stunned by her sudden change in fortune.

"What is it?" her snide friend asked. "You getting pointers from the staff now?"

That brought her back to her senses. "Mind your own business," she quipped. Then, to me, she murmured, "I'll do it."

"Excellent," I said. "You can finish up this game." It was hard to disguise my worry that she'd get sucked into playing all night. "Your passenger will be waiting at your ship in an hour and a half." That should give me enough time to reach the *Red Azalea* after I snuck out of this place.

"Done, done," Captain Hye said. Eyes gleaming with greed, she added, "Get me more gukhwaju." She hadn't even finished her glass yet, but it gave me a reason to head back to the bar.

On the way, I passed Yong. He turned and accompanied me out of the room, whispering sternly, "You should stick to your duties instead of getting friendly with the clients."

"Sorry," I said in a suitably chastened voice. To allay any suspicion, I added, "Those high-stakes players really know how to tip."

He frowned and shook his head. "You're not going to last here long if you give any customer preferential treatment. Nari doesn't like that."

I nodded obediently. "Understood."

Yong pointed to a table where a rotund man was signaling for a drink and said, "Don't keep him waiting," before stalking off.

Just then, I heard a commotion behind

me. Two of the bouncers strode quickly past, toward the high-stakes room I'd just left. I wondered what was going on, but I couldn't investigate — I had to fulfill the man's request for rice wine.

I kept my ears pricked — metaphorically, anyway — while hurrying to the bar. On my way back to the table, I saw that Hye was being escorted to Nari's office.

"I told you, Nari and I have an agreement!" the captain slurred in a loud voice. Was she drunk already?

I intentionally dropped the glass of rice wine I was carrying and bent over to pick it up so she wouldn't spot me.

"Just let me finish my —" Hye was saying as the office door closed behind her.

It looked like she wouldn't be going anywhere tonight.

I waited until one of the other bouncers passed by, then popped up and looked at him with a worried frown. "Is something wrong?" I asked innocently.

"Hye finally bet too much," the bouncer said with a headshake. "Must have gotten overconfident — or desperate.

None of your business, though." He scowled at me, and I hurried over to a table, not coincidentally one close to the parlor's entrance.

Hye would rat me out to Nari any minute now. Time for me to make my exit.

I just had to hope the *Red Azalea* had other crew on board, guarding the ship while their captain was "busy." As long as someone else could pilot it, I still had a chance of getting off-planet.

Then an even worse thought came to me. *Gamble her ship away . . .* Yong had said earlier. What if Nari took the ship as payment for Hye's losses?

I had to get to the *Red Azalea,* fast.

I stepped into the restroom and let my Charm unravel. No more silk, pearls, and gold jewelry for me. I reverted to "Bora" form but gave myself spacer's clothes and a flatter, more average face. I checked the mirror to make sure I looked unmemorable in every way.

Heart pounding, I sauntered out of the restroom, hoping no one would notice me . . .

. . . and walked smack into Yong. He grunted but didn't budge an inch.

"Sorry!" I said automatically. I looked down at the floor as I quickly moved out of his way.

He stepped into my path and took my arm. "No, *I'm* the one who should apologize, miss," he said. "Looks like you're in a hurry."

"Yes," I said, my head still bent. "I'm running late. Must go."

"That's right," he said. "You must go." Then, in a much lower voice, he added, "Go while you can, Min."

I stared up at him. He'd seen through my Charm!

"Fox or no fox," he whispered, "you're too young for this life. I'll escort you out, while Nari is distracted." He pointed toward the parlor entrance with his chin.

When we passed the bouncer at the door, Yong said to me loudly, "And don't let me catch you in here ever again!" Then he made a show of pushing me outside.

The other bouncer didn't even blink. He'd seen it all before.

I couldn't exactly say thank you to Yong while he was throwing me out, but I did flash a grateful smile at him.

As I hurried down the street, the music from Nari's dwindled behind me. It sounded harsh and jangly, and I couldn't believe I'd ever liked it.

I thought of the graffiti I'd seen earlier and wished I had time to add AND DON'T DRINK THE WINE.

Following the spaceport directions I'd memorized previously, I broke into a run toward the *Red Azalea*'s dock. I now had some tip money in my pouch, but I had no idea whether it would be enough to buy my way on board. Too bad I hadn't been able to squeeze a little more out of "Aunt Nari."

A ship rose up before me in silhouette against the night sky, a squat freighter with stubby wings. I bet it was barely capable of atmospheric flight. Under the harsh overhead lights, it looked even more battered than its identifying photo in the kiosk. Still, I sighed in relief when I spotted the painted red azalea on its wing. I was that much closer to getting

111

off Jinju and finding my brother.
Now I just needed a pilot.

EIGHT

It wasn't difficult to convince the dock agent that I was on the *Red Azalea*'s passenger list. By the time she double-checked the roster at my urging, my name had magically appeared on her data-slate. The illusion wouldn't last long, but then, I didn't plan to be around here long, either. With any luck.

I sprinted the rest of the way to the *Red Azalea,* looking around nervously, convinced that one of Nari's goons would nab me any second. She must have noticed by now that I'd skipped out.

Once I reached the starship, I shouted up at it, "Captain Hye's in trouble!" When no response came, I banged on the closed hatch with my fist. Ouch! But, if there was a crew inside, I couldn't see any other way of getting their attention. "Is anyone in there?"

There was a loud, staticky noise; then a deep voice buzzed out of a speaker I couldn't locate. "We're busy. Go away."

"Captain Hye has been detained by Nari for racking up too much debt," I said. "Nari is threatening to claim her ship."

I heard some words that Mom wouldn't have approved of. "I knew it! If you have anything to do with that parasite Nari —"

I thought furiously. "No! Captain Hye sent me to tell you because she couldn't get away herself! She was being too closely watched. If there's a pilot on board, you need to get out of here before Nari shows up. She's got some kind of deal with the spaceport authorities. If you don't go *now* —"

More choice words came from the

speaker. I filed them away for future use so I could sound like a spacer.

"Captain Hye had more instructions," I said. "I'll tell you if you let me up. It's best that we speak privately."

Once inside the ship, I'd be a step closer to my goal. Maybe I could use Charm on the crew to convince them to take me along.

There were a few moments of silence, then a grudging sigh. "All right. You'd think Hye would know enough to stay out of trouble, but no. . . ."

The hatch lowered, forming a ramp. I scrambled up, banging my head on the rim of the opening in the process. A short, heavyset man awaited me. He looked much less like a stereotypical spacer than Captain Hye did, although if he was watching the ship, he had to be one. Instead of a sleek uniform, silken robes drooped from his shoulders and trailed onto the deck. He must have been pretty confident of the *Red Azalea*'s artificial gravity to wear an outfit like that.

"Nari never changes," the man muttered. "But taking a spacer's ship? That's low. Especially when all she ever does is sell them to scrappers."

"You can't let her do that!" I blurted. I needed this ship!

"I don't intend to," the man said, looking at me quizzically. "So, you were going to give me further instructions from the captain?"

I gulped and used Charm to appear confident. "She, um . . . she said to go to Gingko Station as originally planned." That was the starbase near the Ghost Sector. If the *Pale Lightning* was in the area, there was a chance I could track down my brother from there. "Besides, she owes me. She promised me passage there in exchange for getting word to you."

Hye *did* owe me — for the surprise drink, if nothing else. The man continued to watch me with raised eyebrows, so I kept talking. "Nari's minions were watching Captain Hye too closely — I was the best she could do. Besides" — and this part was true, too — "I also need to get away from Nari."

"Join the club," the man said grimly. He spoke what sounded like code words into a wrist unit, then said to me, "I just told the crew to stay wherever they are on Jinju and keep out of sight until this blows over. I can't wait for those three to get back here, not if the ship's at stake. I doubt Nari will go after them if they lie low — her beef's with Hye." His mouth crimped and he grumbled, "It figures this would happen when I'm the one left babysitting the ship."

"So we can take off now?" I asked hopefully.

"You a good copilot, by any chance?"

I was crestfallen. "No," I admitted. It would be dangerous for me to try to fake that.

My answer didn't faze him. He took the pilot's chair and pointed at the seat next to him anyway. "Dirtsider, huh? Well, some of the ship is automated, but you might as well learn the basics. Strap yourself in. I'm Byung-Ho, by the way. You?"

I stuck with my cousin's name. "Bora," I said as I fiddled with the strap.

"Okay, Bora. First, check the life-support and engine panels. With a cranky old ship like this, there are signs of stress to look for, but we'll keep it simple for now." Byung-Ho pointed at the various illuminated digital graphs on the display panel as he spoke. "Basic principle is, you want to make sure these indicators stay in the blue zone. *Blue for heaven,* as they say. If any of them dip toward red, something's wrong, and you'll need to consult the diagnostics. The computer will guide you."

It sounded doable, although I was sure he was glossing over the details. I studied the graphs carefully. After all, I realized with a sickening feeling, if anything happened to Byung-Ho, I'd be on my own. I liked working with machines, but I'd never flown before, and this system was new to me.

"Now," Byung-Ho said, his hand hovering over a large gold button, "we power up the ship's maneuver drive. This will get us past the atmosphere until we're far enough from local gravity to Gate out." He hit the button.

A red light came on above a completely different button. "Did something break?" I asked.

He laughed. "No, but be prepared for some bluster." He pressed the button under the red light.

A loud, heavily accented voice squawked from the communications system. "*Red Azalea,* you are not cleared for takeoff. What is going on?"

"Aren't you going to say something?" I whispered to Byung-Ho.

He ignored the annoyed voice on the comm system and answered me instead. "There's nothing to say. I'm not going to hang around here and let Nari's thugs take the ship. Captain Hye's good at talking her way out of trouble. She can take care of herself until I come back for her."

The loud voice spoke over Byung-Ho. "*Red Azalea,* power down your maneuver drive. You cannot depart until you have filed the proper documents. If you do not comply within one minute, you will be subject to fines under Regulation 138.8.2."

"I wish them luck collecting *that,*" Byung-Ho said with morbid cheer. "I locked our account as soon as I noticed Hye starting to dip into it." With that, he entered a set of coordinates, then settled his hand on a complicated-looking joy-stick.

"But won't they — ?"

Before I could finish my question, I was flung back into my seat as the ship tilted up and blasted toward the sky. The pressure increased, and I saw spots before my eyes. The loud voice threatened us with more fines.

We pierced a murky veil of clouds and angled ever upward. I could no longer hear what the voice was saying because of the roaring in my ears. My stomach dropped. My seat — no, the whole flight deck — vibrated, which I hoped was normal. It didn't seem to bother Byung-Ho.

After a few dizzying minutes, the acceleration eased and we were soaring through space. The sky bloomed black before us, lit by the pinprick fire of stars. My breath caught at the unexpected beauty of it, as well as the knowledge that, for the first time in my life, I was free.

"We got away without even a warning shot?" I asked as soon as I'd recovered from the takeoff.

"You've been watching too many holo shows," Byung-Ho said with a dry chuckle. "If they shot down everyone who had to leave a step ahead of the authorities, no one would bother touching down on a backwater planet like Jinju. I made sure we were paid up this morning. They save their defenses for real threats."

The voice from the spaceport was still lecturing us. Byung-Ho reached over and flicked off the communications channel. "There," he said. "The navigation system will alert us if we're about to smash into anything, so there's no need to endure that."

I couldn't believe how quickly we'd catapulted beyond the thin veil of Jinju's atmosphere. We swerved past a moon, and in the distance I could see one of the system's swirly green-blue gas giants as a distant disc. In reality, I knew it was many times larger than Jinju.

"Now tell me," Byung-Ho said, "why are you going to the Ghost Sector? Do you have gambling problems of your own?"

I glared at him.

"If it's not that, it's gotta be something just as seedy," Byung-Ho said, making a placating gesture with one hand. "Like looking for treasure, or smuggling for mercenaries, or dealing with traders from the Jeweled Worlds. I've heard it all."

"I would never!" I said indignantly. Raiders from the Jeweled Worlds attacked the Thousand Worlds from time to time, but that didn't stop less scrupulous people on our side of the border from illegally buying goods from their traders.

"Whatever it is, you must be one tough cookie. Either that, or desperate."

He was right about the desperate part. I didn't dare tell him about my brother, though. I had no idea what kind of trouble Jun had gotten himself into, or whether he really did know where the Dragon Pearl was. I definitely didn't want to lead a stranger to such an important artifact, even if that stranger happened to be helping me.

"It's for my family," I told him, because I had to say something. "We're poor, and I want to do my part to help." I said it like I was ashamed of it, which grated on me — maybe because it was true and I *was* ashamed of it. I'd finally gotten away from home — Jinju was dwindling to a speck behind us — but the memories of omnipresent dust and threadbare clothes and worn-out furniture would always haunt me.

Byung-Ho nodded. "Well, you're not the first adventurer to go into space seeking her fortune," he said. "And the *Red Azalea* has friends at Gingko Station. There's no direct Gate there, but the fastest route will take us there in two hops."

Even steaders like me knew the basics of space travel. In order to cross vast distances, you had to use a special stardrive to punch your way through a local Gate. Each Gate only connected to a handful of nearby ones, so voyages could involve a lot of hopping. Plus, starships had to be recharged between jumps. For this reason, spaceports had sprung up near Gates to cater to travelers. Jinju's Gate didn't see much activity; right then I was grateful it existed at all.

"I'm warming up the jump drive," Byung-Ho added.

"How bad will it be?" I'd heard stories

123

of what it was like to pass through a Gate. Some people got sick. Others were tormented by dreams that were reputed to be half prophecy, half nightmare. Seasoned spacers got used to the visions over time, though they tended to become superstitious about them. Certain Gates had reputations for causing more unpleasant experiences than others. Jinju's Gate was supposedly one of the worst.

Byung-Ho shook his head. "You'll see soon enough. Try not to be too loud, if you're a screamer."

"I *never* scream."

He wasn't paying attention. "Drive's ready." He pointed to the blue flashing indicator on his panel.

I couldn't shake the feeling that the battered freighter was eager to make the jump. In the old stories, older even than the Thousand Worlds, a humble carp could become a dragon by leaping up a waterfall. If a fish could dream of upgrading, I didn't see why a starship couldn't, in its secret crystal heart, have ambitions, too.

"Here goes nothing," Byung-Ho said. He pulled a lever and the ship surged forward.

At first I thought nothing had happened. The ship seemed to freeze in place. Then a great swirl of shimmering rainbow colors, like on an abalone shell, spun around us. I closed my eyes, but the colors followed me, as though they had seeped behind my eyelids and pressed their patterns into my brain. If I concentrated on the patterns, I could almost read them.

I saw faces, indistinct at first. Then one of them drifted close, smiling sadly. I gasped as I recognized it from the silk portrait I'd lost earlier that day. Dad! He opened his mouth as if to say something, and I leaned forward, eager to hear it.

Instead, his mouth gaped wider and wider, and his teeth grew longer and sharper, like knives. His face sprouted fur with orange and black stripes, and his brown eyes turned amber. He'd morphed into a tiger. He lunged for me with a snarl.

I shrieked and jerked back.

"Bora?" Byung-Ho said.

So much for my not being a screamer.

I opened my eyes and stared out the viewport. "I'm okay," I said weakly. No trace remained of the gorgeous swirling colors, or my father's face, or the ferocious tiger. Instead, there was only a dead staticky gray. *Just nerves,* I told myself. Still, I couldn't help wondering if the vision had been a warning.

While we were Gating, we wouldn't be able to exit the ship, not even to make repairs. Gate space was harmful to living creatures. I hoped the *Red Azalea* wouldn't choose now to break down. There had to be repair robots on board in case of an emergency, but I didn't want to have to find out.

"Bora!"

Byung-Ho had to say it twice to break me out of the trance, because I still wasn't used to going by my cousin's name. "Good," he said roughly. "I was starting to worry."

"About what?"

"Some people get lost in the patterns," Byung-Ho said, "and they don't come back. It's not as common as the rumors claim, but it's worst the first time you enter a Gate. You looked like you were drifting away."

I shivered, remembering the tiger about to bite my head off.

"Well," Byung-Ho said, "we'll be recharging for a while now. While we wait, let me show you around the rest of the ship. Maybe you can make yourself useful."

I should have known that even in space I couldn't escape chores.

I'd already seen the cockpit. The *Red Azalea* also had a tiny office in the ship's midsection, which Byung-Ho said I wasn't supposed to enter; cramped living quarters with bunks for four; a kitchen and a dining area; an engine room, which I also wasn't supposed to mess with; and a cargo hold in the rear.

The stacks of crates in the hold made me curious. Byung-Ho hustled me past them and set me to scrubbing the deck in the dining area. I stifled a groan, especially since some of the marks on the floor and walls weren't dirt. They looked like blaster burns, and I was pretty sure no amount of elbow grease would get rid of those. On the other hand, I wasn't going to volunteer to paint the whole deck, either.

I scrubbed at the scuffs and stains for an hour, until my back hurt so much I couldn't take it anymore. Byung-Ho didn't check on me the entire time. At home, someone would have nagged me about doing a better job. It was nice not to have to live up to my relatives' standards anymore. But I would have preferred to spend the hour learning how to operate the ship. I guessed Byung-Ho didn't want me to know too much.

I returned to the cockpit. Byung-Ho reclined in his chair, snoring peacefully. I slid into the copilot's seat and took the opportunity to explore the help system. I knew I couldn't master everything overnight, but I had to start somewhere.

In the middle of puzzling out the engine-status symbols, I, too, slid asleep. I couldn't help it. I was used to working long hours, but today had been longer than most, and it had included way too much excitement.

I dreamed of dragons snaking from red to blue and back again, of worlds spinning topsy-turvy in the deep black of space, and of the Gate swallowing us in a swirl of pearly colors. The dragons led me down to a planet wreathed in white mist, making me shiver even in the depths of sleep. White was the color of death and mourning. I glimpsed Jun at a cliff's edge in the distance, staring up at the sky, and I ran after him, shouting his name. He turned and waved, but I never managed to get any closer. . . .

Despite my disconcerting dreams, it would have been a refreshing sleep if I hadn't woken to an alarm so loud it gave me an instant headache. "Go away, Bora," I mumbled, forgetting that *I* was supposed to be Bora.

My annoying cousin would have been an improvement over reality. "Wake up!" Byung-Ho said, sounding worried. "The first hop went without any problems, and we've just completed the second one."

"Isn't that a good thing?" I said. My strange dreams must have resulted from our entry into the second Gate.

He gestured at the sensor panel, which showed four rapidly approaching red dots. "Not likely. We're stuck in-system until we're charged up, and unless I'm mistaken, those are mercenaries. I hope you spent some time familiarizing yourself with the weapons system."

"I couldn't, because —" My retort died in my throat when Byung-Ho suddenly jerked a lever and the *Red Azalea* shuddered to one side to begin evasive maneuvers.

"Too late now," Byung-Ho said. "You're going to have to learn on the fly."

NINE

Byung-Ho was busy with the ship's controls after that. "At least they're shooting to disable, not destroy," he muttered. Before I could breathe a sigh of relief, he added, "Don't get too comfortable. They'll zap us both if they board."

My stomach clenched and my palms felt clammy. Four ships against one were bad odds if they caught us unable to Gate. Even I knew that. And the *Red Azalea* wasn't exactly a battle cruiser. The fact that the enemy fought as a quartet was a bad omen as well. Four was an unlucky number — it signified death. Mercenaries went around in groups of four to strike terror into their victims.

"Can we signal for help?" I asked.

"Already done," Byung-Ho said. "There ought to be a battle cruiser on patrol near this Gate. I just hope they're not busy elsewhere."

After scanning the onboard computer's help guide, I located the cockpit controls for the *Red Azalea*'s defense systems. They had to be better than nothing. As far as I could tell, I would just need to flip some levers, tell the system which target to prioritize, and let the computer do the calculations.

"This isn't so bad," I said to Byung-Ho when our defenses took out an incoming missile in a bright flash. Even though I knew better than to expect to hear anything in space, it was mildly disappointing when the explosion was silent. The scan system only emitted a sad little blip to mark the occasion.

"Check our ammunition level," Byung-Ho said tersely. "The *Red Azalea* has upgraded defenses, but mercs are faster and meaner. They can afford to wait for us to exhaust our antimissiles. At least they're not likely to destroy us — a bucket like this is worth more to them intact."

So we were sitting ducks. My hands clenched and unclenched as I searched the dash for a display that would tell me how much ammo we had left. Found it! To my dismay, the bar was draining toward empty at a frightening rate.

"Don't we have any shields?" I asked.

Byung-Ho hesitated. "We do, and they're on, but they've tended to glitch ever since — Yikes!" He shoved a lever to one side. Dizziness overcame me as the *Red Azalea* veered away from the latest burst of fire. The ship's maneuvers got worse before they got better. I wondered if I'd ever get used to the sudden accelerations.

"Oh no!" I cried as a burst of violet fire hit us in the side. Several alarms went off, deafening me. Five different emergency status screens came up on my control panels. I inspected the reddest one, which claimed that our life support had been hit.

Byung-Ho swore when he saw that. "We'll have to do some quick repairs. Go back to the engine room and get the computer to help you put it into Emergency Mode. The automated diagnostics will take it from there. I'll tell the system to give you access."

At least the name "Emergency Mode" would be easy to remember.

"And use the handholds, or you might get knocked about. Good luck!" After that he had no more attention to spare for me.

I gulped as I unharnessed myself from the safety restraints. I didn't know what scared me more: the *Red Azalea* getting blown up, or our being boarded. If only I could will the ship to fly faster, away from the mercenaries' clutches.

My head swam. Our artificial gravity was fluctuating. And I'd magicked up regular boots, not magnetic ones, out of habit. While I could have fixed that, I didn't have time to get used to walking in magnetic boots.

I caught one of the handhold straps just before the ship moved again, but still got bruised when I was abruptly flung into a wall. I concentrated on gripping the handholds and placing my toes in the footholds so I didn't get knocked around some more. My clothes were drenched in sweat by the time I made it through the ship's midsection to the engine room at the back.

A hatch separated the room from the rest of the ship. Behind it I could hear an almost musical thrumming. I pressed my palm against the keypad, worrying that it wouldn't accept me. It would be ironic if I couldn't do my job because I couldn't get in. Byung-Ho had been as good as his word, however. After a hair-raising shriek of metal on metal, the door slid open.

The engine room was the loudest part of the ship, although not in an unpleasant way. I almost released a handhold because I was gawking at the fantastic arrays of crystals and the rows of glowing display screens like the ones in the cockpit, only more elaborate. The crystals gave the ship the ability to open Gates and protect itself while in Gate space. The more mundane fusion reactor powered the maneuver drive and everything else on the ship, including life support.

"Computer," I said, "how do I put the engine in Emergency Mode?" I clung like a burr to the side of the room as the ship rolled. I was starting to get used to the sudden maneuvers, though that wasn't exactly a good thing.

One of the panels lit up. "Damage has occurred to the life-support, shield, and navigation subsystems," the computer said in a friendly voice. "Which subsystem would you like to prioritize?"

"Life support, please," I said.

Another alarm joined the ones that were already going off. I could barely hear myself think. "Uh — could you make those less loud?"

"I'm sorry," the computer said, still in that friendly voice, "alarm volume parameters are fixed according to Thousand Worlds starship standards by the Fifth Accord of —"

I was sorry I'd asked. "Never mind," I said. "Just tell me how to deal with life support."

The computer jabbered a list of procedures to follow. I had to tell it to slow down and give me an overview of what went where. I hated the delay, but randomly pressing buttons wouldn't be useful, either.

Captain Hye, or Byung-Ho, or whoever normally dealt with the engine, had stowed a toolkit in a side compartment. I opened the kit eagerly and hooked it to my belt loops so the tools wouldn't drift away or, worse, rain down on my head during maneuvers. Most of the gadgets looked familiar. For the first time, I was grateful for all the things around home that had always needed fixing.

I narrowed down the problem to one regulator that had been damaged by the mercs' fire. The details were a little murky, but the more I tinkered with the regulator, the more I realized the basics weren't so different from those of the ecofilter system we used in our dome back on Jinju. Given how often it had broken down, I'd had a lot of experience with it. Maybe I wasn't a qualified technician, but I knew a few tricks.

I wondered if we'd ever escape the mercenaries. My work settled into a nerve-racking routine. Every time something broke, I'd follow the computer's instructions, tunneling down through menus, rerouting damaged functions to backups, and so on, all the while hanging on so I wouldn't get smashed when the ship jerked. My fingers ached. Still, I couldn't afford to relax.

The comm system crackled to life. "Good work," Byung-Ho said over the speaker.

I appreciated the compliment, but I wasn't under any illusions that I'd fixed everything wrong with the *Red Azalea.* I'd just bought us a little more time. Whether it would be enough for help to reach us was another question.

"What would have happened if I hadn't?" I asked Byung-Ho.

He didn't answer, and I gulped. Had something gone wrong in the cockpit? Were we now drifting aimlessly, easy pickings for the mercs?

It didn't take me long to make my way back to the front of the ship now that I'd gotten used to moving around in flickering gravity.

Byung-Ho waved a hand when he heard

my approach and sat up straighter. He kept his attention fixed on the screens. I retook the copilot's seat.

"I managed to turn on the shields again after they glitched," Byung-Ho said. "That'll keep the mercs at bay for a while." He turned to look at me. "Seriously, good job back there. You sure you've never been on a ship before?"

I glowed at his praise, but we didn't have time for chitchat. With my fox's nose I couldn't escape the rank stench of his nervous sweat. He was trying to mask his fear — for my sake.

"Has anyone responded to our call for help?" I asked. Communications frequencies were much slower than travel via Gate and only reliable for reaching people in the immediate vicinity, which was why long-distance messages were conveyed by courier. The local space station should have heard us and relayed the distress signal, but it was an open question as to whether anyone in a position to help had detected it.

"No luck yet," Byung-Ho said.

That "no luck" sealed our fate.

Another blast took the *Red Azalea* from

behind, according to the displays. The shield strength indicators flickered red, then plummeted almost all the way down to zero. Through the viewport I glimpsed sparks flowering out ahead of us. If our situation hadn't been so desperate, it would have looked beautiful.

The attack itself had made no noise, but then we heard a *bang* from the engine room. My stomach dropped when the musical thrumming of the engines sputtered, then stopped. "What was that?" I whispered.

Byung-Ho blanched. He didn't hide the truth from me, which I appreciated. "Maneuver drive's down. We're just drifting now, thanks to inertia. They've herded us away from the Gate, and they'll be boarding us next." He triggered a command, and the hatch to the ship's midsection slid closed. It would give us a little time. "Quick — do you know how to use a blaster?"

I hesitated at the thought of killing. On the other hand, I didn't want to die.

"Point and shoot — that's all there is to it," Byung-Ho said. "With our luck, they'll have personal shields, too. But I refuse to roll over for them."

He unholstered a blaster from his belt and handed it to me. "That toggle is the safety. Point it *away* from me when you flick it off — yes, like that. I keep it fully charged, but in a firefight you may run out of juice."

"What about you?" I demanded. After all, he'd just given me his gun.

"Don't worry about me," Byung-Ho said. "I'll use the plasma rifle. It's temperamental. A beginner's better off with a simple blaster."

He retrieved the rifle from a compartment behind the pilot's seat. It looked so large and bulky that I doubted I could have wielded it well, temperamental or not. I was strong for my usual size, thanks to all the menial labor I did, but I wasn't going to win any wrestling matches. I had good reflexes, though. Maybe that would help.

While we waited for the intruders to arrive, I glanced out the viewport, suddenly resenting the distant stars and the colorful smudges of nebulae. We continued to float along peacefully. The mercs, knowing we couldn't escape, had stopped

firing. Byung-Ho had guessed right —
they'd get more valuable scrap out of the
Red Azalea if they didn't shoot it up too
much.

Then the ship shuddered, as though
something had bumped into us at low
speed.

"That'll be the boarding party,"
Byung-Ho said. "Crouch behind the seat
and get ready to fire if you see anything."

My sharp ears picked up the sounds of
the mercs aligning one of their ships with
ours and forcing the hatch open, then
the whine of the airlock cycling. I tensed
up. How many of them would come for
us?

"Stay steady," Byung-Ho said. "All that
matters now is taking them out and hoping that friends arrive soon."

He didn't have to tell me that the situation looked dire. On the other hand, I
wasn't going to let my quest end here,
not if I could help it. My palms started
to sweat, and I shifted my grip on the
blaster.

The mercs were eerily quiet. In the
holo shows, boarding parties always

yelled threats or fired randomly ahead of themselves. I hadn't expected this total silence.

That didn't last long. The smell of ash and sparks and scorched metal caused me to wrinkle my nose, and I peeked out from behind my seat. I heard a *thump,* then stared in fascinated horror as the mercs started torching their way through the hatch. A cutout panel fell forward with a *clang,* showering white-hot sparks.

I spotted a flicker, a shadow edging into the *Red Azalea*'s kitchen. Without thinking, I brought up the muzzle of the blaster and squeezed the trigger. The blast shot out, a straight line of fiery red. Someone with a deep voice snapped orders in jargon I didn't understand.

The shadow pulled back. Byung-Ho grabbed my arm and dragged me down behind the copilot's seat. Great timing: A bolt sizzled over me, where my head had been just a second earlier. My heart jumped up into my mouth as I realized how close I'd come to being barbecued.

While I could shape-shift into an inanimate object to fool the mercenaries into thinking Byung-Ho was alone, I didn't want to abandon him mid-combat. It would only delay the inevitable anyway. Being stuck in the shape of a crate or wrench wouldn't get me where I needed to go.

Two more bolts flew over my head. I peeked around the side of the seat and fired once at the first shadowy figure I saw. I heard a yelp. Five more people joined the first. Hastily, I withdrew behind cover again before the hostiles could roast me.

Byung-Ho's rifle bolts crackled down the length of the *Red Azalea,* throwing up sparks whenever they hit home. He was trying to force the intruders back. There were more of them than there were of us, though, and we were pinned in the cockpit.

Still quiet, the mercs advanced. I wished they would yell curses or threats, mock us, anything. In their sleek jointed suits, they scarcely looked human. One of them darted out and flung a small spiky canister at us: a stun grenade.

Byung-Ho yelled, "Duck!" He shoved me to the side. I hit a wall and yelped as all the breath was knocked out of my lungs.

Seconds later, the grenade went off. The flash blinded me, but I remained standing. I fired wildly, again and again, as I heard Byung-Ho's bubbling scream.

This is it, I thought. *I'm going to die in the middle of nowhere and Mom will never find out what happened to me.*

I heard a noise. I aimed at the source of the sound and fired, only to hear the blaster give a discouraging whine. It had run out of power.

Still, I'd hit someone. I heard a curse followed by a dark chuckle. *I'm done for,* I thought, and then I slid out of consciousness.

TEN

I woke in an unfamiliar, well-lit room. I smelled antiseptic and herbs: a medical bay. Someone had transferred me off the *Red Azalea* and placed me on a cot. I shoved off the blanket and sat up, then winced as all my muscles protested. My skin itched as though I'd gotten sunburned all over. And then I remembered the grenade. Oh no, what had happened to Byung-Ho?

"You're not dead," a hollow voice remarked.

I almost leaped out of my skin. I hadn't realized there was someone standing next to my bed. It was a boy, maybe fifteen years old, in the dark blue uniform of a Space Forces cadet. His name tag said BAE JANG. Three things about him were off, though. He had no smell, for one. Also, his face flickered as though it were a kaleidoscope of shadows. Finally — the real clue — his hair hung in long, disheveled strands around his face.

My injuries might have affected my sense of smell. The shadows might have been a trick of the light. The hair, though — no one in the Space Forces would have hair that long.

Not unless they were a ghost. In the tales, they always had hair like that.

I scooted back on the pallet, heart thumping in my chest. I remembered the stories my aunties had told me. Ghosts weren't necessarily unfriendly, but many of them became vengeful over time, especially if the unfinished business that bound them to the world of the living went unresolved for a long period.

"What do you want?" I asked in a low voice, wary. Curtains shielded the rest of the medical bay from my view, but I could hear doctors and nurses speaking authoritatively.

"It was such a stupid way to die . . ." Jang said, almost as if he hadn't heard me. "I got winged by a merc just as my personal shield failed. No one had seen him hiding." He smiled sardonically. "Faulty equipment, just my luck."

"I'm sorry," I said, still cautious. Would fox magic work on a ghost? Shamans exorcised ghosts as part of their job, but I didn't have their powers. And I wasn't sure if trying to Charm Jang would only make him mad. On the other hand, since he had appeared to me, I assumed he wanted to make a bargain. I remembered that much from my aunties' lore. "Do you need something from me?"

His smile twisted. "We were saving you and your friend when I got injured. The physician tried his best, but I died just half an hour ago."

My heart fluttered. "We didn't mean to get you killed." *But we wouldn't have been there if it weren't for me,* I thought guiltily.

"You owe me," Jang said. "The mercenaries are all dead, but my training cruise is over."

I thought fast. "What ship are we on?"

"The *Pale Lightning*," he said.

The *Pale Lightning*! What were the odds that I would end up on Jun's ship?

But how had I gotten here? Jang and the rest of his team had boarded the *Red Azalea* after the mercs, I guessed. I didn't remember that at all. I had passed out by then.

I had to take advantage of this stroke of luck. "We can help each other. I need a reason to stay on this ship" — no need to go into detail, as I doubted a ghost would care — "and I can do that if I pose as you. I can continue your training cruise *for* you."

Jang's eyebrows shot up. "How are you going to manage *that*?"

I cast my eyes down. "I'm a fox." It felt odd admitting it to a stranger.

"Huh," he said after a moment, looking thoughtful. "Never heard of a fox in the Space Forces, but why not?"

Interesting reaction. Maybe ghosts were

more open-minded than the living.

"There are a few supernaturals on this ship," Jang added. "The captain tolerates them. But most of the crew is human."

If Jang had never heard of a fox cadet, then Jun must have kept his true nature hidden from everyone. That figured — he'd always been the more obedient of the two of us. While the captain was open to some kinds of supernatural cadets, I bet that he, like most folks, didn't trust fox spirits.

"It is true that your kind can shape-shift?" Jang asked.

I demonstrated by growing my hair, then returning it to its original length. He grinned appreciatively.

"I really am sorry about what happened to you," I added, biting my lip. I'd never dreamed that by hitching a ride on the *Red Azalea* I would cause someone's death.

"It was over quickly," he said without emotion. "The mercs are really the ones to blame." Then: "I accept your proposal. You can be me. And while you're at it, you can find out more about the mercenaries who killed me."

"It's a deal," I said, wondering if I was being reckless.

"Swear it on the bones of your ancestors," Jang said.

I gulped. That wasn't an oath I could wriggle my way out of. Also, I worried that taking on this detective work would distract me from my real quest of finding Jun. But I needed Jang's help. "I swear on the bones of my ancestors," I said, and shivered.

"All right," Jang said, apparently satisfied.

"By the way," I started, "did you know a cadet named — ?"

"Someone is approaching," Jang said, cutting me off. "You'd better be convincing." With that, he faded out, leaving a wintry chill in the air.

I heard footsteps. Focusing on my memory of how Jang looked, I shifted into his shape. The face involved some guesswork, because the shadows had obscured some of the angles, but at least I had a pretty good idea of what a regulation haircut looked like from news clips

151

of Space Forces soldiers in parades.

Before I had time to lie back down on the pallet, a curtain drew aside to reveal a tall woman in a slightly more elaborate version of the uniform Jang had worn, carrying a battered slate and stylus. She had short-cropped hair streaked with white and the demeanor of a bemused crane. From her round gold lapel pin with the symbol for longevity, I guessed she was the ship's physician. I hit her with a dose of Charm to muddle her wits so I could convince her that Jang had survived and "Bora" hadn't.

"Water?" I croaked, figuring that was safe. My new lower voice sounded odd in my ears, but I would just have to get used to it.

"Not until I've checked you over, Cadet," the woman said. Her brow furrowed as she looked at my face, and I threw more Charm at her. She shook her head and pushed me down onto the cot. Her fingers traced lines in the air above me. I didn't know much beyond first aid, but my late grandmother used to talk about the meridians, the body's lines of energy, from which you could diagnose injuries and illnesses. Just as veins and arteries carried blood throughout the body, the meridians carried life force. Any damage to the mind or body would be reflected in its flow.

I stared up at her, trying not to show how intimidated I felt. As a doctor, she knew the human body inside and out, and there I was, a fox impersonating a human of the opposite sex.

"Good thing my shield took the worst of the hit," I said so the physician had a plausible story for my survival. "By the way, what happened to the pilot of that freighter?" I asked, recalling Byung-Ho's last scream.

"Him? He's still in one of the healing pods," she said, "but he'll make it."

I breathed easier and pushed with Charm again. "Too bad the girl didn't." I'd never used this much magic on a single person before. I'd expected it to be harder. My body ached, but that was from the grenade blast.

How much pain was Byung-Ho in? I wondered. He'd taken that grenade for me.

"Can I see the pilot?" I asked the physician before I'd thought the matter through. There was no reason Jang would have made such a request.

The doctor clucked. "You won't do him any good. He's in a medi-coma." She traced another meridian. "But you're in satisfactory condition. As soon as I fill out the forms, you can return to duty."

While she input some information on the slate, I wondered how I could get a map of the ship. I had no idea where I was supposed to go. Too bad Jang had faded away before giving me tips about how life on a battle cruiser worked. Maybe I'd get a chance to quiz him once I had some privacy. And at some point I wanted to get a real uniform to replace my magical one, especially if I was going to be stuck here for any length of time.

The physician was frowning over something on the slate. "I could have sworn . . ."

I looked innocently at her even as I began to sweat. "Yes, Doctor?"

"There's an error in the database," she muttered. "It lists the girl on that freighter as having survived."

I definitely didn't want *that* info getting

around. I closed my eyes and directed my Charm at her again.

"Poor thing," she said. "Still, that's easy enough to fix." Without any more hesitation, she edited the database.

Whew! Close call.

"All right, Cadet Jang," the physician said, "off you go." She strolled over to her next patient.

"Thanks, Doctor," I said, getting to my feet.

What I didn't say was *Go where, exactly?*

ELEVEN

It took me a couple of tries to locate the medical bay's exit. I emerged into a passageway wide enough for four people side by side. Unlike the *Red Azalea,* this ship's deck had a slight concave curve to it, so it felt like I was moving along the inner surface of a cylinder. There were hand- and footholds not only on the sides, but also on the floor and the ceiling — in case the artificial gravity went out and magnetic boots weren't enough, I guessed. The ship could probably be spun all the way around its long axis to simulate gravity.

I picked a direction — there were only two to choose from — and started walking in as military a fashion as I could manage. The ship was full of strange smells. Some I recognized from my brief time aboard the *Red Azalea* — metal and rust and smoke. Some scents were human. And some had a distinctly supernatural flavor.

The Space Forces accepted the "more respectable" supernatural creatures, such as dragons and celestial maidens — and even tigers, if they could control their violent tempers — as long as they confined themselves to human form. Dragons, in particular, were enormous in their true manifestations. It was easier to design starships for human shapes and sizes and have everyone else adapt.

I had just enough time to wonder how to trace Jun's trail, when a nearby door whooshed open. Another cadet barreled out of it and crashed into me. I emitted a strangled yell when the person's knee accidentally connected with my crotch. I was going to have to be more careful about guarding that part of my body! Assuming the shape of a boy might not be any weirder than turning into a table or a teacup, but I had to remember that it didn't make me immune to pain.

The other cadet's eyes went wide. "Jang!" The person's name tag told me they were called Sujin and that I should address them as gender-neutral. I recognized them immediately as a dokkaebi, one of the goblin folk. While I'd never met one before, the small horn protruding from the middle of their forehead was a dead giveaway. Otherwise they had a smooth tawny human face, with black hair and brown eyes, like those of most citizens. Goblins were known for their strength, magical wands, and invisibility caps. I couldn't help peeking around Sujin for a glimpse of their hat, but I didn't spot it. Which made sense.

"Wait, what?" A second cadet emerged from the same doorway. She was taller than the dokkaebi, and she, too, was a supernatural. The name on her badge was HANEUL, which would be easy to remember. It meant *sky.* Even if it hadn't been for her blue-tinted hair, which was pinned up severely, I would have smelled the sea on her. She had to be a dragon. They had an affinity for air and water. "Jang, I didn't think you'd be up and about so soon!"

When I'd hastily adopted my disguise, I hadn't taken the other cadets into account. At least some of them would know Jang — they were all training together to be officers, after all. Yikes! What if they asked me questions only he could answer? I'd talked with his ghost for just a few minutes, so impersonating him convincingly would be difficult. But it was too late to back out. For now, I'd have to rely on magic to get me through. Later I could try to find Jang and grill him. In the meantime, maybe these cadets knew something about Jun. . . .

"It's me all right," I said. "I have a headache, but otherwise I'm fine." The headache might help excuse any gaffes I made. Cautiously, I nudged both of them with Charm. If they detected that I was a fox and ratted me out, I'd be toast. My powers should keep them from realizing I was another supernatural, but I would have to be careful. I'd never had the opportunity to test Charm on a goblin or dragon before.

My stomach chose that moment to growl. I hadn't eaten in a long time, and using Charm so much was making me hungrier than usual.

"I'm so glad you're not as badly hurt as we thought," Sujin said.

"Yeah, I was knocked out for a while there," I said. "I only just woke up. You're the first people I've spoken to."

"Where were you going?" Haneul asked with a frown. "Shouldn't you report in to Lieutenant Ju-Won?"

Of course. I couldn't just wander anywhere I liked, not if I was supposed to be a cadet. Perhaps talking to the lieutenant would give me a better idea of how to fit in while I figured out how to continue my investigations.

"Sorry," I said, feeling stupid — as well as a little faint. While the doctor had declared me fit for duty, I could tell I wasn't at full health. "I forgot."

Sujin looked alarmed at that. "You must really be out of it! Haneul, let's take him to the lieutenant."

Haneul studied my face, and her stern expression softened. "Yes," she said. "You don't need any more bad luck after what you went through on the *Red Azalea.* Everyone said it was going to be a routine rescue mission, safe enough even for cadets."

"Come on," said Sujin, turning me around. "If we keep the lieutenant waiting, she'll put us all on report."

I followed them, trying not to gape at the surroundings. One of the passageways featured a grand engraving of a white tiger with a lightning bolt in its mouth. Along the right-hand side, fine calligraphy declared the ship to be the Space Forces battle cruiser *Pale Lightning.*

Jun must have passed this way many times. Had he, too, stared in wonder at the engraving? Did he stop noticing it once he'd grown used to being on the ship? The thought made me miss him even more. I had to find his trail — and soon, before my ruse was uncovered.

We passed officers in dark blue uniforms bright with gold braid. I'd have to study the insignia so I'd be able to identify people's rank on sight. I only knew the cadet emblem that Haneul, Su-jin, and I were wearing. For now, I saluted smartly whenever the two of them did.

"There she is," Sujin whispered as we approached a broad, worried-looking woman.

The lieutenant might have heard that Jang was badly injured. Time for more Charm. I was desperate to get away and scrounge for food — surely even military food couldn't be worse than what I'd grown up eating — but I had to take care of this first.

Lieutenant Ju-Won was overseeing a group of enlisted spacers pulling bundles of wires from behind a large, dented panel. From time to time she consulted a slate and barked orders. I itched to join them, because I could already tell that one of them was damaging the internals with rough handling, but I bit my tongue just in time.

I peered curiously at the wires. The patterns they were in reminded me of the body's meridians, which made sense. The ship wasn't alive like a person or an animal, but like any object, it had an energy flow, or gi, of its own. For its systems to work properly, all its components needed to be placed in harmony with its gi. I'd learned that from repairing things back home.

"Cadet," Ju-Won said. The worry lines between her brows deepened. "I thought you . . . Never mind." Her eyes scanned me up and down. "Who let you out of the medical bay with your collar crooked like that?"

I should have checked it over earlier, but I'd been too disoriented by the whole situation. By this point I was about ready to fall over. "Sorry," I mumbled.

Her worried expression changed to a glare. "What did you say, Cadet?"

Sujin mouthed, *Say "ma'am"!* Haneul shook her head ever so slightly at me.

"Sorry, *ma'am*!" I said hastily.

"Sloppy, Cadet," Ju-Won said. "Are you sure you don't need to go back to Medical?"

"I'm fine, ma'am," I said. I didn't want to get stuck in the sick bay.

"Very well," she said. "Why don't you report to level two and help them with inventory? Check in with me again if you don't feel well, though."

This time I had the presence of mind to salute and say, "Yes, ma'am!" I must have sounded too enthusiastic, because she frowned at me some more.

"Cadets Sujin and Haneul, I assume you know where you're supposed to be? Good. Dismissed, the three of you."

Once again, I had no idea where to go. Too bad foxes didn't know divination magic. I saluted and picked a direction. I had a 50 percent chance of being right, after all.

"*That* way, Cadet!" Ju-Won said in exasperation, pointing down another corridor.

"Oh, of course, ma'am!" I lied. I saluted a third time for good measure and marched off in the correct direction this time.

Sujin and Haneul accompanied me, although the latter cast anxious glances back to Ju-Won to see if she was watching us.

"Hey," Sujin said in an undertone, "you look terrible. Let me get a snack into you before I report to my station."

That sounded wonderful. "Thank you," I said, smiling at the goblin.

Sujin herded me into a side passage. Haneul shook her head and said, "We're so dead if we're caught shirking."

"I can't let Jang faint from hunger," Sujin said reasonably. "Anyone coming?"

Haneul sighed, then peered around the corner. "No, you're clear."

Sujin pulled out a spork with a flourish.

Wait, a spork? Really? My nose tickled, and I suppressed a sneeze. That wasn't any ordinary utensil. Dokkaebi were known for carrying magical clubs or wands. I'd never heard of one coming in the shape of a spork, though.

Sujin waved the spork, and a box of chocolate-dipped cookies magically appeared. I tamped down another sneeze. The goblin snatched it out of the air before it fell to the deck. "Eat these," they said. "They'll perk you up."

Haneul shook her head disapprovingly at Sujin. "You're not supposed to mess with the rationing system."

"Are you going to tattle?"

"No," Haneul said with a sigh.

I tore open the box and practically inhaled the cookies. Too late, I realized I should have been polite and offered some to my companions. Oh well. Maybe they were used to Jang being rude. I snuck a glance at the others. Indeed, Sujin and Haneul looked more worried than offended.

After I'd finished, I considered my options. I needed to find out whether Sujin and Haneul knew Jun — they were a likelier source of information than the lieutenant. But I didn't want to ask outright, because it might make them suspicious. It would be better if I got to know them first — which would be tricky, since we were already supposed to be acquainted.

"Thank you," I said to Sujin. "That'll keep me going until dinner."

Haneul frowned. "You already missed mess!"

Mess. I forgot that was what they called meals around here. Jun had used some military terms in his letters home, but I hadn't absorbed them the way he would have as a cadet. Great, I was going to have to learn all the jargon, too. I wondered how long it had taken Jun to adjust to life in the Space Forces. Of course, he hadn't been thrown in the deep end immediately like this. . . . Or had he?

Sujin ignored my slip. "I wasn't thinking," they said with chagrin. "I should have conjured up something more substantial for you. At this point, you'd probably be better off filching something from the galley, though. Snacks are the best I can manage."

"Please," Haneul said with a sniff. "You'd live on nothing but cookies and shrimp crackers if you could, Sujin. We have nutritional guidelines for a reason, you know!"

"I'll take shrimp crackers," I said, my mouth watering at the prospect.

I'd already figured out that, of the two of them, Haneul was the stickler for following the rules. That could work in my favor. At least she knew what the rules *were,* and I could lean on her until I got a chance to corral Jang's ghost. In the meantime, I didn't care how unhealthy shrimp crackers were — I just wanted something to fill my aching belly.

Sujin waved their spork and a box of the promised shrimp crackers materialized in thin air. This time my nose only tickled slightly, maybe because I was getting used to the goblin's magic. "Giving him junk food's better than letting him starve, right?"

It took me a few moments to react. I was going to have to get used to people referring to me as a *him.* "Right," I said with a weak chuckle, opening the package. It didn't look like I would be able to get rid of Haneul or Sujin anytime soon, so I figured I might as well eat while I had the opportunity.

Sorry, Jun, I thought. *I'm on my way, I promise.* I may not have found out much yet, but I *had* managed to reach his ship. New clues were sure to come to light if I kept my eyes and ears open. I gobbled down all the crackers, knowing I was going to need my strength for the days to come.

TWELVE

That first day aboard the *Pale Lightning* seemed to stretch on forever. While on my way to the restroom after inventory duty, I got an officer's rank wrong and he assigned me toilet-scrubbing duty to "help" me remember. At least toilets, while smelly, didn't care how I addressed them.

The battle cruiser had unisex bathrooms. Another cadet came in while I was busy working and did her business. With Charm I confused her enough that

I could ask some quick questions about the *Pale Lightning*'s layout. She answered, all right, by using a grease pencil to draw diagrams on the floor I had just scrubbed clean. While she explained the elevators and their codes, I kept straining to hear if anyone else was about to come in. Luckily for me, no one did. After she left, I had to memorize everything before getting down on my hands and knees to erase it. By the time I was done, my back ached terribly.

From the outside, the *Pale Lightning* resembled a tube with a ring around its middle, which the ship spun when it had to generate artificial gravity the hard way. The ship's levels were concentric cylindrical shells around that ring, which explained the curved passageways. A series of elevators connected the different levels, and there were backup maintenance shafts in case of power failure.

It was useful information. Unfortunately, learning it all meant that I reported back to the barracks late. I was thankful Haneul had let it slip that Jang slept in Bunk 12 in Barracks 5, like she and Sujin did, or I would have been even later.

The senior cadet in charge of Bunk 12 didn't seem to care that I'd wandered in past lights-out; he waved me listlessly to the only empty bed. Sujin and Haneul were both asleep. If I hadn't already figured out that Haneul was a dragon, her snoring would have given her away.

When Lieutenant Ju-Won swung by to check on us, I found out that the senior cadet had reported me for being late.

"You're going to have to do better, even if you're not feeling back to normal yet," Ju-Won said to me as I slid under my sheets. And she assigned me more toilet scrubbing, starting two hours before mess the next morning.

Despite the fact that I could have used the extra hours of sleep, I did a better job of cleaning the bathroom the second time. I suspected I wouldn't be sleeping in anytime soon, not while I was on this ship. But Jun had served on it, too, once. If he had survived the experience, so could I. Had he ever been unfortunate enough to be stuck with latrine duty? I wondered.

I kept hoping Jang would pop up so I could consult with him, but no such luck. Maybe he was discouraged by the fact that people kept coming in to use the restroom. He hadn't seemed eager to reveal his presence to his former comrades.

Once I was finished with the cleaning, I washed myself up, then ran to the mess hall for our level, slowing down only when I heard others approaching. I thanked the ancestors for my fox senses, because the others were officers. Cadets were at the bottom of the pecking order, and anything I did wrong in the officers' eyes might mean more demerits — and chores.

A wide door opened into the mess hall, which was filled with tables and benches bolted to the deck. I spotted Haneul first, thanks to her distinctive bluish hair, and hurried to take a seat across from her. Sujin was there, too, idly toying with their spork.

"Put that thing away," Haneul told Sujin. The air around her felt staticky, like a thunderstorm was about to break out inside the ship. I made a note never to anger her. I didn't want to get zapped by any lightning bolt she might summon by accident.

Sujin grumbled. "The food here's terrible."

"You didn't sign on to be a restaurant reviewer," Haneul said. "And you can't magic up enough candy to make everyone happy, so it's best you keep that opinion to yourself."

The mess officer called us up by tables to collect our food. I got in line behind Sujin and Haneul, picking up a tray, chopsticks, and a spoon, all made of plain gray metal. The spoon handles were engraved with the Space Forces' flower-and-spear emblem. The chopsticks featured an elongated version of the same thing.

A pair of girl cadets behind me whispered to each other as they cast sly glances at Sujin and Haneul. With my fox ears, I could hear them quite distinctly. "Don't you think it's weird how he's hanging out with the supernaturals?" one of them was saying. "He's just as human as we are."

I realized with a shock that she was referring to me. I kept my expression neutral while continuing to eavesdrop, curious.

"Maybe he's practicing his sucking up," the other girl said snidely, "so he'll be ready for the captain."

The exchange left a sour taste in my mouth. What was their problem with supernaturals? Sujin glanced back at me when I fell behind, and I made myself smile reassuringly. Haneul and Sujin had been kind to me, and those girl cadets had no idea that I was really the lowest of the low, a distrusted fox.

I wondered if Jun had run into this kind of prejudice. Was that what had made him run away?

No, that couldn't be it. I couldn't imagine him ever revealing his true heritage, and Jang had been shocked to see me, a fox, on the ship. Besides, my brother wasn't the sort to be discouraged by a few nasty remarks.

It was a relief to make my way back to our table. I was glad the two mean girls sat far from us. I was famished from all my exertion coupled with not eating much the day before. But Sujin was right — the food was dismal. Rice gruel with a few small pieces of abalone, underspiced gimchi, and oversalted fiddleheads. I did savor the abalone, which tasted like the real thing, not vat-grown protein. I'd had it once at a festival, as a treat, and I'd never forgotten the chewy texture and mild meatiness.

"What comes next?" I whispered to Sujin. "I know I should remember, but my head is still a little foggy. . . ."

Lieutenant Ju-Won hadn't told me what to do after I finished with the toilets. I doubted that meant I could spend my time doing whatever I wanted. Until I saw a good opening to ask people questions about Jun, it would be best for me to keep trying to fit in.

"You're in luck," Sujin said brightly. "We have class with Lieutenant Hyosu. She said we'd learn about the weapons systems today."

Considering how miserably I'd held up against the mercenaries on the *Red Azalea,* that sounded useful. Granted, a battle cruiser as large as this one would normally keep pirates at bay, but the fact that Jang had been critically wounded on his rescue mission told me we weren't entirely safe, either. The more I knew about our defenses, the better. Besides, I had to stay in the mix. I'd promised Jang's ghost I'd find out more about what had happened to him. And while I was at it, I could also listen for any gossip about people going AWOL, including a certain cadet.

The mess officer dismissed us by tables. In spite of myself, I felt a pang of homesickness. Sure, I'd had chores and lessons there, too, but I'd also had more freedom. Life on this ship was so strict, with rules for every little thing. I even missed squabbling with Bora over the best food scraps.

Stop complaining and do your best, I could almost hear my brother say. Jun had chosen this path, hoping to rise in the ranks and use his influence to help Jinju someday. I had always wanted to follow him into the Space Forces, and now I had, two years sooner than I was supposed to. But it was hard to care about that when I didn't know where Jun was.

Twenty of us marched to the ward-room, where Lieutenant Hyosu, a woman with a round, friendly face and black-framed glasses, was waiting. She smiled at us, and I couldn't help smiling back. "Hello!" she practically sang out when the last cadet had entered. "Go on, take your seats. Today's the fun stuff."

"You think everything's the fun stuff," Sujin said under their breath, although they were smiling, too.

Haneul rolled her eyes at Sujin.

Lieutenant Hyosu made us follow the rules, but she wasn't too exacting about them, and she was a pretty good teacher. She introduced us to the *Pale Lightning*'s armaments, from its point defense system to its missiles and laser cannons. By the end of the lesson, my head ached from all the figures I had memorized. Not surprisingly, everyone else in the class was far ahead of me. As long as I was here, I'd have to study hard. The merce-naries had caught me unprepared on the *Red Azalea.* I didn't want that to happen again.

"Here's the part you've all been wait-ing for," Hyosu said. "Simulator time!"

Everyone sat up straighter. It seemed that this was everyone's first time, which was a good thing — my lack of experience wouldn't be as obvious. Besides, I was dying to see how well I would do, even if it was "just" a sim.

Hyosu briefly explained how the simulator worked. It tested how a pilot and a gunner would cooperate in a battle situation. The targeting system sounded similar to the *Red Azalea*'s: The gunner designated target priorities, and the computer did the rest. Put that way, it sounded deceptively easy. But after my battle experience on the freighter, I knew better than to take the job for granted.

"It's almost as good as the real thing," the lieutenant said, "except you don't die if you mess up." Then her tone became serious. "Remember, I'm recording everything you do so I can help you improve."

A door from the wardroom opened into the sim chamber. Hyosu had shown us holos of the *Pale Lightning*'s bridge, and the room resembled the area where the pilot and gunner sat, except this was grimier. I wrinkled my nose at the reek of nervous sweat that emanated from it, coupled with the harsh smell of disinfectant, which, for a fox, never canceled out scents — it just served to further irritate the nose.

Hyosu paired me with one of the gossipy girls from lunch. Her name was Gyeong-Ja. She didn't look happy about being separated from her friend.

"Hello," I said. "What's your preference, pilot or gunner?" I figured that was a safe topic.

She laughed. "Pilot, of course! I want to be a navigator, and I'm good at the math."

That suited me fine. I would much rather try my hand as a gunner.

Gyeong-Ja sneaked a nervous glance toward Haneul and Sujin, who'd been assigned to each other, then lowered her voice. "Do you find them easy to work with?"

"They're pretty nice," I said. "Haneul snores, though."

Gyeong-Ja grinned. "Dragons! I guess they can't help themselves."

We were up next. We climbed into our

seats while Hyosu scolded the exiting pair about their inability to work together. I resolved not to make the same mistake, even if I wasn't thrilled about being partnered with someone who didn't like supernaturals.

Gyeong-Ja and I strapped ourselves in and adjusted the seats so we could reach the control panels. I wondered if the real panels on the bridge were all scratched up like these.

The overhead illumination dimmed as Gyeong-Ja's fingers flew over a series of buttons. All the lights turned blue, and the chamber hummed in a way that reminded me of the *Red Azalea*'s engines. "Preflight check looks good," she reported.

Hastily, I inventoried the weapons, which ranged from lasers to missiles and mass drivers that used electromagnetism to fling metal projectiles. I had blue lights across the board — *blue lights for heaven,* as Byung-Ho would say — and I hoped Hyosu wasn't about to hit us with inventive equipment failures.

An alarm screamed. "Incoming!" Gyeong-Ja cried, and she began listing coordinates as her hands triggered evasive maneuvers.

I could see the enemy on my own displays. "Got 'em," I said, before realizing that was too informal. "I mean, *acknowledged.*" I remembered that the session was being recorded for Hyosu to review, and I winced.

The targeting system showed two hostile fighters. I checked the tactical scanner, which told me the ships had identical capabilities. I marked the closer one as the priority — it would be best to concentrate my lasers and take it out of the fight first. If I shot at both of them haphazardly, both would be able to return fire and do more damage in the long run.

The fighters, fast-moving red blips on the display, swooped and soared. The blips formed green afterimages behind my eyelids. I was almost hypnotized by the complex patterns my chosen target was tracing. As it accelerated away and its partner darted in to attack us, I realized just in time what was happening: The first ship had been a decoy, distracting me with its fancy maneuvers! I called a warning to Gyeong-Ja, who rolled us out of the path of some missiles. I over-rode the priority system and let loose a salvo of antimissile fire, then engaged the lasers. They connected, and the second fighter tumbled away. The original target fled, and I couldn't help feeling disappointed that my prey had escaped.

A chime sounded and the lights came back up to tell us that the scenario was over. I found myself soaked in sweat. Gyeong-Ja didn't look much better.

We emerged from the seats, blinking at the bright lights. Hyosu beamed at us. "You two work well together," she said. "Jang, your reaction time is the best it's ever been. Good job!"

I hadn't stopped to consider that Jang would have slower reflexes than me, but it made sense — he was a human, and I was a fox. Fortunately, Hyosu hadn't leaped to the conclusion that I was an imposter. So far, so good.

Gyeong-Ja and I stood to the side of the chamber while the next group of cadets underwent the exercise.

"Not bad, eh?" I whispered, still glowing from Hyosu's praise.

"Nice to see you actually *try* for a change," she said with a sniff.

I felt insulted on Jang's behalf. I nudged her with Charm and took a gamble. "I bet Cadet Jun would have been great at sim." After all, he had good reflexes, just like me.

"That dirty deserter?" Gyeong-Ja said. "I can't believe he ran off with the others like that."

The others? I thought Jun was the only one missing. I *knew* that investigator wasn't telling the truth!

Who were the rest? If only Jun had named the "friends" in his message . . . Perhaps that was a clue in itself. Had "the others" threatened him so he'd had no choice but to go along?

I started to ask Gyeong-Ja for specifics, but then I caught Hyosu frowning at me. I'd mistakenly assumed she was busy giving feedback to another pair of cadets.

"If you pay attention, instead of distracting classmates with your gossip, you might learn a thing or two, Cadet," Hyosu said.

"Yes, ma'am," I said contritely. So

much for that opportunity.

Disgusted, Gyeong-Ja edged away from me. I wouldn't be getting any more information from her.

While I was confident my brother had no reason to go AWOL, I couldn't say the same for whomever he had fallen in with. If I learned more about them and their motives, that might lead me to Jun. Unfortunately, I wasn't having any luck wheedling information out of the other cadets, not yet. It was time to talk to Jang.

THIRTEEN

After lessons, I was assigned to scrub a bulkhead next to a maintenance shaft. As soon as no one was in sight, I whispered, "Jang! Where are you?"

No answer. Where did ghosts go when they weren't haunting, anyway? That was one thing my aunties' lore hadn't covered.

But after a few moments, a cold breeze swirled nearby, unnatural in the controlled environment of the starship, and I shivered. Jang materialized next to me, his long, unkempt hair at odds with his neatly pressed uniform. He looked at the sponge in my hand and smiled ironically. "Having more trouble than you expected?"

"There's so much to learn," I whined. "Where do I even start?"

"You can always access the cadet handbook from any of the workstations in the barracks," Jang said.

"That's good to know, thank you," I said sincerely.

"But don't waste too much time studying," said Jang. "You're supposed to be looking into what happened to me, remember?"

His eyes glowed. Was I imagining it, or had the temperature dropped further?

"Yes, yes, of course," I assured him. "I'm on it." Then I thought of a way to get what I needed. "Maybe your mission had something to do with the disappearance of that cadet, Jun . . . ?"

"I don't think —" Without finishing his sentence, he vanished.

I looked around frantically. "Wait! What were you going to say?"

An officer was looming above me. She cleared her throat. She did not look impressed.

I snapped to and saluted, but it was too late.

"Lost in a daydream, Cadet?" the officer asked, scowling. "Weren't you the one who was cleaning the bathroom earlier? Perhaps you need to stick to that until you figure things out."

I suppressed a sigh just in time and instead said, "Yes, ma'am."

Each time I cleaned the toilets, I got a little faster. I had to, as a defensive measure. As soon as I finished, I headed back to the barracks and straight for an unoccupied workstation. One of the other cadets was lying in his bunk reading an old-fashioned book made out of real paper. I was dying to know what it was about, but I didn't want to draw his attention. In any case, he didn't look up as I passed him.

A holographic data screen appeared in front of me as soon as I sat down. Just when I was starting to worry about how to gain access to the system, the handbook popped up. I guessed they wanted it to be easily accessible to the cadets so they wouldn't forget the rules. I skimmed it as quickly I could, hoping some of the information would stick. One part of the code of conduct leaped out at me: *Anyone caught impersonating a Space Forces cadet or officer will face court-martial and, if found guilty, imprisonment or capital punishment.*

Welp. I can't let them catch me at this! I thought. *I'd better study hard.*

I was going over rank insignia, muttering under my breath as I tried to memorize them, when someone behind me said disapprovingly, "Shouldn't you know all that by now?"

I squeaked involuntarily. "Don't sneak up on me like that!"

Haneul chuckled. Maybe she had a sense of humor after all. "I didn't know your voice could go that high!"

If only you knew, I thought. "I just wanted to review a few things," I said, hastily closing the handbook file.

Sujin came up next to Haneul. "You haven't been studying, have you?" they asked. "Isn't it enough that we have classes all day? This is leisure time. You're supposed to be doing something fun."

I wavered. I had so much to learn, but I was getting awfully tired. Surely a break wouldn't hurt. "Any suggestions?" I asked.

Sujin grinned slyly at me. "You could help me with another taste-testing."

Uh-oh. If this was a regular occurrence, it would look fishy to turn them down. "Why?" I asked, stalling for time. "What do you have in mind this time?"

"It can't be any worse than the last concoction," Haneul said to Sujin. "I don't know what possessed you to combine spinach with plum tea!"

I made a sour face just thinking of it. "Maybe something that doesn't have spinach in it?" I suggested.

"Aww, you're no fun," Sujin said. "You're not willing to taste my cinnamon-spinach-egg masterpiece?"

"Um . . ." I looked pleadingly at Haneul.

She crossed her arms. "You're going to have to get out of this one yourself, Jang."

"C'mon," Sujin said. They produced their spork and waved it right under my nose.

The spicy fragrance of cinnamon mingled with the smell of sodden spinach and fried eggs wafted from the spork. I gagged and leaned away. "Uh, I'm not so sure. . . ."

Sujin withdrew the spork, smiling even more broadly. Haneul's eyes twinkled. I realized they were both teasing me. On an impulse, I stuck out my tongue at them, and we all dissolved into giggles.

After dinner, when I got another moment to myself, I went through Jang's personal effects for clues about his family and friends. Jang materialized and looked on, his eyes dark and sad. He came from a large family on one of the more important space stations. I found a digital photo frame that cycled through pictures of smiling people in formal clothes, each person helpfully tagged. I memorized their faces. It had to be a wealthy family, if they could afford professional portraits.

"You must miss them," I said, tilting the frame so Jang could get a good view of the pics.

As a ghost, he was trapped between the world of the living and the world of the dead, unable to visit loved ones in either realm. Most ghosts were bound near the site of whatever had felled them, although I wasn't sure how that worked when he'd died in space. Before he could move on to his eternal rest, he needed to know what had happened to him.

Jang reached out with insubstantial fingers. They passed through the frame, and he grimaced. "I knew I was signing on for a long tour, but I don't want it to be *eternal.*"

"I'm sorry," I said inadequately. I felt bad for ever thinking of him as a distraction.

He drew himself up, and the chilly breeze that always accompanied him swirled by me in a rush. "Just find out more about who killed me." He gave the photo frame one last look, then vanished.

The next day, I was back to scrubbing toilets again. I'd failed morning inspection for not making my bed properly. I was getting the distinct impression that

Lieutenant Ju-Won didn't like me.

At least I had a helper this time: Sujin. The goblin had gotten caught fiddling with the seasonings in the galley. As Sujin had put it, "The officers don't appreciate experimental chemistry."

The chore seemed a lot less tedious when there was someone to talk to. "Tell me, Sujin," I said as I stretched my aching back, "why is it that on one of the Space Forces' most modern battle cruisers, as Hyosu is so proud of pointing out, we have to scrub things by hand, instead of relying on robots to do the job?"

"Don't you know?" Sujin asked sarcastically. "It's supposed to 'build our character.' "

"How does becoming intimately familiar with the restroom make me a better person?"

"It's a process," Sujin said. "Work hard, and maybe someday you'll graduate to scrubbing a different part of the ship. Then you can become intimately familiar with that instead."

"Do I dare to dream that big?" I asked with a sigh, and we both laughed.

After a brief silence, Sujin said, "You haven't talked about it at all."

I had to keep from wrinkling my nose at the smell of their worry.

"Talked about what?"

"The attack."

My stomach twisted. All this time I'd been so preoccupied with trying to impersonate the Jang everyone knew, I'd never stopped to consider how the experience on the *Red Azalea* would have affected him if he'd survived. I'd been trying to act normal, to fit in. I hadn't wanted to seem like a coward, or to draw attention to myself. But now it looked like that plan might have backfired.

While I didn't know anything about what Jang had experienced in his final moments, I did remember how afraid I'd been when the mercenaries came for Byung-Ho and me. "I was sure it was going to be the end," I said with perfect honesty. "I try not to think about it."

"If you ever do want to talk —"

I made myself smile at Sujin. I was tempted to reach out and squeeze their hand in thanks, but I'd learned from observation that people in the Space Forces didn't casually touch each other. "I'm fine, really."

"That's good," Sujin said, although they didn't sound entirely convinced.

Now for the tricky part. It was finally time for me to test our friendship. I nudged Sujin with a bit of Charm and asked, "Did anyone ever find out anything about that cadet who took off with his friends? You know — Jun?"

Once again, my timing was bad. The restroom door opened behind me, and Sujin scrambled to their feet. The goblin jabbed me in the ribs, then snapped a salute. "Captain Hwan!"

Hwan? Where had I heard that name before?

I turned to see a tall, bearded man with amber eyes regarding us with a frown. I saluted, too, gulped, and tried to keep the panic off my face. The ship was so big, and I was so lowly, I never thought I'd run into the *captain.* Yet I had — in the restroom no less — and I was impersonating one of his cadets.

And something else was putting my

nerves on edge. He smelled supernatural. Specifically, I detected the prickly scent of . . . *tiger.*

Then I remembered. One of the guards back in the Market District had mentioned a tiger captain. This was him!

"Cadets," Captain Hwan said. His voice was low and rumbling with a hint of a growl in it.

I straightened in spite of myself, wishing I hadn't caught a glimpse of his teeth as he spoke. They didn't look sharp, which surprised me, but they were unnaturally perfect and white. Like most other supernaturals, tiger spirits could assume human form whenever they wanted to. They sometimes adopted the guise when they were hunting, to fool their prey. But they couldn't shift into other things the way foxes could.

Captain Hwan fixed me with his stare. "How have you been feeling, Cadet Jang? Lieutenant Ju-Won informs me you've been distracted lately."

Oh no. I'd performed so poorly that I'd come to the captain's attention. If he figured out I was a fox in disguise, I'd be in real trouble. And I knew better than to use any additional Charm around a tiger. Given his predator senses, it would be a dangerous proposition.

"I'll work harder, sir," I said, hating the way my voice trembled.

His brows drew down. Next to me, Sujin held very still. "Cadet Jang," Hwan said, "what do you think serving in the Space Forces is about?"

"Protecting the Thousand Worlds," I said. Not an original answer, but a safe one.

Hwan smiled wryly, as if he could read my thoughts. "That's *one* of our functions. We spend most of our time defending our territory against the Jeweled Worlds. But we are also tasked with keeping the peace *within* our own worlds."

I nodded, not sure what he wanted me to say next.

"Sometimes local rulers seek to grab power," he went on. "They rarely do so openly, of course. Even the rashest members of the Dragon Council or the Pearled Halls know better than to risk getting caught if they want to play such games." He leaned closer and pointed a finger near my chest. "There are plenty of mercenaries, though, who will carry out raids for anyone who can pay them. Haven't you wondered why we were patrolling this area when we came across the rascals who wounded you?"

An odd chilly dizziness gripped me. "Listen closely," Jang's voice whispered in my ear.

Neither Hwan or Sujin showed signs that they'd heard the ghost. If only I had Jang's memories, I could respond to the captain with more confidence. Charm didn't work that way, though.

Cautiously, I said, "I figured mercenaries were looking for easy prey with that unlucky freighter, sir."

"There *has* been a lot of mercenary activity lately," Hwan acknowledged. "And the raids are becoming bolder. Those pirates knew we were in the area and yet they still went after the *Red Azalea.*" His mouth compressed as his eyes bored into me. "They're looking for something specific, and they're getting desperate. They seek the Dragon Pearl. It's important that we keep it out of their hands."

The Dragon Pearl. A snippet of the investigator's conversation with Mom came back to me: *According to his captain's report, your son left to go in search of the Dragon Pearl.*

Hwan was that captain. He knew when my brother had gone missing, and he thought he knew why. I was getting so close to finding out the truth!

I couldn't speak without the captain's permission, so I just nodded again to indicate Jang's understanding. If I wanted Hwan to trust me, I had to convince him that I remained a reliable member of the crew, despite my screwups.

"At least it doesn't seem that the Pearl has been found yet — the Space Forces' shamans would have detected its reappearance," the captain said, continuing to look at me to gauge my reaction.

I wondered why the captain was telling me all this. Had he known Jang well? As for Sujin, they were still frozen in place.

Then I realized what was going on. Hwan was concerned that Jang had been shaken up by his encounter with the mercs.

"The pirates who attacked that freighter might have been able to tell us more, but unfortunately, none of them survived our skirmish," Hwan said. "Sooner or later we'll capture someone and force them to tell us what they know. In the meantime, I'm hoping to get intel from the sole survivor of the freighter's crew."

My breath caught. By *sole survivor*, he meant Byung-Ho. The girl, "Bora," was dead. Even though I'd wanted everyone to think that, hearing him confirm it made me feel odd. Thankfully, it didn't sound like the captain thought Byung-Ho was going to die. I hoped my pilot friend would wake from his healing sleep soon.

I was allowing myself to get distracted. I hated taking the risk, but I had to ask, and Hwan seemed to be in a talking mood. "Permission to speak, sir?" I ventured.

"Yes, Cadet?"

"Sir, does any of this relate to the cadet who vanished with his comrades? Cadet Jun?"

His eyes turned to slits, and I knew I'd made a mistake. "Have you been listening to gossip, Cadet?"

"I'm worried about him," I said.

Beside me, Sujin groaned slightly.

"The whole group of them went AWOL," Hwan said curtly. "It's none of your affair."

I gulped. "Yes, sir," I said hastily.

Something was wrong. When I'd mentioned Jun's name, I'd caught the distinct stink of alarm. Hwan was definitely hiding something.

"Carry on with your duties, Cadets," Hwan said, and he moved on, leaving me wondering how a mere cadet could get information out of their captain.

FOURTEEN

"Whew," Sujin said once the captain was out of earshot. "I'm glad he didn't detain us for long. You should have known better than to bring up the deserters, though. Captain Hwan's been furious about them ever since they vanished."

"You're right," I conceded. "That was stupid of me."

"Why do you care about Jun, anyway?" Sujin asked.

"Just curious," I said, shrugging and throwing a little Charm Sujin's way to make them believe me.

I was torn. On the one hand, maybe, if I hadn't choked, I could have come up with a way to salvage the conversation with Hwan. On the other hand, I was relieved he was gone. Having a tiger stare at me with those amber eyes made me nervous. There was no higher predator, after all. I was grateful he thought of me as his crew member and not his prey.

Our next duty was a shift in the robot maintenance room. The senior cadet in charge looked bored as he pointed to a gleaming laundry robot standing against the wall. It had a head like an overturned wash bucket, two long arms as well as a scrub-brush extension, and a ridged washboard surface on its torso.

Sujin grimaced as they ran through the diagnostics in the robot's rear control panel. Despite its shiny metal exterior, the robot refused to move or respond to any of the test commands. Instead, a single red light blinked wanly from its forehead area.

"This one's no good," Sujin said, banging on the robot in frustration. A front panel fell open to reveal a fold-down ironing board.

"Don't do that," I said automatically, although sometimes giving a machine a good thump was exactly what you needed to do to get it working again. "Here, let me try."

It didn't look too different from the household robots I'd occasionally had to repair back home — it was just a newer model. Sujin watched while I pulled out the battery pack. I counted to sixty, then put it back in. The robot chimed, its lights cycling back to blue. "See?" I said. "Always try a reboot first."

"I'll remember that," Sujin said. "The more robots we fix, the less laundry we'll have to do the old-fashioned way!" The goblin smiled at me, and I smiled back, relieved that my asking about Jun hadn't made them suspicious.

We rushed to lessons and made it just in time. Haneul was already there, tapping her foot impatiently. Lieutenant Hyosu hadn't assigned us seats — another nice thing about her class — which meant I could sit near Sujin and Haneul, the cadets I knew best. I felt bad about deceiving them by pretending to be Jang.

The more I got to know them, the more I liked them.

That day, Hyosu was instructing us on the ship's internal security system. She called on one of the older cadets and asked him, "What can you tell us about the ship's meridians?"

"They're lines of mystic energy that run throughout the ship," he said. "If they get blocked, the ship will malfunction, just like a person gets sick when their gi is disrupted."

I remembered the physician examining me, checking my gi — life force — for any signs of blockage.

"Correct," said Hyosu. "When an engineer interfaces with the ship's energies, we call that Engineer's Trance. If the meridians are compromised, engineers can get injured because their gi is synced with that of the ship."

Gyeong-Ja raised her hand. "How would a meridian get compromised in the first place?"

"Good question," said Hyosu. "We have external shields to protect us from regular attacks — missiles and lasers and so on. Most of the meridians are *inside* the ship, but sabotage is still a possibility — from hackers overloading the systems or subverting the maintenance robots. Mercenaries are getting more and more clever."

The mood in the room turned somber as the lieutenant continued. "Normally a battle cruiser like the *Pale Lightning* is more than a match for mercs. But in the Ghost Sector, things have become more dangerous. It has always been a base of operations for raiders, because sensible people don't want to go anywhere near the Fourth Colony. Lately, though, violence has escalated. High Command wants us to intimidate the mercs, and the pirates are striking back any way they know how."

Another cadet raised her hand. "Why are mercenaries tolerated at all?" she asked.

"It's complicated." Hyosu sighed. "They serve a convenient role for the Thousand Worlds' major factions. Individual worlds and space stations aren't allowed to have private armies — that would threaten the peace. But planets and factions get into feuds anyway. Since they can't declare war outright, they raid each other instead, and the mercenaries are the ones paid to do the dirty work."

I couldn't help asking a question of my own. "Don't the mercenaries have to get their supplies from somewhere, though? Couldn't people shut them down from that end?"

"They could," Hyosu said, "if enough people worked together. Unfortunately for us, a lot of planetary governments find the mercenaries so useful, they look the other way when the mercs come around for repairs or resupply."

"Excuse me, Lieutenant," I said, "but why haven't the Space Forces cleaned out the Ghost Sector earlier? Why leave it until now?"

Someone behind me snickered, and I flushed.

Lieutenant Hyosu spoke sternly to the rude offender. "Don't be so quick to laugh, Cadet. All questions are valid." Then she turned to me. "The short answer is that the Space Forces rely on all the Thousand Worlds for funding. The mercs use the Ghost Sector as a base of operations. If we offended individual planets by shutting off their access to mercs, they would hit us in the budget. Battle cruisers aren't cheap, you know."

Hyosu looked around seriously at all of us. "Space Forces Command believes that the Dragon Pearl has surfaced in the Ghost Sector. That's why we're breaking the status quo. The mercenaries are all looking for it. We have to get to it first."

I tried not to squirm in my seat. I didn't want to reveal my interest in the artifact.

Luckily for me, Gyeong-Ja asked about it. "Is the Pearl that important?" she asked. "I mean, the stories are two hundred years old. Is it even real?"

Hyosu pursed her lips. "The Dragon Pearl might not be as powerful as the legends claim, but we can't risk it falling into the wrong hands. Think about it, Cadet. If the Pearl *could* transform an entire barren world, give it forests and seas and make it suitable for habitation, it could just as easily *destroy* a world, turn it into a lifeless desert. That kind of magic needs to be controlled by the proper authorities, not sold to the highest bidder."

I shivered at the thought of someone using the Pearl's magic to lay waste to a living world. All planets deserved to exist, even one as shabby as Jinju.

"What I'm trying to say here," Hyosu continued, "is that our cruise around the sector has already proven more dangerous than usual, and it may get more dangerous yet. That unlucky freighter docked in our bay won't be the last victim of greedy pirates. There could be more rescue missions — missions that involve cadets."

I felt everyone in the class turn to look at me, but I held my head up high and refused to meet their gazes. I wondered if Jang's ghost had heard any of this lesson, because it explained a lot.

Hyosu returned to the topic of the meridians and how to protect the ship's energy flow. We spent the rest of class memorizing the locations where the gi was most vulnerable. While the *Pale Lightning* had officers who specialized in overseeing the meridians and making sure the gi was flowing properly, we cadets might be called upon to help defend key locations in the event the ship was boarded by hostiles.

My head swam with all this new information. Hyosu was a good teacher, but it was a lot to absorb. I'd taken notes on my assigned slate, which I'd have to review later. After all, I knew from experience that raiders were a real threat.

Had Jun and his friends joined their ranks, hoping for a chance at the Dragon Pearl? Had he turned into a soldier-for-hire? I couldn't imagine that. I *refused* to imagine that. No, it had to be something else. But what?

I was too tired to puzzle it out. Pretending to be someone else was exhausting. I knew how I was going to spend my free time that afternoon — conked out on my bunk.

Both Jun and Jang would have to wait.

FIFTEEN

"Hey!" Sujin whispered just as I closed my eyes.

"Hmm?" I said, not wanting to get up and face the world. I smelled moisture in the air, which meant Sujin had brought Haneul with them. Only a dragon could make it rain in the closed world of a starship. If I annoyed her too much, Haneul could drench me.

"Have you forgotten about our regular game of baduk?" she asked. "You keep swearing you'll beat me, and you haven't yet."

Uh-oh. I'd have to play as Jang, and I didn't know how good he was. I was decent at the game, and at home I used to watch professional matches on the holonet when I could snatch some free moments. If Jang always lost to Haneul, maybe I wouldn't have to scare up skills I didn't have.

"Why?" I asked, keeping my tone light. "What handicap are you going to give me today?" I didn't know if she typically allotted Jang extra pieces to even things up, but I'd soon find out. . . .

"I'll give you five instead of four," she said, "seeing as how you had a tough time on your rescue mission."

I relaxed inwardly. My question hadn't raised any suspicions. "Fine," I said, and sat up. Maybe I could quiz her about my brother while we played. I gestured for her to lead the way, and Sujin and I followed.

Haneul took us to the lower recreation room, which contained equipment for games like table tennis and geomdo, or fencing. Two soldiers were sparring in one of the corners with their swords of split bamboo. I sneaked a glance, fascinated. Both of them wore traditional-style armor and helmets, but I still couldn't imagine standing up beneath those heavy blows. Foxes were known for cleverness and trickery, not brute strength.

A few other people were playing board games. One unoccupied table had a baduk set atop it, and Haneul slid easily into a chair. I took the seat opposite her. Sujin sat between us and brought out a slate. I glanced at what my goblin friend was reading. . . . A chemistry text? Well, it took all kinds.

Baduk was played on a grid of nineteen by nineteen lines, and the stones — black for me, because I was supposedly the weaker player, and white for Haneul — were placed on the intersections of those lines. The object was to capture the most territory by setting down pieces to form boundaries. Since Haneul had given me a handicap, I started with five stones already in play.

Haneul frowned, then picked up a white stone, gripping it between her forefinger and middle finger in the proper manner. She snapped it onto the board. I responded after a moment, and we exchanged moves without speaking for a time. I was starting to get rattled, because even with the handicap stones I was struggling to keep up.

"You're doing better than usual," Sujin said at last. I hadn't realized they were paying attention in between reading about chemistry.

I laughed nervously. "Lucky today, I guess."

"Haneul never gives *me* a handicap," Sujin muttered.

"You don't need one," she retorted. "As for you," she said, turning back to me, "never count on luck. You used up almost all of yours in surviving that attack!"

I didn't want to talk about that — it was too dangerous, because I didn't know what had happened during Jang's last moments. I decided to distract her by asking questions, which I needed to do anyway.

"It could be worse," I said. Time for some more Charm. "At least I didn't end up missing, like Jun and the rest. . . ." I apologized mentally to Jun for bad-mouthing him. But how else was I going to find out what was going on?

Haneul glanced around the room. The air grew crackly with static, as in an electrical storm, and the players nearest us scowled and got up to leave. I was starting to understand why dragon folk rarely went into spy work. She lowered her voice and asked, "Do you believe the rumors?"

I pounced on the opening. "Which ones?" I asked.

Haneul squirmed. "It wasn't like any of us younger cadets knew Jun well, but he seemed solid enough. I was surprised when the captain declared him a deserter. Some of the others, like Corporal Hyun-Joo, sure. *She* was always so sour-faced, I'm not surprised she was up to something. But Jun was a good soldier."

At least Haneul remembered my brother. That was a start. "I bet pirates got him while he was on a mission," I said, because gossip about mercs was so common no one would think twice of it.

"Well, from what I heard, he and his

comrades weren't on a regular assignment," Sujin said in a whisper. "They really did leave on their own."

I tried not to reveal my shock. So Jun actually *was* a deserter!

"I wonder whose idea it was, and why they were all so desperate to get away," Sujin went on.

Haneul studied the board, narrowing her eyes at a pattern in the center. Finally she placed her stone. "It can't have been *Jun's* idea," she said in a hushed tone. "I mean, one of the people with the group was a lieutenant. And everyone said *she* was loyal. Even if it's true what people are saying — that they decided to chase after the Dragon Pearl — it doesn't make sense."

So my theory that Jun had been forced into going might be right. I remained convinced that Jun's motives were pure. He'd never cared about money. . . .

"I don't know about that," Sujin said, cynical. "A lot of people are eager to get their hands on that thing. I know you don't like hearing about it, Haneul, but the Dragon Society in particular would pay handsomely for it. If they control all

215

the ways to do terraforming magic, they can raise their fees as high as they want and no one can do anything about it."

"The Dragon Society wouldn't stoop so low," Haneul said stiffly. "Besides, it's a wild-goose chase. The Pearl probably got destroyed long ago."

Sujin shook their head but didn't press the point.

I forced myself to relax. I couldn't let them see how much I cared about this. "Let's say a soldier deserted and somehow retrieved the Pearl," I said. "What would they do? They'd be a fugitive the rest of their life." I glanced over the board, then placed my stone to keep one of my groups from being captured. Haneul might be beating me, but I was determined to make her work for it.

"That bothered me, too," Haneul said. "Maybe they have debts we don't know about and are really desperate."

I thought of Captain Hye at Nari's gambling parlor and grimaced at the memory.

"If so, Jun, for one, hid it well," Sujin said. "He worked hard. Even when some of the other cadets made nasty remarks about his steader heritage, he kept his cool."

I had to keep my mouth from twitching into a smile of pride.

"The ones in Bunk Two straightened up fast after he vanished," Sujin went on. "I mean, they got questioned more than anyone else about what happened."

I made a note of that information. While I didn't get much chance to talk to people outside of class, it would be easy to look up which cadets had bunked with Jun. Figuring out a good excuse to approach them would be harder, even with the aid of Charm.

I finally plunked down a black stone on the game board. It was a weak move, and I knew it. Fortunately, Haneul's mind wasn't on the match anymore. The air crackled again, and a small wind swirled around us. I hadn't realized this topic would bother her so much.

Haneul caught me staring at her and blushed. "Sorry about that," she said. She closed her eyes and recited a chant under her breath until the energy in the air dissipated.

"Do you think we'll ever catch up to the deserters?" I asked after Haneul had calmed down.

"I hope so," she said. "They need to face the captain's justice."

"They probably just heard a rumor about the Dragon Pearl's location, got greedy, and struck out on their own," Sujin said. "But if that's the case, it's odd that the captain didn't try harder to locate them. . . ."

The more I thought about it, the more it didn't make sense. If Jun had known something about the Dragon Pearl, he should have told the captain. Unless he couldn't trust Hwan for some reason. . . . I winced involuntarily.

Luckily, Haneul misinterpreted my expression. "We shouldn't keep talking about mercs in front of Jang," she said to Sujin.

"It's all right," I said hastily. "I'll double-check any personal shield I use in the future!" I meant it, too.

In the back of my mind, I heard Jang's dry chuckle. So he was somewhere nearby. I wondered what he thought of this conversation.

Sujin wasn't done talking about the deserters. "The other strange thing," they said, "is that we should have been able to track the shuttle pretty easily. Shuttles can't outrun a big battle cruiser like the *Pale Lightning,* and they shouldn't be able to hide from one, either."

I hadn't thought of that before, but the anomaly bothered me, too. Had someone covered for their escape? If so, they must be lying low. No wonder Captain Hwan was touchy about the subject.

For the rest of the baduk match, those questions distracted me. Haneul defeated me handily, which meant that I had to pick up some of her chores. I didn't care — I was too busy dreaming of ways to dig up more information.

Afterward, I made my excuses and went back to the barracks to think. For a change, no one else was there.

No one, that is, except Jang.

"Hello," I said awkwardly. "I've been making progress. Did you hear what Lieutenant Hyosu said about increased merc activity — ?"

"You made me a promise," he said. Cold air whirled around him, making me shiver, and his long, ragged hair fell about his face. "You keep getting distracted by the deserters. I don't care about them."

I suppressed a growl. Jun wasn't a distraction. He was the whole reason I was there! But I had to appease Jang. "Yes, I understand," I said in my most soothing voice. "I won't let you down."

"You'd better not," he said, "or you'll regret it." He laid his hand on mine, then vanished, leaving behind a chill that went all the way to the bone.

SIXTEEN

At mess the next morning, I accidentally dropped my chopsticks on the floor, and while I was retrieving them, I knocked my head on the table and spilled my gruel.

Sujin asked, "What's wrong with you today?"

Jang's threat weighed heavily on me. I needed answers for him and had no more time to waste. "The mercs who almost fried me," I asked, "how much do we know about them?"

"None of them survived, if that's what you're wondering," Haneul said. Her eyes softened as she regarded me. "This has been bothering you for a while, hasn't it?"

"Yes," I said, which was close enough to the truth. At the least, it was bothering Jang — the real Jang. "These pirates looking for the Dragon Pearl . . . are they all working together?"

"Oh, there's no chance of *that*," Sujin said. "If the pirates joined forces, they'd be a real threat. But it's impossible for individual merc captains to trust each other. They'd rather sell each other out for a quick profit. That's what our officers always say, anyway."

"Why were they foolish enough to attack that freighter," I asked, "when they knew we were in the area?"

Haneul stirred her gruel, thinking. "They might have thought its captain was another pirate with new information about the Pearl."

Byung-Ho, a pirate? Just in time, I stopped myself from saying that out loud. I didn't think he had it in him.

But then I remembered something: All

those crates that had been stacked in the hold. Were those smuggled items? Could one of them have contained the Pearl? He hadn't wanted me to see them. . . .

Sujin and Haneul were staring at me, because I'd been quiet for too long. "Yeah. They must be desperate for leads," I offered.

"I'll say." Haneul glanced up at the clock on the wall. "Hey, we'd better clean up if we're going to make it to class on time."

That day's lessons were on engineering. Afterward, Hyosu took me aside. My friends shot me worried glances as they left me behind.

The lieutenant peered down at me over her glasses. I tensed, thinking I was about to get lectured, but instead she said, "You've been studying hard, haven't you?"

"Y-yes, ma'am," I stammered. What was I going to say, no?

Hyosu beamed at me. "Well, keep it up. You're doing much better than the last time we discussed the subject."

So engineering hadn't been Jang's strong suit. I wondered what he *had* been good at. It really didn't matter anymore, though. I had to get by with my own strengths and weaknesses now.

I thanked her and made my way toward the mess hall, where I had KP duty. I took one of the less frequented corridors. "Jang," I called softly. "You around?"

He appeared, his hair even longer and more disheveled than the last time I'd seen it. Maybe it was my imagination, but the unnatural breeze that usually accompanied him didn't feel as cold as usual.

"I overheard your conversation with Haneul and Sujin," he said.

I blinked. "You were there? I didn't notice."

"It's easy for me to hide my presence around Haneul, especially when she's upset," Jang said, sounding wistful. "No one notices a ghost-wind when she's accidentally summoning a miniature storm in the same room."

"So you heard that the people who killed you are dead," I said, hoping that would satisfy him.

"Yes, that was a very interesting detail."

Wasn't that enough? I wondered. His eyes still looked . . . well, *haunted.*

I had an idea. "Would you prefer to speak to Sujin and Haneul yourself?" I asked gently. "We could explain the situation — that I'm pretending to be you. Hopefully they'd understand." Truthfully, I didn't want to do it. I felt I had to make the offer, though, because of his pitiful expression.

Jang was already shaking his head. "No," he said, "it's better not to complicate things." He looked away for a moment. "If they found out I'm dead, they'd be obliged to report you. And they might try to exorcise me so I don't bring bad luck to the ship. Then I'd *really* be gone. I'm not ready for that quite yet."

"I'll keep your secret if you keep mine," I said.

Jang smiled thinly. "Fair enough."

"Sorry I'm not living up to your reputation as a slacker," I teased gently, thinking back to Lieutenant Hyosu's compliment.

"That's the one nice thing about this arrangement," Jang said. "Not having to study anymore."

I stuck out my tongue — his tongue, which must have been weird for him to see.

Jang started to fade away. "You have KP duty next, don't you? You should get going."

I wondered when I would see him again. It was unnerving to know he could eavesdrop on me without my knowledge.

After the first week, I was starting to take to life as a cadet. It felt almost like I wasn't pretending anymore. I was getting better at following the complicated military regulations. Saluting whenever an officer showed up had become second nature. My posture was the best it had been in my entire life, which would have made Mom proud. It even impressed me. Considering how much of my life I'd spent scrubbing things, I'd thought I would always be hunched over.

It took me by surprise the first time I was excused from toilet-cleaning duty. One night Lieutenant Ju-Won regarded me sourly and said, "Your comportment is adequate, Cadet. See that it stays that way."

I didn't expect my good luck to last, though. As much as I was enjoying my taste of life in the Space Forces, training to be a soldier wasn't my true purpose. I was there to find my brother.

The next morning, I woke early by force of habit. Truth is, I hadn't exactly gotten many opportunities to sleep in when I lived at home, either.

I padded quietly past the other bunks. Haneul was snoring the loudest, as usual. Good thing I could sleep through anything after growing up with my cousin Bora's snoring and snuffling. Sujin lay curled up on their side, their horned brow slightly creased. I wondered what kinds of dreams they were having. In mine I sometimes saw Nari and my mom sitting side by side, eating sesame cookies and chatting. They looked almost like real sisters, Nari with her sly eyes, and my mother smiling more easily than I'd ever seen before.

I'd left all that behind on Jinju, though. Until I found Jun, I couldn't go back.

My feet took me to Bunk 2. The door opened for me readily enough. The first thing I heard was several people snoring, one of them even louder than Haneul at her worst. They didn't smell like a dragon, though.

I looked around, letting my eyes adjust to the darkness. Then I walked softly around the room. My nose picked up the smells of soap, sweat, synthetic fabrics, plastic, and metal. I couldn't detect any trace of Jun, and my heart sank, even though I'd anticipated that would be the case.

They wouldn't have left Jun's personal effects here. My best guess was that they were locked up somewhere as part of the investigation into his desertion. How could I get access to them?

I hadn't learned anything useful by sneaking in there. I retreated back into the corridor . . . and almost collided with a sergeant.

I bit down on a yelp. Unfortunately, I didn't have enough presence of mind to nudge her with Charm to dampen her suspicion.

"You're up awfully early, Cadet," the

sergeant said, eyeing me with distrust.

I scrambled for an excuse that wouldn't stick in her head. "I was having trouble meditating because of all the snoring," I said. "So I went for a walk."

The sergeant harrumphed. "Well, you shouldn't be wandering around like this. I'm going to have to put you on report."

"Yes, Sergeant," I said, swallowing a groan.

"In the meantime, you should catch up on sleep," the sergeant said. "Go."

I hurried off, wondering what my punishment would be. So much for avoiding toilet scrubbing.

SEVENTEEN

My punishment turned out to be something else. After breakfast mess, Lieutenant Ju-Won informed me that I was to report to Hydroponics with Haneul and Sujin. "You can help with inspection," she said.

"Inspection?" I asked before I could stop myself.

The lieutenant shook her head. "What's the matter? You don't remember how to perform that duty? Well, the other cadets can remind you."

I wasn't sure what *inspection* meant. Hopefully it would be like gardening in our dome back home. *At least it doesn't involve toilets,* I thought, but I kept that to myself.

By pretending I was prepping her for a quiz, I got Haneul to explain the setup to me. The ship's hydroponics facility grew food to supplement our rations. Hydroponics on a ship the size of the *Pale Lightning* was something of a misnomer. Not only did it include vast, brightly lit gardens where vegetables were fed nutrient-rich water, it also contained gruesome vats where slabs of cultured meat grew. A separate section contained saltwater tanks, in which unshelled abalone meat clung to the walls.

My task, once Haneul had oriented me, was to go through the gardens' rows and check for signs of mold or rotted roots. The computers were supposed to monitor the plants, but they weren't foolproof, and no one wanted to take chances when it came to our food supply.

Another ensign entered my row and started working alongside me. I smiled cautiously at him. He was broadly built,

231

and I recognized him as one of the sleeping cadets from Bunk 2. Once upon a time, he had bunked with my brother.

"Sorry this is taking me so long," I said. "I haven't done this in a while."

"Not a problem," he said. "I thought you could use a hand."

My spirits lifted. "I'm Jang," I said. If this charade went on much longer, I wouldn't remember my real name.

He bowed formally. "I'm Woo-Jin," he said. Then he let out a laugh. "You thought I wouldn't remember you? We humans have to stick together." His smile took the sting out of the words, and I reminded myself that I had to act like I was, in fact, human. "We may outnumber the supernaturals," he said, "but I've always suspected that the captain treats them better, because he's one, too."

Woo-Jin double-checked some of my work and turned up a couple rows where I'd missed some rot. I flushed at the mistakes. Even though I was an imposter, I was determined to do well.

I glanced around. Haneul had her hands pressed up against one of the saltwater tanks and was frowning in intense concentration, blessing the water so the abalone would stay healthy. Sujin was busy checking the ratios of chemicals in the nutrient mix.

Woo-Jin caught my look. "Do you ever wish you could do things like that?"

"What, chemistry?" I said. "That's Sujin's specialty." I didn't have any crushing desire to spend my free time reading chem textbooks.

"Yes, goblins have a better intuition for that stuff," Woo-Jin said.

"Humans make better shamans and scholars," I said, repeating what I'd heard from the holonet.

He grinned at me. "Yeah, except here we are, being neither shamans nor scholars."

That wasn't entirely true. We may not have been surrounded by books and scrolls on the *Pale Lightning,* but all the cadets — humans and supernaturals alike — did have to study hard. We needed to understand the basics of the geomantic arts — the flow of gi and the cosmic balance of the universe — and engineering to keep the ship running. I couldn't help feeling a little proud that even though I was a "lowly fox" and two years younger than everyone else, I was keeping up. For the most part.

With Woo-Jin's help, I finished early. I looked around again. Haneul had moved on to the next water tank, and Sujin was preoccupied with some adjustments to the nutrient mix. No one was paying attention to us.

"Hey," I said to Woo-Jin, leaning on Charm, "was it weird in Bunk Two after that boy deserted with the rest of the team?"

Woo-Jin frowned. "I wish I knew what really happened. I already told the captain everything I know."

So Hwan had done the questioning personally. That wasn't surprising. It was inconvenient, though. I already knew that I needed to ask the captain some questions. But how was I going to do that?

"Everyone was on edge for a while," Woo-Jin was saying. "I thought things were settling down, but . . ." He bit his lip. "I could almost swear that the captain's covering for —"

"You two done over there?" the warrant officer yelled at us.

I bit off a curse. "Yes, Officer." Was Woo-Jin suggesting that the *captain* was involved in the team's disappearance? Why would he — ?

"Well," the warrant officer said, interrupting my musing, "see if you can help Cadet Haneul."

The dragon was tugging a stray lock of hair in frustration. "This isn't working the way it's supposed to," she muttered when I reached her.

"What isn't working?" I asked.

"The ship's gi is concentrated at this point to help the plants grow," Haneul said, "just like there is a focal point at Medical to encourage people to heal more quickly. I've heard some engineers say that the energy flows have been shaky ever since we rescued the *Red Azalea*."

Oh no. That couldn't be because Jang was still lurking on the ship, could it? For all I knew, he was watching us now, maybe out of longing to be near the friends he'd had in life.

"Do they have any idea what's causing

it?" I asked. That ought to be a safe question.

"They've been working on rebalancing the flow," Haneul said, "but Engineering told me that someone hacked one of the key meridians. The ship's been cranky ever since."

"Which meridian?"

"The one that runs through Deck Three." Haneul frowned at the water tank as if she could fix everything by staring the hapless abalone into submission. "We're hoping the bad luck doesn't spread to Medical — it's on the same level."

I was starting to hatch an idea. When I needed to leave this ship — and it would be *when,* not *if* — a little careful sabotage might buy me some time to escape. Guilt washed over me, because I'd gotten to like the rest of the crew, and it would cause them trouble. But once I figured out who was behind the mercenaries who had killed Jang, and where Jun had gone, I wouldn't have any reason to linger.

At the end of our shift, the warrant officer hemmed and hawed before declaring that we'd have to return during the next day-cycle. "You're getting faster, Cadet Jang," he said to me. "But you need to be more careful in your inspections."

I swallowed. "Yes, Officer."

After mess that day, I claimed to have a stomachache and begged off watching a fencing match. Sujin looked disappointed, but only said, "I hope you feel better soon. Are you sure it's not because you're still hungry?"

"Leave him be," Haneul said. "And don't give him shrimp crackers — they never help stomachaches. He's probably suffering from one of the 'experiments' you conducted while on KP duty."

While they argued over that, I slipped away.

I headed toward Deck 3. I wanted to examine the damaged meridian for myself. I didn't have much experience with energy flows, and I was curious to feel one up close.

According to the old lore, energy flows could bring whole civilizations to ruin or grant good fortune. Just like you could have flows of good or bad luck in a room, depending on how furniture and ornaments were arranged, there could be flows of good or bad luck across star systems and beyond. The Thousand Worlds hadn't yet gotten to the point where we could rearrange the stars for our own benefit, but I'd heard that some of the more ambitious dragon masters dreamed of making that happen.

I was so wrapped up in my own thoughts that I took a wrong turn and had to retrace my steps. *Don't walk too quickly,* I reminded myself. *Act like you belong here.*

I passed several soldiers and technicians on the way. By now, I had perfected the worried, borderline sullen look of someone trying to get his job done before having three more assigned to him. I no longer minded getting extra chores, though. When people gave you work to do, you stopped being a person and became a part of the scenery. Sometimes that was convenient.

A guard stood watch at either end of the corridor that contained the damaged meridian. The nearest sentry started to frown at me. I pushed some Charm in his direction to convince him I belonged here. He blinked watery eyes, then muttered to himself and looked away. I let out a breath I hadn't realized I'd been holding and hurried past. I threw Charm at the guard on the far end, too, to make him too drowsy to notice me.

In class, Lieutenant Hyosu had shown us a diagram depicting meridians as glowing lines flowing through the ship. In reality, meridians didn't glow. But as soon as I entered the corridor, I felt a prickling on my skin, and I saw a flickering in the air, like the shimmer of a heat haze. That much was normal. What wasn't normal was the way my eyes stung, or the way the air chilled my skin. A healthy meridian shouldn't cause pain, or feel like a ghost-wind.

One of the floor tiles was warped. I tripped on it and went sprawling. Despite all the drilling exercises I'd done with the other cadets over these past few weeks, I still hadn't gotten used to my higher center of mass, or my heavier body. I yelped as I rolled to soften my fall. I ended up bruising my elbows and hip anyway.

Oh. Of course. The fall wasn't due only to my newfound clumsiness. The flow of bad luck had affected me. I started to appreciate why fixing meridians was so important, and why the repairs required a delicate touch.

Unfortunately, this also meant the bad luck would persist as long as Jang's ghost did. I wasn't sure how I felt about that. Would our luck worsen over time if his ghost wasn't laid to rest? How would it impact the ship's mission, or my own?

Helpfully, the repair crew wasn't around; they must have been on break. The restricted area had been marked off with red tape — red for good fortune, even though the color looked like the bright splash of new blood. I approached slowly, being careful of how I placed my feet. Despite my best efforts, my ankle twisted and I fell across the tape.

I shut my eyes, panting. This close to the broken meridian, I could feel the energy flow like a knot in the pit of my stomach. Now I really *did* have a bellyache.

I heard footsteps approaching from behind. Getting caught here wouldn't do me any favors. Wincing in pain, I levered myself up, then glanced around. I saw a supply closet door and didn't have to think twice. I palmed it open and found emergency suits hanging inside. I shoved myself in among them, trying not to gag at the overwhelming stench of metal and chemicals. Besides the footsteps, I now detected voices, one male and one female. Frantically, I yanked the door shut, grimacing at the noise it made. Had they noticed?

No one burst in on me, and the conversation continued.

". . . don't like it." The female voice belonged to Lieutenant Commander Ji-Eun, the executive officer. "The engineers can't figure out what's causing the damage here."

The male voice had a hint of a growl in it: Captain Hwan. "I know what's going on," he said. "The ship has a ghost."

My stomach pain flared. He was onto me and Jang.

EIGHTEEN

"I was hoping it was something else," Lieutenant Commander Ji-Eun said wearily. "Don't tell me we're being haunted by some of those accursed mercenaries. . . ."

The *mercenaries'* ghosts?

I'd assumed the captain was talking about Jang, but I supposed I couldn't rule out the possibility of additional spirits on board. Just because I'd only seen Jang's ghost didn't mean there weren't more around. Could apparitions detect each other? I'd have to ask Jang the next time we spoke.

I leaned closer to the door to hear better, flinching when one of the suits creaked. My thoughts were racing. If ghosts were causing ill fortune, how much of it could a battle cruiser endure? Sure, the *Pale Lightning* had a lot of firepower, but all the weapons in the world can't save you if your luck is bad.

Drat. I'd missed some of their conversation. I needed to focus.

"None of the pirates died on this ship," the XO said. "Besides, even if they came to the *Pale Lightning,* the shamans' chants should have laid them to rest. What I'm more worried about is the fact that we can't seem to fix this meridian."

"You're sure no one tampered with it as a prank?" There was just a hint of tension in Hwan's voice. I wondered if the XO could detect it.

"Of course not!" she said, indignant. "I've had guards on watch twenty-four-seven. If they'd seen anything, I would have notified you immediately. Besides, even the unruliest of the cadets wouldn't dare."

I almost squawked in surprise at the captain's laugh. "I don't know about that. Cadets are notorious for playing pranks."

"Not when it comes to something this serious," the XO said. "They're terrified of you, anyway. Convinced you'd court-martial them if they sneezed in your presence."

Captain Hwan huffed. "I'm not *that* unreasonable. Cadet silliness is one thing. The deserters, on the other hand . . ." I held my breath, silently begging him to drop a clue as to where my brother had gone. "Too bad we haven't been able to retrieve them. It would be the galaxy's fastest court-martial if we did."

I gulped. An entire section of the code of conduct was devoted to courts-martial. The most severe penalty for a military infraction was execution. Jun would have known this even better than I did. Whatever had caused him and his comrades to leave the ship had been serious enough for them to risk death.

The two lapsed into silence for a while. I had an itch between my shoulder blades, but I couldn't try to scratch it, because I might make too much noise.

"All right," Hwan said at last, "you'd best go check on the bridge. I want to examine this meridian a little longer. Who knows, maybe one of the pirates' ghosts will come by and say *boo.*"

"As you wish, sir," the XO said in a subdued voice.

I held my breath, partly because the emergency suits' reek was still making me gag, partly so I could hear the retreating footsteps more clearly. Only one pair. I wished the captain would leave, too, so I could. . . .

"All right, Cadet," Hwan said. "You can come out now."

Oh no. He'd known I was here all along! I couldn't shape-shift to escape his notice, because, as a predator, he would sniff out any surge in my magic. And my cowering in the closet wouldn't impress him, so I shoved the door open. I tumbled out and offered a clumsy salute.

The captain looked even taller and more imposing than before as he loomed over me. "At ease," he said. "What are you doing here? You must know this area is off-limits. The meridian has been compromised. Hasn't Lieutenant Hyosu told you its 'bad luck' can hurt you?"

Bad luck was right. It couldn't be mere coincidence that I'd stopped there just when the captain and his executive officer had decided to inspect the damage.

I bowed my head and blurted, "I was just curious about it, sir."

Maybe it was a mistake to say anything at all. The captain's amber eyes darkened, and I flinched at the smell of his sudden anger.

"Tell me, Cadet Jang, how did you manage to get by the guards?"

Yikes. I couldn't tell him about using Charm, and I couldn't try it on him, either. I had to tell the truth.

"I . . . I distracted one of them, sir, and then snuck past. I hid in the closet when I heard someone coming." It wasn't a lie, just not the complete truth.

He regarded me coolly, testing, waiting. I started to sweat.

"I don't sense that you're lying," he

said finally.

"I'm not, sir. I'm sorry, sir," I mumbled, "I won't do it again."

"You're how old, Cadet?"

I knew the correct answer, thanks to my research. "Sixteen years old, sir, from Clover System." Also not entirely a lie. Jang's body was that old.

He growled in the back of his throat, and I tensed. "Did you come up with this idea on your own?"

He was asking me to rat out pranksters. Fortunately, I didn't know of any. "It's just me, sir." I kept my eyes downcast.

"Look at me, Cadet."

I didn't want to do it, but I couldn't ignore a direct order from the captain. Looking him square in the eyes would have been too bold, so I settled for staring awkwardly at his chin.

"Do you think sneaking around is the best use of your training cruise?"

"No, sir."

The captain was still peering down at me. What did he want?

Inspired, I burst out, "I — I also did it

because . . . because I needed to be alone. I don't want anyone to know how afraid I am." I could feel my cheeks heating with the admission, which, again, was true. "I almost died on that freighter. . . ."

I hadn't allowed myself to really think about it until now. I *had* gotten hurt on the *Red Azalea.* The grenade had knocked me out, left me helpless. Like Jang, I, too, could have died.

Hwan's face changed. The expression in his eyes wasn't sympathy, exactly — I doubted that a tiger felt sympathy often, if ever. It was more like a grim understanding. "The first time is always like that," he said. "We can send you to all the classes in the world, but none of them will prepare you sufficiently for real battle."

I took advantage of his change in mood, for Jang's sake. "I still see the pirates in my dreams," I said. I didn't have to fake the quaver in my voice, although it was caused less by the memory of the attack than by the thought of getting munched by the captain if he caught me lying. "I know the Dragon Pearl is valuable, but they shot me down like I didn't even matter."

"The stakes are higher than ever," Hwan acknowledged. "Everyone thinks the Pearl is within their reach, and they will do anything to get it. Those pirates might have been working for the Dragon Society, which will pay a high price to maintain their monopoly on terraforming."

"I could have died over that," I said quietly.

"Yes. But you have to gain experience in the Space Forces sooner or later. The initial brush with death is always hard," he said. "I wasn't much older than you when someone first died in front of me."

I kept silent, sensing that he wanted to tell me more.

"I'll never forget it," Hwan said. "It was my comrade, back in the early 1480s. If she'd lived, she would've made captain before I did. But the blaster burned her life short, and that was all there was to it." He grimaced. "It was a completely unnecessary sacrifice on her part, too. By the time we fought that battle, the peace had already been negotiated. It was a secret mission, so we didn't hear about

249

the treaty until afterward."

I shivered inside at the shadow of anguish in his eyes. But I remained wary. Was he trying to manipulate me the way I'd just tried to play him? If so, that meant he might know about me and Jang. I couldn't let my guard down, no matter how authentic his story sounded.

"You'll understand as you grow in your years of service," Hwan said, sensing my discomfort. He nodded at me. "Go back to your bunk, Cadet."

"Yes, sir." I saluted and turned, suppressing my desire to run. The spot between my shoulder blades itched again as I walked away. I didn't dare glance back to see if he was watching me or if he had returned his attention to the broken meridian.

My instincts told me that his story had been true. I'd never thought of the captain, or any officer for that matter, as someone who'd suffered their own losses. What did it feel like to hold command of a military ship? Did the captain grieve over every crew member who died?

Once the captain was safely out of sight and I'd ducked past the guards, I felt that familiar winter swirl of cold air around me.

"Not bad," Jang's voice said in my ear. I couldn't see him. "He practically admitted that he knowingly sent me to my death."

I looked around before replying. No one was there to hear me. "He knew the mission wasn't safe at least," I said. "And he mentioned the possible connection to the Dragon Society — did you hear that part?"

Jang's ghostly form started to materialize, his long locks swaying as he nodded thoughtfully.

Seeing him reminded me to ask, "*Are* there other ghosts on this ship?" I had to get that out of the way.

His wispy face registered surprise. "Not that I know of. And especially not pirates. The ship's shamans would have laid their spirits to rest to prevent them from cursing the *Pale Lightning.*"

So the XO had been right. Then something else occurred to me. "You wouldn't do anything like that, would you? Curse the ship?"

"Of course not." But the answer came after a pause.

By the time I thought to ask about his hesitation, Jang had vanished again.

NINETEEN

Later that day, I shared a shift on the bridge with Sujin. Miraculously, the captain hadn't reported me to Lieutenant Ju-Won. If he had, I would have been stuck with something much less appetizing, like scrubbing toilets again.

Lieutenant Hyosu had explained that we needed to be on our best behavior when we were on the bridge. "We hope this will never be necessary," she had said, "but everyone needs to be familiar with how the bridge operates in case there's an emergency and the rest of us go down. Of course" — she had grimaced — "if, as a cadet, you're the last person standing on the ship, good luck. . . ."

Thanks for the friendly reminder, I thought.

Sujin and I walked toward the elevator that would take us to the bridge level. The goblin was more subdued than usual, and it made the distance seem to stretch forever. Had they heard about my run-in with the captain? If so, I wished they'd just ask me about it and end the suspense.

The elevator was big enough to hold a good dozen people, but it was just the two of us. Sujin leaned over the panel with its glowing buttons and punched in the elevator code. The security measure wouldn't do more than slow down an attacker, yet I supposed it was better than nothing.

This would be my first time on the bridge, although I couldn't let that slip. Would Hwan be there? My heart was beating too fast, and I was breathing so hard that Sujin noticed.

"What's the matter?" they asked. "You

seem antsy. Didn't you like it last time? Or did you like it *too* much?" they added with a smile.

I shrugged and tried to look nonchalant. "It's no big deal. We're just observing, right?"

"Sure," Sujin said. "But people get superstitious about time on the bridge. They think they'll advance faster if they linger there."

It wasn't exactly a consideration for me, because I was an imposter, but I could see why some cadets might have felt that way. It was the closest they got to seeing officers in action.

The elevator arrived and we stepped onto the bridge. The executive officer sat on a raised dais in the middle of the room. The other crew members were arranged at various stations in a semicircle around her. No captain in sight, I noted with relief.

"Cadets Sujin and Jang reporting for duty," Sujin said crisply as we saluted.

I wondered, if I ever returned home, would I accidentally salute my aunties when they called my name? Of course, whether I'd recognize my own name at all was an open question at that point.

"You're on time," the XO said, so dryly that it sounded like a criticism. "Today you'll be shadowing Navigation." She waved a hand toward one of the stations, where an ensign gestured for us to take up positions to either side of his seat. We'd have to stand the entire shift, but I didn't mind.

I stared in wonder at the navigational display. Far bigger and more complex than the one we'd had in the sim module, it showed a holographic map of the region and the Gates we were passing through. Inhabited star systems, which burned like fierce white points, were labeled, while Gates showed up as purple spheres. On either side, additional digital indicators in blue and red reported the status of the ship's shields, engines, and so on, just like in the *Red Azalea*'s cockpit.

"All right, Cadet Jang," the ensign said. "What do you remember about this?" He pointed to a shimmering shape on his control panel. At the moment the circle glowed a calm violet.

I knew the answer to this one. "That means we're traveling through a Gate," I said. "Blue means we're in regular space."

"And why is it important to keep track?" the ensign asked Sujin.

"We can't carry out certain maintenance operations while the ship is Gating," Sujin said.

"Give me an example," the ensign urged.

"Well, for one, we can't go out onto the hull while we're in the Gate."

The ensign kept prodding. "What happens if there's a hull breach?"

Sujin winced at the thought.

"Go on," the ensign said. "It's a possibility we have to be prepared for."

"If there's a hull breach," Sujin continued, "the ship is at risk of getting stuck in the Gate and never coming out again. That's why we have to be absolutely certain the hull is in good shape before we Gate."

"Correct," the ensign said. "But sometimes you don't have much choice." His mouth twisted. "As long as the shields stay up, most battle cruisers are tough beasts. But if there is a shield malfunction and the ship is compromised by enemy fire, even minor hull damage can prevent a ship from Gating to another location for safety. And once it's trapped, predators can move in."

The ensign turned to me. "Cadet Jang, tell me another problem with being stuck in a Gate."

"We can't depart the ship," I said. I'd been thinking about this ever since I'd heard of the deserters. "No extravehicular activity — no leaving on shuttles or in escape pods, nothing."

"That's right."

Something didn't add up. Jun and his comrades couldn't have left while the battle cruiser was in a Gate. They would've had to plan their escape for sometime when the *Pale Lightning* was on patrol in normal space. But if the crew hadn't been preoccupied with Gating, how did no one notice a departing shuttle? Was security that lax? And why did the captain leave the area instead of trying to retrieve and punish the deserters? Especially deserters who might have had information about the location of the Dragon Pearl . . .

What was going on?

I tried to concentrate on what the ensign was telling us about other navigational maneuvers, but it was almost impossible.

I needed different information — information he couldn't provide — and I knew what I had to do to get it.

TWENTY

I had to get into the captain's quarters. For the next several days, I planned my approach. I glided by his door a couple times whenever I found an excuse to be on the senior officers' deck. The door had a lock, of course. Could I pick it without tripping an alarm? While locks weren't my specialty, they couldn't be much more difficult than any other electronic system.

The cadets' barracks only had simple locks that opened in response to passcodes. Many of the cadets didn't bother covering their hands when they punched in their numbers, and most of the crew was similarly trusting. By simple observation I had learned a scattering of passcodes all around the ship, even to areas where a mere cadet shouldn't have access.

The senior officers' deck was another matter. *Their* locks didn't just have passcodes — they also required fingerprint identification. Ironically, the fingerprint was going to be the easiest part for me to get around. I didn't have a lot of practice making tiny, subtle changes to my body, but I thought I could manage it.

"What do you want with that litmus film?" Haneul asked me when she caught me with a small roll of the stuff in Hydroponics. Watching Sujin use it to check the acidity of a nutrient solution had given me the idea. I bet the film would take impressions of fingerprints just fine.

I grinned at her and stretched a piece of it back and forth, like thin taffy. "I like playing with it."

Haneul rolled her eyes. "Do you ever take anything seriously? And don't try eating that. Technically, it's edible, but it'll taste awful."

I mimed putting it in my mouth, and she made a face and walked away. Once she'd turned her back, I pocketed the roll, smoothing my jacket over it so it wouldn't stick out too obviously. One obstacle down.

I didn't get much time to celebrate, however. A little while later, just as I'd stashed the roll with my — Jang's — personal belongings, an alarm went off. The blaring siren made it almost impossible to think. For a heart-stopping moment I thought that someone had unmasked me, and I jumped.

Then my brain caught up with the rest of me. Stealing litmus film would look weird but not suspicious. Not in the way I was worried about, anyway.

I tore off a couple strips of film and stuffed them in my pocket, then shoved the rest of the roll back with my stash.

Just then, Sujin ran in. "Come on!" they cried. "We have to get to our assigned stations."

It was a good thing Sujin had come to

get me, because I'd blanked on where my assigned station was. It didn't take long for me to figure out we were headed toward Engineering, along with a cluster of other crew members.

"What's going on?" I asked breathlessly as we hurried toward the elevator.

"Shh!" Sujin hissed.

The alarms quieted for a moment. I relaxed, but only for a second, because an announcement followed over the loudspeakers. "This is Captain Hwan." I couldn't tell whether the growl in his voice came from a fault in the speakers or his emotional state. Maybe both. "We un-Gated at Sycamore Station per our orders to survey the area. Unfortunately, it turns out that an unauthorized force of approximately ten ships has gathered here. All hands to battle stations."

My stomach dropped. I wasn't ready for this. I was just a stowaway!

"Ten ships?" I whispered to Sujin as we waited for the elevator to reach our deck. "That's bad news, isn't it?"

"It depends," Sujin said, also in a hushed voice, even if no one was around to overhear us. The goblin smelled rank with dread. "Are they big ships? Little ships? Ships tricked out with upgrades from some rogue station?"

I was sorry I'd asked.

We made it to Engineering in record time. The moment we showed up, one of the warrant officers took us in hand. She told Sujin to help monitor the state of the engine. I didn't envy that work, which was both tedious and important.

As for me, I was assigned to an engineer who was busy trying to put a hotfix on an unstable meridian before it became an issue.

I frowned. "I thought the broken meridian was on Deck Three," I said.

"It is, but all the ship's meridians are connected, and the damage has impacted other areas." The engineer sighed. "You've never done this before, have you?" he grumbled. "Well, here's your chance. Can't say it's not likely that you'll make it worse."

I bristled a bit but tried not to take his attitude personally. After all, there was a lot at stake. Everyone's life depended on the ship staying in one piece.

"How bad is it?" I asked, thinking of all the warnings I'd heard in class, and the possibility that Jang might be the cause of the problem.

The engineer was silent for a moment. "I was hoping we'd have a good long spell to fix it before we had to gallop around the sector some more," he said. "I was against Gating as much as we already have. If we have to Gate again in a hurry, it won't be pretty. But the captain wants what the captain wants." He shook his head.

"What do you need me to do?" I asked.

The engineer didn't trust me with the master flows, of course. Some meridians were bigger and more important than others. He set me to work with the smaller, less crucial ones. "Don't think it isn't important," he said when he saw my dismay. "It's good practice, and luck in small matters builds luck in large matters."

I took the seat he indicated. At first I had difficulty concentrating. I itched to be on the bridge so I could see what was going on outside the ship. Then I glanced over my shoulder at Sujin, whose station was across from mine. They were hard at work, and I felt ashamed. If they could do this, so could I.

In its way, redirecting flows was like sewing — gathering up the lines of gi and guiding them to their proper channels. When I'd mended clothes at home, my mother had often criticized the crookedness of my stitches, much to my annoyance. Here, I sweated to make the flows as even as possible.

In my imagination, the ten ships crowded closer to us. I listened for explosions, waited for the deck to shake beneath my feet. But no alarms went off; the ship sounded remarkably normal. I almost wished there were some evidence of the attack. It was hard to take it seriously when I was walled up in Engineering with no view.

Then I heard shouting and a string of curses. Sujin jumped back from their workstation, clutching their side. An enormous burning line of light had seared the goblin from the neck all the way to their waist, as though someone had slashed them with a whip of fire, severing their safety harness in the process. Sujin struggled to remain upright, then slumped to the deck, unconscious.

Without thinking, I rushed over to my friend. The status indicators in their station flashed a garish red. "Cadet Sujin needs help!" I cried.

"Take over Sujin's work for now," the engineering chief said tersely.

As I sat in Sujin's chair, I could hear the chief calling Medical for assistance. I hoped they'd be able to revive the goblin and do something for those burns, which stank of charred flesh. Meanwhile, my engineer mentor swore and assumed the functions I'd been overseeing.

I could tell at once what had happened. Something had damaged Meridian 3, and the resulting backlash had burned Sujin along the corresponding meridian of their own body. Suddenly I appreciated how dangerous engineering work could be. By taking up Sujin's station, I was risking my life in the same way. But I was acting the part of Jang, and I couldn't let down my friends, or the rest of the crew.

The next minutes passed in a haze as I

frantically wrestled with the lashing currents of gi. I kept flinching from the task, remembering the livid burns inflicted on my friend. It didn't help that I could hear their ragged breathing behind me.

Yet the longer I managed the flows, the more natural the task felt. Whenever I wasn't sure what to do, I just trusted my instincts. Sure, it might have been dangerous, but it was producing good results. I could almost see the flows as a tapestry I was weaving.

Finally, an orderly arrived to take Sujin to Medical. I could only spare the goblin a glance as the orderly hoisted them onto a hover-pallet. *Don't get distracted,* I told myself.

As I became more confident in my work, I was able to listen to the others' terse conversations with half an ear.

The chief engineer was in constant touch with Captain Hwan on the comm channel. "We'll either have to run soon, or figure out some clever way to outfight the remaining nine ships," she was saying. "The gi is stable for now, but I can't guarantee that the current state of affairs is going to last."

"You're going to have to do your best," Captain Hwan said from the bridge. "We need to take them alive if we can."

"Take them — ?" The chief engineer swore at him. "You don't ask for much, do you?"

"Do your job," the captain said calmly.

"You *requested* this mission," the chief engineer said bitterly. "Even knowing this entire sector is bad luck, and it's only going to worsen the closer we get to the Fourth Colony."

"I said, *do your job,*" the captain repeated, more menacingly, and the chief engineer shut up.

I flinched as if Hwan had addressed me. The gi currents bucked and trembled, and I scrabbled at the controls, worried that I hadn't reacted in time. But the flows steadied, and I sighed in relief.

I'd relaxed too soon. The gi snarled again like fouled thread, knotting up dangerously. What had I done wrong? I gasped as my insides clenched, feeling as though someone had punched me in the gut. Not just that: A burning sensation roared up through my body, and my vision swam.

Luckily, one of the warrant officers had been keeping an eye on me — probably because she didn't trust me to get things right, but at the moment I didn't care about that. She ordered someone to key in an override from another station.

"Stay alert!" she snapped at me. I had to remind myself that my embarrassment was unimportant when the ship's safety was at stake. "That wasn't your foul-up," she went on. "That was an attack getting through the shields. And if the shields are going down . . ."

I swallowed. Had that burning sensation meant that the ship was in real trouble?

"You feel the connection, don't you?" the warrant officer said in a low, relentless voice. "That's good. Give yourself over to it."

The chief engineer started arguing with the captain again. The racket was giving me a headache. Nevertheless, I forced myself to focus on the warrant officer's words.

"You were starting to go into Engineer's

Trance," she said, "synchronizing your gi with the ship's so it's like a part of your own body. See if you can do it again."

"But isn't that dangerous?" I asked. "Cadet Sujin just —"

"Sujin wasn't in control," the warrant officer cut in. "For you it would be different. You seem to have a knack for this, and you'd be going into a trance deliberately. It'll make guiding the gi flows come more naturally."

I'd just had a small taste of what it felt like to be in sync with the ship, and I wasn't looking forward to more of the same.

On the other hand, I did want to know what was happening to the *Pale Lightning.*

"I'll do it," I said, nodding firmly even though I was shaken.

The warrant officer clapped me on the shoulder, making me wince, and turned her attention to some new emergency.

I took a deep breath and focused once more on the control panel, which showed pulsing lines of light. I concentrated on them, carefully mapping each of the ship's meridians to its equivalent in my own body. As I worked with the gi flows, my breathing slowed, and my pulse along with it. After a while, I could detect the ship's wounds. Two shots had gotten past the shields; one hole was already being patched up. My muscles and joints ached as though I'd been sprinting pell-mell and making sudden starts and stops.

I found myself in two places at once. One version of me sat in front of the panel, adjusting the controls with more certainty than I'd had before. I knew what to do without having to think about it.

The other version of me was flying through deep space. Before, I'd always thought of space as cold and empty. But as the ship, I felt at home there, and I could sense other ships moving through the dark. I knew where the local star and its planets were, and I could detect the pulsing gravitational knot of the nearby Gate, the grand sweeping paths that connected star systems to each other like a skein of ever-shifting constellations.

The *Pale Lightning* gathered itself and fired its mass drivers. There was a burst of white light behind my eyes.

Then something slammed into my body.

"You went too deep!" I heard someone cry from a distance, but I didn't understand the words. Everything dissolved into static, and I plummeted into blackness.

TWENTY-ONE

I woke up on a pallet in Medical. I'd been dreaming of Jinju — the red skies, and the dust that got into everything — and of my mother shaking her head at me. Then I remembered where I was, and who I was. Who I was pretending to be, that is. I looked down at my body and saw with relief that I was still in the guise of Jang.

I was a bit groggy, but I didn't appear to be injured anywhere, and my body didn't hurt. Perhaps I had only fainted.

Or maybe they had injected me with a painkiller. If so, I was grateful it hadn't interfered with my fox magic. The aunties had told me once that ordinary medicine wouldn't do that. Still, I didn't trust drugs, and I preferred not to spend any more time in the medical bay.

Since the ship was still in one piece, another of the engineers must have taken over for me when I passed out. I winced, remembering the sensation of the *Pale Lightning* taking fire. I'd been so deeply linked with the ship that I'd felt the assault as if it had happened to me.

This time, I knew my way around and, with the aid of Charm, it didn't take long for me to sneak out. With everyone so preoccupied by the attack on the ship, it wasn't difficult to persuade anybody I came across that I was no one significant.

I already knew where I was going. I would never get a better chance to check out the captain's quarters. Because right then I was guaranteed that Captain Hwan would be on the bridge dealing with the battle.

Is it really worth it? I wondered. *They think you're Jang. They're counting on you*

275

to get back to your station and help.

But I'd only be gone a little while, long enough to see if the captain had secreted away any information about who was behind the mercenaries or where the deserters had gone. I couldn't forget my promise to Jang or my quest to find my brother.

Like a heart-stab, an image came to me — Jun pointing out the local constellations on the nights we snuck out to stare up at the sky. I remembered the way we'd stolen a single honey cookie from the pantry — Auntie Areum saved up for honey to make them, on account of her sweet tooth — and we passed it back and forth, nibbling each time we could name one of the Thousand Worlds. We'd drawn out the process as long as we could, but even so the cookie disappeared quickly.

Somewhere in the Thousand Worlds there must be people who would be willing to help restore Jinju, Jun had said. *If I have to, I'll visit every world to find them.* I'd believed him then, and I believed him still.

I paused for breath on the way to the elevator. My heart was pounding too hard. My body didn't like the way I was pushing it, and I wasn't even walking all that quickly.

I slowed down until my heartbeat eased. I would have to take it easy while being careful not to get caught. The delay was aggravating, because I had no way of telling how long the battle would last. Part of me wanted the *Pale Lightning* to emerge victorious quickly, of course. But another part wanted as much time as possible.

The corridors of the *Pale Lightning* seemed to stretch out forever on either side. On the few occasions I passed people, I relied on nudges of Charm to keep them from looking at me too closely, even though wielding magic caused my head to swim. I was used to the ship being busier, but everyone was at battle stations.

The elevator ride to the officers' deck felt like it took longer than usual. My skin was clammy with sweat, even though I hadn't walked any great distance. I leaned heavily against the side of the elevator, clinging to the rail. I wondered if the engineers had had any difficulty with the ship when I fainted. I shuddered at the thought. Nothing I could do about that now, and I hoped that Captain Hwan, as much as I distrusted him, had matters under control.

I made a beeline to his quarters. The lock on the door — a number pad combined with a fingerprint reader — glowed intimidatingly red. I studied it with narrowed eyes.

First, the easy part. I fished the litmus film out of my pocket. Fortunately, it hadn't gotten too crumpled. I pressed the central dot on the purple film for three long seconds until it turned transparent to indicate that it was ready. Careful to handle it only by the edges, where it changed to pale red in response to the acidity of my skin, I placed it over the fingerprint reader and pressed it there for just a second.

The reader beeped forbiddingly, and I snatched the film away. I listened for alarms. None went off. I let out my breath in relief.

I'd been counting on this. The locks weren't so sensitive that they responded to every chance touch. If they did, false alarms would go off every time someone tripped and fell against a door, or tried the wrong door by mistake. I didn't intend to push my luck, though. The next time I touched the reader, it would have to be for real.

The film had done its job. Several overlapping fingerprints showed up on it in sharp lines of red. I squinted at the whorls and ridges and concentrated on changing the tip of my index finger to match. Then I stopped and cursed my stupidity. If I copied this view, the print would be *reversed.*

I flipped the transparent film over so I wasn't looking at the mirror image anymore. Then I gathered Charm again. The good thing was that this wasn't my real body to begin with, so making small adjustments to it wasn't hard. I would just have to remember to use this process again to change my fingerprint back to Jang's.

Now for the hard part, which was figuring out the passcode. I scowled at the keypad. I knew that people often got lazy and used the dates of anniversaries or graduations. Even if Captain Hwan was the lazy type, though, I didn't know enough about his past history to guess what he might have picked.

Or did I? Come to think of it, he had mentioned that time when his comrade died. *In the early 1480s,* he had said. It had sounded like he'd respected her greatly. Did I want to gamble on that, though?

Another idea occurred to me. There was a way to check first. . . . I pulled out a second strip of litmus film. The buttons that the captain pressed would have a residue of skin oils. If the film had reacted to the fingerprints on the reader, it would react to the fingerprints on the buttons, too. And I doubted the captain was in the habit of randomly fiddling with any buttons he didn't need to press. That would help me narrow things down.

The red marks showed me that the captain had pressed four different buttons: 1, 3, 4, and 8. If the number was indeed a year, only one of those combinations would make sense.

I took a deep breath, then pressed my index finger to the reader. It lit up blue, which was a good sign. It had accepted my fingerprint. I exhaled in relief, and then carefully entered the numbers one by one, my hand trembling: 1-4-8-3.

Nothing happened for a beat. I held my breath, hoping an alarm wouldn't sound. Then the lock snicked open. I'd done it! I darted inside and then nearly whimpered when my body reminded me it wasn't in the best of shape.

The door closed behind me as the lights flicked on. I looked around, blinking. Captain Hwan's outer office featured an impressively white carpet — I knew how hard it was to clean stains — and an immense desk bolted to the deck. I hated to think of how much it would hurt if it came loose during maneuvers and slammed into me.

An old-fashioned sword in its sheath hung on the wall, fixed in place by several ornamented brackets. I sniffed the air, then drifted closer to the sword, eyes narrowing. Was that — ? I knew that smell. Just as I recognized it, I sneezed, only barely covering my mouth in time. Someone had used fox magic in here, so much that it lingered. My brother.

"Jun?" I whispered in spite of myself,

glancing quickly around the room for any sign of him. Nothing. Yet the trace of fox magic was undeniable.

I tracked the smell. It wasn't strong by any means, given the weeks that had elapsed, and the general cleanliness of the room — just the faintest trace. I doubted anyone else would have been able to detect it.

Jun had touched the sword's hilt. Despite the oils sunken into the leather, and the captain's own intimidating musk, which had undertones of fire and metal, I could still pick up Jun's scent on it.

My alarm grew. What had Jun been doing with the sword? Had he just been fooling around? Or had he threatened the captain with it for some reason? My mouth felt dry. Could Jun have been trying to defend himself . . . ?

Another possibility came to me — something I'd seen in holodramas, during ceremonial moments. Had Jun sworn an oath on the sword? An oath to the captain? But if that were the case, why had Jun deserted? And why would the captain take a cadet into his confidence in the first place?

The captain's predator smell was everywhere, and it made my skin prickle with nerves. I needed to get a move on. Jun's scent trail didn't extend beyond the office, so I guessed that any other clues would be in here. They had to be.

I started with the desk drawers. At first I thought they'd be locked, too, but no. All I had to do was hit the buttons on the latches to make them slide open. Like the bolts holding all the furniture in place, the buttons must have been another precaution, in case everything got tossed around during combat.

I was surprised to discover that the captain kept some old-fashioned paper logbooks. They were nestled in the top drawer, along with some pens. The other drawers contained various personal effects. A faded, fraying handkerchief embroidered with a magpie for good luck. A stained calligraphy brush with splayed bristles, although there were no inkstones. And the most technologically advanced item — a photo frame that was either broken or out of power. I wondered what these things meant to the captain, but I doubted I would be asking him anytime soon.

I dug out the notebooks and sniffed again, giving thanks to my ancestors for my fox heritage. I tried to detect traces of Jun's scent, and also something more — *emotion.*

The captain's scent was all over the notebooks, of course. But I could tell that some had been handled more recently than others. One in particular reeked of desperation. I snatched it up and leafed through it, skimming the passages of vertical text. I hadn't seen this kind of writing since the aunties had taught me old-fashioned calligraphy, as part of our "cultural heritage." Back then I'd thought it a waste of time. Most humans didn't learn it anymore, because everyone used digital slates. Now I was glad I could decipher the writing.

The captain had legible handwriting, but it looked like he wrote quickly, with heavy strokes. A passage caught my attention because of the texture. He'd crumpled the page at some point.

The Dragon Pearl is vital, Captain Hwan had written, *but not in the way those fools in the Pearled Halls think. The scholars would lock it away and study its religious significance, while the Dragon Society would use it to make the wealthiest worlds even wealthier. I doubt they would allow it out of their hands to benefit others.*

My hand spasmed, and I carefully unclenched it to avoid wrinkling the page. The thought of the Pearl being used to make the wealthy core more fertile, more vital, made me scowl.

The Pearl could win wars for us, he went on. *As a weapon, it would be the ultimate threat, able to devastate an entire world as easily as it could make it blossom.*

I didn't like where this was going. I'd always thought of dragon magic as benevolent. But deep down I knew it wasn't that simple, as Haneul could have told me. True, you could use dragon magic to terraform worlds so life could flourish on them, or make the weather pleasant, or encourage crops to grow. That same magic could, as the captain suggested, destroy worlds and turn them into wastelands. It made sense that Hwan would think of the Pearl's benefits in military terms.

The next several pages contained terse

notes about disciplinary matters on the ship. Under other circumstances I would have lingered over them, but I had more important things to worry about than gossip.

Then I found another passage about the Dragon Pearl. And this one revealed an interesting detail.

The cadet is a fox. He will be useful.

I bit my tongue against a gasp. It had to be Jun! But why had he revealed his gumiho heritage to the captain? And "useful" how? I didn't like to think of my brother as a pawn.

I continued flipping through pages, looking for more mentions of Jun or the Pearl. Another sentence jumped out at me: *I can't make a direct approach to the Pearl's site until the ship is in good repair.*

So Captain Hwan knew where the Dragon Pearl was! That explained why the *Pale Lightning* was lingering in this area. But we couldn't land anywhere yet. Last I'd heard, the engineers were still working on Deck 3's damaged meridian.

If only I had more details about the location. Myung was only able to tell me so much before her untimely demise. It's a pity her family didn't know more about their ancestor's plans.

Could Myung be the comrade Hwan had mentioned to me earlier? I remembered the captain's words: *The blaster burned her life short.* Whose blaster? Had she known too much for her own good? Was her ancestor the shaman who had vanished with the Dragon Pearl? It all sounded very fishy. . . .

The next words caused ice to run through my veins.

The fox cadet is aware of the risks. Short of myself, no one has a better chance of helping the team survive.

Jun and his comrades hadn't deserted after all! The captain had sent them on a secret mission.

The investigator had implied that Jun had shamed our family. I had to find my brother and bring him home. Then Mom would have her son *and* the truth.

I flipped ahead a few pages, didn't see anything more about the site, then backtracked. My heart skipped a beat when I read a line I'd missed the first time.

287

We are reasonably certain Charm will work on the dead.

The dead? *Ghosts,* I realized, with a sickening feeling.

This could only mean one thing. Captain Hwan had sent Jun down to the world from which the entire Ghost Sector took its name. The Fourth Colony, better known as the Ghost Colony.

And if I wanted to retrieve my brother, I'd have to go there after him.

TWENTY-TWO

Heart hammering, I flipped through the rest of the notebook. I didn't spot anything else obvious in the writing. But a folded sheet of paper had been slipped into the back. I took it out, opened it, and saw that it was a sketched map. The captain had written a set of planetary coordinates on it. He'd also marked a landing site, and a destination.

For a moment I was tempted to take the map with me, but the captain would notice if it went missing, and I didn't want to make him more suspicious. Anything that caused him to step up security would make it harder for me to do what I needed to. I studied the sketch with narrowed eyes, committing it to memory.

My vision grew blurry, and nausea was starting to creep in. If the captain caught me in his quarters, my throwing up all over his carpet wouldn't help my case. Time to get out of there.

I made sure to gather Charm around me like a cloak of whispers. I'd hate to have gotten this far only to get caught now. I replaced the notebook in its drawer, making sure the latch closed properly, then padded across the expanse of carpet and out the door.

When the panel had closed behind me, I let out a breath I hadn't known I was holding. I wanted to lean against a bulkhead, maybe even nap standing up, but I couldn't stop, not there. I forced myself to keep moving, putting one foot in front of the other as though I were walking a tightrope.

I must have been in worse shape than I thought, because a crew member hurrying through the passages with a crate stopped dead a few feet from me and frowned in my direction. Sweating as I drew upon Charm, I thought at him, *I'm not here. There's nothing interesting to see.*

He slowed and shifted the crate in his arms, glancing this way and that. His eyes didn't focus, though, even when he was looking right at me. He gave a puzzled headshake and continued on his way.

After what seemed like hours, I slipped back into Medical. They'd given my bed to someone else while I was gone. I hoped they didn't keep track of who went where during the confusion of battle.

I recognized the head physician with her white-streaked hair. She was busy consulting a chart, and she had one stylus tucked behind her ear and another in her hand. I eased my way across the room until I came to an empty pallet, and climbed up onto it.

I had only dozed off for a few minutes, when someone prodded me awake. I sat up and mumbled, "Ma'am?" out of habit. For a second I thought I had missed the morning reveille and was going to get lectured for sleeping through an exciting session of scrubbing floors, or possibly helping out in the galley. The thought of the latter made my stomach protest, and I barely kept myself from retching.

"Don't sit up," the physician said, half a second too late.

Gratefully, I sank back down, feeling miserable.

The physician was studying her slate. "You're Jang. But I thought . . . No matter. We'll just have to give you your dose a few minutes late. More than a few minutes. I wonder . . ."

"Dose of what, ma'am?" I asked to distract her from the question of scheduling. My voice came out as a croak. I didn't want any medicine in my system, even though I would have welcomed relief from the nausea.

She smiled thinly. "More painkillers. I keep telling those fools in Engineering that they shouldn't be asking cadets to enter Trance without a lot more training. Open your mouth." I did, and she dropped a couple of foul-tasting orange pills into it. "Here." She brought a cup of water to my lips.

I faked swallowing, and, as soon as she

turned away to make a notation, I spat the tablets into my hand. Quickly, I stuffed them into a pocket. I'd just have to live with feeling awful.

I said, "It was an emergency at the time."

The physician harrumphed. "It's always one emergency or another in Engineering."

That sounded like a long-standing argument, and one I didn't want to get involved with. "Please — is Cadet Sujin all right?"

The physician relented enough to say, "They're healing nicely. Don't fret about them. You should get some rest yourself, Cadet."

She moved off, and I closed my eyes again. Although I meant to plan my next move, I fell asleep.

Some time later, I woke to a familiar voice. Not Haneul's or Sujin's, or even the physician's, but Byung-Ho's. I opened my eyes and peeked in his direction. He was propped up in a nearby pallet with a tray of rice gruel before him. One of the human medics was fussing over him. He had obviously recovered enough that they could remove him from the healing pod. Or maybe they needed the pod for someone hurt even worse.

I almost called out to him before remembering that he wouldn't recognize me, not in Jang's guise. I used my keen sense of hearing to eavesdrop on what he was saying.

"You were in a healing coma for quite a while," the medic informed him.

"I appreciate all the help, don't get me wrong," Byung-Ho was saying to the medic, "but there was someone else on the *Red Azalea* with me. A girl about so high." He held out his hand to indicate height. He went on to give a description, which didn't sound like me. Then I remembered that I'd been going around as Bora. I wondered if half the reason my mom was so dead set against using Charm was how hard it was to keep track of all the details.

The medic shook their head in bafflement. "Sorry," they said. "You're the only one who made it."

Byung-Ho's face sagged. "If only you'd shown up a little earlier . . . Not that I'm complaining about the rescue, but she was too young to die like that."

The medic's face cleared. Comforting people was something they were used to. "That's always hard," they said automatically and launched into a standard soothing speech.

It made me squirm inside, realizing that my welfare was the first thing Byung-Ho had asked about upon waking. Without his help, I would never have made it this far. I wanted to let him know that I was all right. On the other hand, I didn't want to blow my cover.

I waited until the medic moved on. Then I gathered up some Charm, which was getting easier with practice. I got out of my pallet, focused on convincing everyone in Medical that the bed was still occupied, and tiptoed over to Byung-Ho. My nausea had passed, and I was so hungry that even his watery gruel smelled tasty.

"Hello," I said.

The Charm I was using made him look not at me but at a spot over my shoulder. "Hello," he said distantly.

"The medic, they were wrong. The girl

from the *Red Azalea* . . . she didn't die. She's all right," I said, stumbling over the words. It felt weird talking about myself as though I was some stranger.

Byung-Ho frowned. "I got her in trouble."

More like I'd gotten myself into trouble. I was honest enough to admit that much. "She's fine," I assured him.

"That's good," Byung-Ho said slowly, as though he was having difficulty concentrating. He smelled faintly puzzled. "Say, if you get a chance, there's something I didn't get to tell her. . . ."

I'd been about to head off, but he'd piqued my curiosity. "Yes?" I said, trying not to sound too eager.

"Tell her she should pursue engineering," Byung-Ho said. "Wherever she learned how to do repairs, she's good. Really good. A talent like that shouldn't go to waste."

I couldn't help blushing. Back home, my family had taken my tinkering with machines for granted. But this was the third time someone on the *Pale Lightning* had complimented my skills. I silently thanked my father for them.

"Don't think about her anymore," I said in a choked-up voice.

"All right," he said, his frown easing.

I made him forget so he would no longer feel guilty about something that wasn't his fault. As I watched his face relax, I experienced a pang, like I'd lost a friend. But it was too late to change what I'd done. I smiled nervously and returned to my pallet.

A couple of hours later, a loud tone came over the sound system. I sat bolt upright as though someone had zapped me with lightning. "What's going on?" I demanded.

The corporal in the pallet next to mine yawned hugely, then cracked her knuckles, making a show of not caring. Her entire leg was in a cast, and I wondered what had happened to her. "Battle must be over," she said. "If the chief physician isn't yelling at everyone, the situation can't be that bad."

I wasn't so sure about that. She'd vanished into her office earlier in response to a call from the captain and still hadn't emerged. I kept eyeing the door nervously, wondering what they were discussing.

The corporal must have seen me flinch, because she laughed, not unkindly. "Don't be so nervous, Cadet. Any battle you live through is a good battle."

The physician chose that moment to come out. Her brows lowered. "You," she said to the corporal, "should take things more seriously."

Silently, I urged the corporal not to argue with the physician, who looked like she was in a bad mood. I could understand why a doctor wouldn't enjoy seeing so many people injured. Had anyone died? I hoped not, but I might have missed something while I was sneaking around in the captain's quarters.

As if my thought had summoned him, I heard the captain's voice over the announcement system. "All hands, stand down," he said. I glanced at the clock on the wall, and my eyes widened. The battle had lasted almost seventeen hours. And I had been unconscious for a good chunk of it.

When the physician turned to examine the corporal, I felt cold air whoosh against my skin. Jang.

"Captain Hwan thrives on combat," he whispered in my ear. "Other captains wouldn't have fought this long and risked more casualties, or losing the battle entirely."

"We have prevailed against the hostiles," the captain went on. "Fortunately" — his voice deepened into a purr that made my hair stand on end — "we have captured some of them. I do not anticipate any further threat at this time. However, we will need to put in for repairs. Our next stop will be the shipyard at Abalone Spire." He went on in this vein for a while.

I was thinking that our good luck was the captives' bad fortune when the captain's words penetrated. *Repairs.* That meant we weren't headed directly to the Fourth Colony.

What did the captain expect to find out from the captives? Were they after the Dragon Pearl, too? If so — my pulse quickened — then I wanted to learn what they knew.

Captives would be kept in the brig. I'd never been stuck in it, thank goodness, but I knew where it was. I had to get down there.

"Excuse me, ma'am," I said to the physician. It would be better if she discharged me so I could save Charm for what was to follow. "I'm feeling a lot better now. Do you think it would be all right for me to go back on duty?"

The head physician smiled humorlessly at me, but she obliged me with a quick examination, long fingers testing the air above me as she traced the meridians to check for any lasting damage. She followed that by poking and prodding my body with quick, impersonal touches. "You recovered awfully quickly," she said. My heart seized up, thinking she might have detected my use of fox magic, but she didn't seem to be suspicious — yet. "You're cleared to go."

Behind me, I heard the corporal say, "Must be nice to be so young and eager to go back to work."

"I could swear you broke that leg on purpose," the doctor retorted. "Do you like it here that much?"

"No better place for a nap," she was saying as I left them behind. I was starting to understand the physician's irritation.

I guessed that I was supposed to report in to Lieutenant Ju-Won. Would the head physician tell Ju-Won to expect me? Or would the doctor, trusting that I'd go where I was supposed to, send the report later, after she'd dealt with the rest of the casualties? I gambled that she wouldn't prioritize telling the lieutenant about a single cadet — me — when she had a lot of other patients on her mind.

"Jang," I whispered into the air, "can you come with me and keep a lookout? We might learn something from the prisoners in the brig."

He didn't materialize or speak, but a cold breeze touched my cheek, as if in agreement.

Emboldened, I walked quickly toward the brig. I only slowed when I felt the chill of Jang's presence again, cutting bone-deep this time. That was all the warning I needed.

I emerged into the corridor just as two soldiers marched by — a man and a woman. They scarcely gave me a glance. I was going to need their help to get into the brig. I focused my Charm on them and flashed a smile at the man.

"Yes?" he said, grinning goofily at me as if I was his new best friend. Which, in a sense, I was.

"I'm supposed to do some toilet-scrubbing in the brig," I said in a woeful voice, "but I can't remember the codes to get in there."

Might as well put all my latrine-duty experience to good use, I thought.

My magic was more wobbly than I'd reckoned on, though, because I still wasn't feeling well. "Why would they schedule someone to do chores in the middle of an interrogation?" the other soldier demanded.

Yikes. I invented an emergency and directed more magic at her, even though my head ached. "There was a problem with the plumbing," I said, "and the interrogators were pretty upset about it." I lifted my hands in a gesture of helplessness. "Look, I'm just a cadet. They don't tell me everything."

The nice thing about Charm was that I

didn't need to come up with a great excuse, just one good enough to give the magic something to fix on. A small voice in my head suggested that I stop relying on my magic to solve problems for me, because at some point all of this was going to catch up to me in a bad way. But I didn't see any alternative right then.

The two soldiers exchanged glances. I held my breath and tried to act unhappy about the mythical chore, rather than anxious that they would catch me lying. Then the woman said, "It's four-four-one-two. Better you than me, Cadet."

"Thank you," I said, and continued to the elevator. Since no one was in there with me, I sagged in relief. *Jun,* I reminded myself. *You're doing this for Jun, and Jang.*

But I hadn't seen Jun in nearly two years, and Jang was already dead, and in the meantime I was becoming less and less certain of what I was doing.

The elevator chimed, prompting me to exit on the appropriate deck. I squared my shoulders and walked to the door, then punched in the code. The world swam before me as the door opened. I heard voices yelling: the interrogators.

Jang's ghost-wind swirled against me, a warning to be cautious.

In the holos I'd watched, starship brigs were full of dramatic shadows where the villains crouched with their eyes gleaming threateningly. Sometimes on the cell walls you could catch a glimpse of scratched graffiti, which offered clues to what would happen next. Often patches of fungus grew on the deck.

Here, however, bright light sliced out of the doorway. I slipped through, drawn to the voices. Their words sounded muffled at first. As I tiptoed closer, I heard them more clearly, and I froze.

"Pox spirits."

TWENTY-THREE

Sweat trickled down my back, and my palms felt unpleasantly clammy. Were the prisoners sick? I hoped there was a medic down here, preferably one who was also a shaman, in case our guests had brought any vengeful disease spirits with them.

I had entered an observation chamber, where a pair of crew members with data-slates was looking through an immense window into a well-lit interrogation room just beyond. I cloaked myself with Charm so I would blend into the back wall.

Through the window, which I assumed was a one-way mirror so prisoners couldn't see out, I saw an interrogator and a stooped man sitting across from each other at a table. Two other people, a man and a woman, slouched behind the bars of separate cells on the left side of the interrogation room. The man at the table and the other two captives wore matching plain dun shirts and trousers. I wasn't sure whether those were their uniforms or our prisoner outfits. And without rank tabs to go by, I didn't know which one of them was the most important.

The person being questioned, weasel-faced and of stringy build, met the interrogator's gaze squarely. He didn't look frightened, just resigned. His words came through a speaker in the observation room. "You don't want to go down there," he was saying. "No one has magic powerful enough to deal with that many ghosts. And even if you did somehow manage to get past them, there's a chance the pox spirits still hold a grudge."

Something about his manner of speaking bothered me. I mulled it over while eavesdropping, but I couldn't put my finger on it.

"That's not your concern," the interrogator said. While her voice didn't waver, I caught a faint whiff of fear from her, even through the window. She had to be really worried.

"What killed all those colonists generations ago was no ordinary plague," the man said. "The Fourth Colony was one of the flowers of the Thousand Worlds. They had doctors and magicians and shamans as skilled as anyone you'd find in the core worlds today, but none of them could save the colonists after they neglected to appease the spirits."

Now I knew what troubled me about his voice. Watching the holos had led me to believe that all pirates were ruffians who solved their problems by shooting them, and my experience on the *Red Azalea* had borne that out. But this prisoner spoke with the measured accents of a scholar. He sounded like the narrator of some of the recorded history lectures my mother had forced me to listen to as part of my schooling.

"That's very interesting." The interrogator said this so sympathetically that I almost believed she felt for the man and his friends. "But it doesn't explain why you attacked us. Surely you knew that you couldn't hope to defeat a battle cruiser? If you'd persuaded your commander to stay in hiding instead of ambushing us, you would have avoided this whole mess."

I squinted at the interrogator. She wasn't using magic, but it was a kind of charm nonetheless. The more she befriended the prisoner, the more he would let his guard down around her, and the higher the chances he would let something slip.

For a moment I felt sorry for the man. Since he was already talking to her, he would eventually spill everything. Then I recalled Sujin's cries when the goblin got burned during the attack, and my moment of sympathy evaporated. The sooner this was over, the better.

The man's shoulders slumped. "You're military," he said, "so you can't understand. I'm not brave. I only told my commander what he wanted to hear."

The interrogator raised her eyebrows.

"Being a soldier isn't about never being afraid," she said, still kindly. "It's about doing your duty even when your gut is knotted up with fear. But, you know, unless you're afraid of bones, your commander can't threaten you anymore — he's dead."

Huh. So this man wasn't a pirate, but some kind of informant or advisor? Curious, but it made sense the more I thought about it. A smart pirate would seek counsel from someone who knew the history of the area.

The man averted his eyes for a long moment. "It wasn't like that," he said. "I — I lost a lot to that scandal. My husbands, my children, my reputation, everything. The commander was the only one willing to take me on. It wasn't much of a life, but it was something."

I had to stop my toe from tapping. The cold air that brushed against my skin told me Jang was still with me and feeling as impatient as I was. Presumably they'd discussed this "scandal," whatever it was, before I'd arrived. I didn't care about that. I wanted to hear more about the Fourth Colony.

They went back and forth in that vein for a while, to my increasing irritation. Apparently the scholar — for that's what he was — had, in desperation, made up an entire "ancient chronicle" in the hopes of establishing his reputation. Someone had caught him in the lie, and it had ruined him. The story made me uneasy, not least because it reminded me of all the lies I'd told to get here.

Eventually they wound back to the point. By this time I'd developed a healthy respect for the interrogator, who had been forced to nudge all the information out of the prisoner the hard way, without being able to rely on Charm. I paid close attention to her methods — it would be nice to have a fallback in case I was ever too tired to use magic.

The scholar bit his lip, complicated emotions playing across his face. He was making a difficult decision. Then he said, almost inaudibly, "Our commander was hired by one of your captain's enemies. Councilor Chae-Won of the Pearled Halls."

Jang, did you hear that? I mouthed.

There was no response.

The scholar kept spilling secrets. "She wants the Dragon Pearl so she can reduce their reliance on the Dragon Society. Whoever possesses it will control the next wave of colonization, and the Thousand Worlds' expansion. That's not just an ordinary fortune at stake — that's guidance over our very future, and wealth beyond imagining."

I closed my eyes for a second, flushed with fury. I thought of all the old clothes I'd mended over the years, the countless times I'd worked to repair the environmental filters and suits because we couldn't afford new ones, the dust that got into everything on Jinju. Whoever this councilor was, I doubted she was thinking about people like me and my family, who could use the Pearl's powers to make our lives less desperate. I knew, too, that my planet wasn't the only one in the Thousand Worlds that had suffered from a botched or incomplete job of terraforming, or the only one that hadn't been able to afford the expensive fees to set things right.

The interrogator didn't speak, only nodded. I admired her self-control.

"We were supposed to find and claim the Pearl for Chae-Won while preventing Captain Hwan from getting any closer to it," the man said. "But we hadn't figured out how to get past the ghosts. What I do know is that, long ago, the colonists grew arrogant and stopped making offerings to the pox spirits, and the spirits took their vengeance by wiping out the colony, as a lesson to the Thousand Worlds. The colonists' ghosts, in turn, became bitter and vengeful."

"A lot of people know that much," the interrogator said.

The man laughed painfully. "You mean they know the spooky stories they see in the holos, where ghosts come rampaging from the planet. That won't be far from the truth, if you offend them. And it seems to be what your captain is spoiling to do. It can't end well."

That *did* sound like Hwan's plan, based on what I'd read in his private log. Dread seized me. Had he gotten my brother embroiled with not only angry ghosts but also pox spirits?

To my frustration, the interrogator said, "You sound tired. It's time for you to have a break. Let's get some food into you."

I wasn't about to hang around to watch the man eat, and I didn't want the interrogator to catch me, either, so I hightailed it out of there before the observers could turn and notice me. Jang saved me from taking a wrong turn, and I murmured a hasty thank-you to him.

My thoughts churned as I headed toward Lieutenant Ju-Won's station to report in, however belatedly. Captain Hwan wanted the Dragon Pearl as a weapon of one kind, and his enemies wanted it as a weapon of another. Even worse, getting to the Pearl — and finding my brother — sounded like it would require finessing my way past spirits who'd held a grudge for a couple of centuries. I liked the whole situation less and less. But I couldn't give up now.

"You got lost *again*?" the lieutenant demanded when I checked in.

I fidgeted and did my best to look penitent. Instead of using Charm, I'd settled for trying to persuade her that I'd messed up rather than taken an intentional detour. It probably helped that I looked ghastly, which I knew because I'd peered at myself in the shiny expanse of a polished bulkhead. Despite the reflection's blurriness, I could see that I had dark circles under my eyes.

The lieutenant went easy on me, probably because I was tottering so much she thought I'd keel over. She assigned me to a shift of doing paperwork: helping to compile post-battle damage reports. When I reported to the sergeant in charge, I got the distinct feeling he didn't need or want my assistance. "Be careful," he said gruffly. "If I have to fix even one record because you got it wrong, you're going to have to weld this ship back together by yourself."

I knew he wouldn't literally follow through on that threat. Still, I bobbed a nervous nod to show that I got his point.

I didn't catch up with Sujin and Haneul until mess that evening. By then, even though I'd spent all afternoon sitting at a desk and only occasionally getting up to fetch tea, sweat drenched my uniform and my legs wobbled as I stood in line to get my food. I caught some of the other cadets raising their eyebrows at me, and my cheeks heated. Word must have gotten around about what had happened to me in Engineering.

Sujin had no trace of a burn, but their pallor did look slightly gray. Even their horn had an unhealthy gray tinge. An effect of the healing pod, I assumed. Still, they waved at me cheerily enough.

For once, Haneul didn't lecture me when she saw me. She'd gotten in line right behind me. I realized why when she reached out to steady my tray just before I would have dropped it.

"Careful there," Haneul said, quickly and subtly removing her hand so I could save face.

We sat down, and her anxious eyes studied me from across the table. "You almost look worse than Sujin here. Are you sure you don't need a stint in a healing pod yourself?"

"I don't want to make excuses," I said, more bravely than I felt. "I'm eager to get back to work with everyone else."

Her expression softened. "You have a good spirit," she said, "even if you can be an idiot sometimes. I heard what you did in Engineering."

"Makes two of us," Sujin said, winking at me.

"Yes," Haneul said, "what is it with you two and Trance?"

"The physician said I was very brave," Sujin crowed. "I heard you hung in there a long time, Jang, and you didn't even get burned. That's really impressive!"

I forced myself to smile despite the tremble in my hands. "Anything to avoid cleaning the bathroom."

Sujin laughed. "No kidding."

"You two missed out on the action while you were recovering, obviously," Haneul said, "but we beat the pirates, just like I knew we would." She looked as proud as if she had won the battle singlehandedly.

"I'm glad you're all right," I said to Sujin.

Sujin fiddled with their spork, then made a small gesture, conjuring up a thin rectangular box. "Thank you," they said, with an oddly formal half bow. "For looking out for me." They held the box out with both hands, as though they were honoring me. "I remembered that you like the chocolates best."

"Thank *you,*" I said, accepting the gift.

We smiled shyly at each other. Then I opened the box and passed the chocolates around. They were delicious. The three of us devoured them in silence, but it was a friendly silence. For a change, Haneul didn't chastise Sujin for using magic.

I thought about how much I would miss the two of them when I left the ship. I'd heard from Lieutenant Ju-Won that the *Pale Lightning* would be putting in for supplies and repairs at Abalone Spire in two days. Repairs would take a couple weeks, maybe longer. I couldn't wait that long to go looking for Jun. I needed to depart soon, and I had an idea about how to do it.

"Jang!" Sujin was snapping their fingers in front of my face. Back home, my cousins would kick my shin to get my attention, but doing that here would have earned the goblin a demerit. "Mess is ending. Hurry and have more tea. It'll wake you up."

"Oh, right," I said, feigning dizziness. It wasn't much of a pretense.

Later that night, after the roster of the next day's duties was announced, I reported to barracks and crept into my bunk. I listened as the others' breathing changed to the rhythm of sleep, or, in Haneul's case, snores. It was tempting to close my eyes, but first I had to plan my getaway.

I knew that, once the ship was repaired, the captain intended to head to the Fourth Colony. I had to beat him there. The map I had memorized from his notebook would guide me, but I would need transportation, and I would also have to come up with a way to slow down the *Pale Lightning.*

I had no idea how to pilot a shuttle. Figuring it out on the fly, while being on the run from a battle cruiser, didn't strike me as a great move. No, but there *was* another solution for getting off the ship, if my Charm didn't let me down. . . .

As far as the *Pale Lightning* was concerned, I had learned enough about the ship's meridians to do a little sabotage.

Thinking about that made my stomach clench. If I caused even minor damage to the ship as it journeyed through space, I'd put the engineers at risk of injury. I remembered Sujin's burn and grimaced.

If I tampered with the *Pale Lightning*'s systems while it was docked, however, people wouldn't get hurt. (At least I hoped not.) And it would serve as a distraction while I deserted.

Deserted. I rolled over on my side and shivered, staring into the darkness. I wasn't even a real cadet, and here I was, feeling regretful. Despite all the toilet scrubbing, I'd come to enjoy life in the Space Forces. I had finally gotten used to all the rules and regulations, I'd performed well in the training, and I'd made two good friends.

But none of that mattered. I had come to find my brother, and I hadn't completed that mission yet.

It wouldn't take long for people on the ship to notice that Jang was gone. There was no way I could Charm the entire crew into believing he was taking care of important business elsewhere or he had never existed at all. After he was missing for a while, Jang's comrades would con- clude that he'd taken the coward's way out and left.

I didn't like smearing Jang's character this way. I'd seen how my brother's reputation had suffered after he'd alleg- edly deserted. But what other choice did I have?

Haneul and Sujin would especially worry about Jang's disappearance. I couldn't reassure them in advance, though. Not without revealing what I'd learned about Captain Hwan's secret mission and, more importantly, risking execution for posing as a cadet.

I could get Jang's permission before- hand. It might assuage my guilt a little.

"Jang," I whispered, "are you there?"

Cold air swirled next to my ear.

"I'm going to have to leave this ship in order to get our answers."

The silence was heavy, expectant.

"I can only do it with the help of the mercenaries down in the brig," I said. Then I added coaxingly, "I could get more information for you in the process."

I took it as a good sign that Jang hadn't

stirred up more wind or frozen my fingers off.

"Once we dock at Abalone Spire, will you help me spring them and escape?" I finished.

His voice hissed in my ear. "Yesss," he said. "Maybe this time I'll finally get some satisfaction."

I sighed. Would he *ever* be satisfied? But I knew I shouldn't complain, because he was handy to have around. Hopefully he would be even more so in a couple days' time.

TWENTY-FOUR

Two nights later, I rose at three a.m., when my bunkmates were still sound asleep. For a moment I listened wistfully to Haneul's loud snoring, and the softer breathing of Sujin and the others. I might never see any of them again. But I couldn't delay any longer.

Given the subtle, self-serving consideration with which the interrogator had treated the captives, I doubted she'd be getting them up in the middle of the ship's night for questioning. All I'd need to do was get past any guards and try to bargain with the mercenaries myself. While I didn't like the thought of working with pirates, I didn't have many options if I wanted to get off the *Pale Lightning.*

First things first. I retrieved a blaster from one of the weapons lockers, along with some extra power packs. I imagined I'd have plenty of use for the blaster in the days to come. It took me a few moments to buckle the holster onto my belt, mainly because my hands shook with nerves.

I headed to Deck 3 with its damaged meridian as Jang kept a lookout. He tickled me with cold air whenever he spotted someone. I held my breath as I approached the restricted area, slowing down so I wouldn't fall on my face again. I had wondered if bad luck might also make my timing wrong, but no one else was in the passageway. There was less nighttime activity when the ship was docked.

As I expected based on my previous visit, two guards were stationed at the site. This time they were standing together — probably to keep each other awake — back-to-back and facing opposite directions. I had my ruse prepared. I took a deep breath, then nudged them with Charm to convince them my presence was nothing out of the ordinary. I pretended to be distraught and kept glancing over my shoulder.

"What's the matter, Cadet?" one of the guards asked.

I drew harder on Charm to increase their anxiety. "I saw someone acting strangely down the corridor. One of the privates — a short woman. She had some power tools. I was afraid to stop her because she looked dangerous. Please, you've got to go after her. . . ."

If the guards hadn't been under the influence of magic, they would have called in the incident instead of looking at each other and then breaking into a run. Their footsteps sounded unnaturally loud as they dashed off, and I couldn't help wincing at the racket. Still, I had bought myself a little time while they pursued a false lead.

Time for some real sabotage. My stomach ached as I ducked under the tape and tried to sense the damage to the invisible meridian. It looked like the recent battle hadn't done this area any favors. The floor tiles had warped further. Some wiring spilled out from a panel in the wall. It was black with corrosion, making it resemble the tormented branches of a diseased shrub.

Had the original sabotage been Jang's doing, however unintentional? I still didn't know, and now, when I needed his help, it certainly wasn't the right time to ask him.

I had no idea how the exposed wiring was related to the meridian, but it made a good target, in any case. I backed up, almost twisting my ankle in the process, and drew out the blaster. I aimed it squarely at the wires. The pistol writhed in my hands like a living creature, and I tightened my grip and shifted my stance, taking slow, deep breaths.

I squeezed the trigger. Red fire splashed the wires and the recess beneath the warped tiles. Sparks sputtered as the wires melted, and a noxious vapor rose from them. I gagged and stumbled away, gasping for untainted air, then quickly replaced the blaster in its holster to avoid accidentally frying my own feet.

Good thing the ship is already undergoing repairs, I thought. *They can just add this to the list.*

The pain in my gut intensified. Time for me to get out of there. I headed in the opposite direction from the guards and made my way to the elevator.

By the time I arrived on the brig level, I had a ferocious headache. I wasn't sure whether it was a side effect of what I'd done to the ship, or a result of nerves. Probably both. I should have grabbed some painkillers on my way out of the bunk. Too late now.

This time, I used shape-shifting to imitate Captain Hwan's form. I wasn't used to being so tall, and it took an effort to imitate his confident gait. But I figured the guards would be less inclined to stop the captain, especially if I used Charm to dampen their suspicions.

"Sir!" The guards snapped to attention in a way that would have been funny if the situation hadn't been so fraught with danger. If only they knew who I really was! Of course, if they guessed, this would end messily.

"I'm here to see the prisoners," I said, discomfited by the low growl of the captain's voice emerging from my throat. I couldn't let that show, though. I almost blurted that I had some additional questions for the captives, then thought better of it. The captain wouldn't owe anyone explanations, after all. Too bad I hadn't had the chance to impersonate him before this. It would have made my life easier.

"Of course, sir," said the guard in charge, a burly man. "Right this way, Captain."

It was bizarre to be addressed as "Captain," as if I were a real officer. Then again, *Captain* was just as much a fiction as *Cadet*. I couldn't let a fake rank go to my head.

I nodded, not trusting myself to speak, and followed the guard to where the three captives were being held. "Open the cells," I ordered, "then leave us." I leaned hard on Charm for this one.

Even so, the guard hesitated. "Sir —"

I decided a bluff was in order. "What's

the matter, you don't think I can handle them?" I caught and held his gaze in a way I never would've dared to as Jang.

The color drained from the guard's face. "Of course not, sir."

Did he think I was going to *eat* the prisoners? I'd never heard anyone so much as breathe the suggestion that Captain Hwan followed such ancient practices. But then again, who would, and risk offending a tiger?

Just out of curiosity, I smiled, letting just a hint of my teeth show. They weren't sharp fangs, though it would have been easy to conjure some — and that kind of shape-shifting was something even a tiger could do. I thought it might be overkill.

The guard swallowed visibly. "As you say, sir." He hastened to unlock the cells. I nodded at him, and he fled.

The three prisoners stared at me, frozen. The air was thick with the scent of their terror. It made me uncomfortable, but if it kept them from rushing me, it wasn't all bad.

I'd already gotten a chance to study the scholar, so this time I took a closer look at the other two. The man had a dour, unshaven face and the breadth of a bear. I made a note not to get close to him in a fight. As for the woman, stringy hair almost concealed her eyes, and her thin, scarred hands twitched nervously. I couldn't afford to discount her as a threat, either.

I reached for my blaster, and the smell intensified. "Keep your distance," I said, training the blaster on the scholar, and stepped back. "Out."

"You're executing us?" the woman prisoner demanded. She sounded more outraged than afraid. "An honorable captain of the Space Forces?"

You did *attack us,* I thought, remembering Sujin's burns. But this wasn't the time to seek revenge. "I said *out.*" I narrowed my eyes, directing Charm at her to make her more willing to obey. "I have a bargain for you."

The weasel-faced scholar made a *calm down* gesture at his comrade. Then to me he said, "Fine," in a weary tone. He emerged from his cell, and the other two followed suit. "What do you mean, 'bargain'?"

This was going to be the dicey part. I concentrated, making sure to keep my blaster trained on the scholar, and shifted back into my cousin Bora's shape. (If Bora ever made it out into space, she was going to have a certain reputation and it was going to be my fault. I wasn't really sorry, though.)

The scholar's eyes widened. "Gumiho," he breathed. "I thought your kind was extinct."

The other two were gaping at me as if I'd sprouted fox ears. When I was younger, I would have been tempted to make that actually happen, but I didn't think it would improve my bargaining position. I wanted to keep the scholar's attention on my blaster.

"I'm going to make you a deal," I said. Another bluff: "I'll take you to your captive ship and get you out of here. In exchange, you'll take me to the Fourth Colony. That's where you were going originally, wasn't it?"

The scholar drew a shaky breath, his mouth tightening. After a moment, he said, "I don't see that we have much choice at this point. But I have bad news

330

for you. I can't wield protective magic, and the shaman we hired to exorcise the ghosts was a casualty of the fighting."

"I can deal with that," I said, more boldly than I felt. "I have ways to persuade them to listen. Ghosts are still people" — even if they were dead — "and fox magic should work on them. I'll be able to calm them down so we can negotiate."

The scholar considered it. "I suppose it could work . . ." he said, his fear subsiding a little.

"If that *thing* is really a fox, it might be preparing to *eat* us," the woman said in an undertone, although I could hear her perfectly well.

I couldn't help feeling nettled. I was standing there with a blaster and she thought I was going to use my *teeth*? Besides — and it's not like I would ever do such a thing — I bet she'd taste revolting. "If you *really* don't want to be eaten," I said flatly, "maybe you should get moving like I told you to."

The woman began to protest, but the scholar made another placating gesture and she shut her mouth. The other man, his face pale, remained silent — too dumbfounded to speak, I guessed — but nodded at the scholar.

I changed back into Captain Hwan's shape. Borrowing the captain's authority would help us get by the guards more easily. Once again, the smell of fear wafted from the scholar and his comrades. Fear — and hope.

They didn't have to trust me, exactly, but I needed them as badly as they needed me. I just hoped they didn't catch on to that. In the captain's voice, I growled, "Forward."

When we reached them, the guards startled. "Sir," one of them said hesitantly, "I'm not sure this is the best —"

"Did I ask your opinion?" I said pointedly.

This, plus another dose of Charm, did the trick. The guard subsided. I pushed harder to convince them to skip the usual step of signing out the prisoners. Not only would that slow us down, I didn't want to leave any record of what had occurred.

The female prisoner coughed to catch

my attention. "Maybe we should . . ." She jerked her head toward the guards, who were smiling blankly at an empty stretch of the wall. "You know . . ." She made a throat-slitting gesture.

A growl escaped my throat.

"Suit yourself," she said, "but you know they're going to cause trouble later."

No way am I killing anyone, I thought. *Not unless absolutely necessary.* I would have to keep an eye on the woman, in case she tried anything.

The scholar glanced back at me thoughtfully while I gave him directions to the bay where his captured ship was docked. After I'd Charmed a cluster of crew members into passing us by with glazed eyes, he said in a low voice, "I'd always thought the old stories were exaggerations. Apparently not."

I was dying to ask why, if he was so impressed with my magic, it didn't seem to be having much effect on *him.*

As if he'd divined my question, the scholar smiled. It wasn't a happy expression. "I may not be the best scholar," he said — and I was reminded that he'd got-

ten his position by faking his credentials
— "but some of my knowledge of the old
lore is genuine."

That lore presumably included ways to
resist fox magic. I longed to ask him how
he was doing it, but he had no reason to
tell me. I'd have to see if I could coax it
out of him later. Assuming we all survived.

More guards awaited us at the docking
bay. I practiced my glare some more,
reinforced by Charm. Even if the *Pale
Lightning*'s crew was intimidated by
Captain Hwan, his decision to reunite
the prisoners with their ship was going to
make them hesitate.

While I'd grown more confident in
wielding magic, I was throwing a lot of it
around, and my headache had intensified. *Just a little longer,* I told myself.
Once we got off the *Pale Lightning*, I
could ease up.

"There it is," the pale-faced man
breathed. I wished he would stop sweating so heavily, even though I knew he
couldn't help it.

The mercenaries' starship rested on
several struts. For something that had

caused us so much trouble, it was dwarfed by the expansive space of the bay. It had a blockish, rectangular shape with protrusions for its various missile launchers and laser cannons. Most of them had been melted into blobby shapes like tree fungus. *Good,* I thought vindictively. Then I remembered I was going to be a passenger on it, and I gulped.

The ship's hull was dented and blackened with laser marks. No one had done any repair work on it — there was no reason they should have — and I winced, wondering how reliable the ship would be. But it was my only way off the *Pale Lightning.*

I followed the three mercenaries to their ship. The scholar smelled calm, but the woman swore when she looked it over. "We'll be lucky if we can get the maneuver drive to work," she said as she opened the hatch.

"You're going to have to do your best," the scholar said to her. I gathered that she must be the engineer, or the closest thing that remained.

I glanced about as I ascended the ramp. Considering the amount of damage on the outside, the interior wasn't as messed up as I had expected. Part of the airlock had been sealed off, but that was it.

The woman started toward the back of the ship. When I twitched, she said impatiently, "I need to check on the engine. You want to launch, don't you?"

She smelled sincere. "Go on," I said. I holstered the blaster. I didn't want to be caught unawares, but I also needed to avoid antagonizing the mercenaries too much. I hoped they'd remember that they owed me a favor for releasing them. I leaned on Charm to strengthen their feelings of gratitude.

In the cockpit, we waited tensely while the pale man asked the computer for the ship's status. I held my breath until the comms crackled on and the woman's voice said, "We can make do. Just don't try any fancy maneuvers."

As much as I wanted to let go of Captain Hwan's shape, I held on to it a little longer. It would be useful for confusing the *Pale Lightning*'s crew until we got out of there. I prayed the docking bay's guards would stay Charmed long enough to do nothing.

"Ready?" the pale man — the ship's pilot — said, his glance flicking between the scholar and me.

The scholar looked my way, and I nodded crisply. Time to go.

TWENTY-FIVE

"All systems go," the pilot said. He sounded grimly cheerful, or cheerfully grim. "Everyone strapped in?"

The scholar and I both said yes. The lights on the control panel changed to blue. The glow sheened over the pilot's face and pooled in his eyes, making them resemble windows to another world.

I shivered. It wasn't dread. Rather, I felt the ghost-wind again. Jang must have followed me off the *Pale Lightning* and onto the mercenaries' ship. I hadn't expected that. Ghosts typically stick close to the location where they died. Maybe now, without him around, the broken meridian on the *Pale Lightning* would heal. But would Jang curse my mission with bad luck?

The ship surged forward. A new light came on, this one red. The pilot hit it out of reflex and laughed sourly.

The real Captain Hwan's voice snarled from the communications channel. "Scholar Chul."

The scholar flinched.

"You have one minute to power down your stardrive and exit your vehicle with your compatriots. After that, I make no guarantees for your personal safety."

"Ignore him," Chul said quietly. "There's no going back, not anymore." His mouth pulled up in an expression that would have resembled a smile if not for the exhaustion in his eyes.

"Right," the pilot said. He thrust a joystick, and the ship surged forward.

I bit back a shriek as we headed straight for the docking bay's hatch. A glance at the cameras revealed that two squads of fully suited soldiers had burst in and were opening fire on the ship. Lucky for us that antipersonnel weapons didn't have much effect on it, despite the damage it had already taken. I kept expecting to feel impacts, however small, or hear the *clatter-shatter-bang* of projectiles hitting the hull.

I was worried we'd crash on the way out. But the pilot was prepared. He blew open the hatch with a missile at short range. Red lights flashed crazily throughout the docking bay as air whooshed out into hard vacuum.

Acceleration slammed us sideways as our ship veered hard to starboard, then rolled. Alarms clanged and flashed red, this time inside *our* ship. I narrowly avoided biting my tongue as I clutched the seat's armrests.

"They can't fire at us so close to their own hull," the pilot said, rapid and breathless, "but I can only keep this up for so long."

I started to ask what he recommended doing, then realized he wasn't talking to me.

"Well, you're going to have to buy me a

few more minutes," the engineer's voice snapped from the internal comm channel. "You don't want us botching the Gate."

I had an idea. "Put me on the channel to the *Pale Lightning.*"

To my gratitude, the pilot didn't argue. He punched another button without looking at me. Good thing, too. I wanted him to concentrate on what he was doing.

I thought of how much Captain Hwan intimidated me. I could use that same predatory presence to my advantage. "This is Captain Hwan," I said, pitching my voice low, and adding a growl for good measure. "Stand down immediately."

I heard bewildered murmurs and gasps on the other end. "C-Captain?" someone said.

"Ignore them!" Hwan snapped. "It's an imposter."

The murmurs quieted. I imagined the scene on the bridge. While I didn't think the captain would face an out-and-out mutiny, any hesitation or confusion would work in our favor.

I had thought the pilot would harangue the engineer to hurry up. Instead, he kept silent. I was impressed by his discipline. It made sense: The more he distracted her, the harder it would be for her to get the job done.

In the meantime, I had a part to play as well. "Don't listen to the real imposter," I said, torn between taking pleasure in toying with Captain Hwan from a safe distance and feeling guilty about tricking the cadets and crew members. "Don't you know he's deliberately been sabotaging the ship? You need to stop him." I deepened my voice further on that last sentence.

"Not bad," the scholar said, softly, so the crew on the *Pale Lightning* wouldn't pick up his voice.

Our ship's internal comm channel crackled to life. "Ready," the engineer said tersely.

The pilot stabbed the channel to the *Pale Lightning* closed in the middle of Captain Hwan's answering tirade. I felt a vengeful glow of satisfaction, like when I had slammed the door on my mom's lectures when I was a kid, except better, because this time I was going to get away with it. I hoped.

"Go," the scholar breathed.

The pilot didn't have to be told twice. He pushed the joystick again. I bit my tongue as the ship suddenly rocketed away from the *Pale Lightning.*

The battle cruiser opened fire on us. Our ship swerved, and the pilot grinned fiercely as his fingers danced over the controls. "Thank all the heavens for advanced electronic countermeasures," he said.

He was jamming the missiles' tracking mechanisms. I watched in tense fascination as the missiles swerved *away* from us, fanned out, then doubled back on the *Pale Lightning.* I caught my breath, not wanting the projectiles to hit the battle cruiser and hurt my friends.

My heart clenched. I wished there had been another way for me to find out what had happened to Jun. Could I have gotten help from Haneul and Sujin without lying to them about who I was and why I cared about him?

Too late now.

As we plunged through the silent cacophony of missiles exploding off our starboard bow, the Gate bloomed open before us, a hole of whirling pearly blue-violet light in the black depths of space. The colors captivated me despite the danger we were in. My breathing slowed in rhythm with the pulsing of the light.

The pilot whispered what I recognized as a spacer's prayer that heaven would see us safely through the Gate. The scholar repeated it a heartbeat later. I squeezed my eyes shut, but the Gate's swirls still appeared behind my eyelids. I was dazzled briefly by visions of dragons and tigers chasing each other across a sky in which lightning flickered and crackled.

With effort, I shook myself free of the Gate-visions. For a moment I wondered why my body felt so heavy and unfamiliar; then I remembered that I was still impersonating Captain Hwan.

Since I certainly wasn't fooling anyone in the ship we'd escaped in (whose name I still didn't know), I shifted back into my own human form for the first time in weeks. A sense of pressure I hadn't even been conscious of eased from my bones. I couldn't relax, exactly, but I felt more comfortable.

I'd forgotten I had an audience. The scholar, Chul, was watching me with intent, curiously bright eyes. "I'd heard the old tales," he said, "but I never would have thought that a fox would care about terraforming."

He was referring to the powers of the Dragon Pearl. Once, I would have snapped a retort, thinking of the way plants struggled to grow on Jinju, with its unrelenting dust and its infrequent rain. I didn't trust Chul enough, though, to reveal anything to him about my past. I merely said, "Maybe foxes are more complicated than you think."

The pilot cleared his throat, then called the engine room. "How soon before we can make another Gate, Sh— ?" His eyes flickered to me; then he clamped his mouth shut.

Foxes didn't have the ability to use people's names against them, at least not that *I* had heard of, but I couldn't blame the others for taking precautions. Chul hadn't shown any concern over the fact that I knew his name, so I guessed I didn't possess any magic in that area.

At first all I heard from the engineer was a clattering followed by a string of curses. Then she laughed breathlessly. I wondered if she was quite right in the head.

I peeked over at the pilot's displays, silently thanking Lieutenant Hyosu for her lessons. I might not have the full training of a genuine Space Forces cadet under my belt, but I'd picked up the basics.

We had emerged not far from a star ringed by a massive planet, likely a gas giant where even dragons wouldn't be able to survive without magical protection. Jun had taught me about such things when we were children, spinning stories of all the worlds we'd explore together. While I couldn't see more than a faint ruddy disc in the scan display, I longed for Jun to be sitting in the cockpit, looking at the planet with me.

A station orbited the planet, and readouts indicated that ships were docking and taking off from there. A light flashed: The station was hailing us, waiting for a response. I glanced at the pilot, but he shook his head.

"All right," the engineer said through a burst of static. The laughter had drained from her voice. "Do you want the good news or the bad news?"

"All the news," Chul said.

She snorted. "The good news is that we can manage two more jumps."

"And the bad?"

"That we can manage two more jumps."

I thought furiously. "One jump to get us to the Fourth Colony," I guessed, "and one to get us away. Then we're stuck until we can recharge the Gate drive, and that's when they can attack us."

The pilot arched an eyebrow at me. "Not bad," he said grudgingly.

"We have to try it anyway," Chul said, rubbing his eyes. "As much as I'd prefer to make a run for it, we made a bargain" — he eyed me — "and we're out of money. If we succeed in retrieving the Pearl, we'll at least be able to scare up a loan at whichever station we escape to."

I fought back a spasm of disgust, not

just because of his interest in the money, but because of my own. While it was easy for me to judge him, was I really much better? Chul sought wealth on behalf of the people depending on him. I was doing the same thing, just on a different scale. Sure, I could talk about bringing prosperity to Jinju, but I longed for some of that prosperity for my own family. My mind flashed back to Nari's luxuriously appointed office in the gambling parlor, and how I had thirsted to have something like that for myself.

The pilot and the engineer were arguing over some repair that the latter had jury-rigged. "You realize our luck is going to be bad, the way our gi flows are wobbling right now," she was saying.

I stifled a flinch. The disturbance in the gi flows could be the result of damage the ship had sustained, of course. It could also be due to Jang's presence.

"It can't be that bad if we've gotten this far," the pilot said. "Anyway, we shouldn't linger here. The station is getting suspicious." He grinned at me, not in a friendly way. "Ready for another jump?"

"The sooner the better," I said. Once it was fully repaired, the *Pale Lightning,* with its bigger, more powerful Gate drive, would be able to jump more times than us before it had to recharge. Worse, they knew where we were headed. Our only hope was to retrieve the Dragon Pearl first so we'd have a bargaining chip.

"I agree," Chul said.

He was going along with everything too easily, even though the three of them could easily overpower me now that we were on their ship. Was this a trap? Was there an angle I hadn't thought of? If he was making me nervous, he undoubtedly felt the same way about me.

"Is there anything *you* can do to improve our luck?" the pilot asked me. He was meeting my gaze with an effort, as though he was afraid I might leap out of my seat and eat him.

"I don't have that kind of power," I said. I didn't like revealing even that much about fox magic.

My guess was that Chul would know if I lied. Could he also sense that we had a ghost on board? Wisely, Jang had not revealed his presence other than the occasional wisp of cold air at my side. If the scholar could resist Charm, he might know ways to harm fox spirits or ghosts, too. I didn't want to find out.

"We'll just have to take our chances," Chul said, "and hope the *Pale Lightning* is not already waiting for us at the Fourth Colony."

I doubted it would be, after my additional sabotage, but I kept that to myself, too.

The engineer said, "Things are as good as they're going to get on my end. Do it."

I caught myself holding my breath and forced myself to inhale and exhale normally. It wouldn't do for the others to figure out how nervous I was. I'd come so far from Jinju. I wasn't about to let Captain Hwan stop me now.

"Here goes nothing," the pilot said. His hands moved over the controls, and the ship veered away from the station. One of the lights on his panel was still blinking, indicating that the station was still waiting for us to identify ourselves. I didn't say anything. They were going to have to live with never knowing who we were or what we were up to, and if they reported us to the *Pale Lightning* after we were gone, well, that wouldn't come as any surprise.

As the Gate drive activated, the ship vibrated enough that my teeth chattered. It hadn't done that the last time, and I hoped it wasn't a bad omen. My fingernails dug into the arms of my seat as I prepared for a rough jump.

The first sign that something had gone wrong was the color of the Gate itself. I'd gotten used to the beautiful purplish swirls of light. This time, the Gate was a white sharper than snow, keener than knives. It stabbed my vision. Even though I closed my eyes, I was terrified that all I'd be able to see forever after was that piercing white abyss.

I peeled one eye open, then the other. The pilot had paled. Despite his calm face, Chul's hands were clenched on the armrests.

"Let me guess," I whispered. "It's not supposed to look like that."

"Good guess," the pilot said.

Normally I would have reacted to his

sarcasm, but I couldn't blame him for his anxiety, not when I shared it.

Through the viewports all we could see was that uncanny white light. Shadows were hard-edged, shapes reduced to riddles. It was so bright I could barely distinguish colors from each other anymore.

Then the light shuddered out, and we emerged near the Fourth Colony, home of the ghosts.

TWENTY-SIX

We shot out of the Gate into orbit around the Fourth Colony. The planet curved beneath us, its surface violet-green. Whirling, eerie white clouds hid some of the land and ocean from view. If those were storms, I didn't want to get caught up in them.

The black backdrop of space and its scatter of stars looked innocent enough. I let out a sigh of relief over the fact that I didn't spot the *Pale Lightning*'s bulk, even though I knew logically it wouldn't be there.

That jump wasn't so bad.

The thought didn't last long. Suddenly, sparks sizzled and leaped from every display in a shocking cacophony of light and foul black smoke. I caught a glimpse of the monitors blackening and cracking, and I cringed from the sound. Then everything went dark.

We'd been hit. I was sure I was dead. I'd made it almost all the way to the Fourth Colony just to be smudged into oblivion by a missile. I was torn between terror and outrage at the unfairness of the whole situation. No wonder ghosts lingered to haunt the living with their complaints.

Then the smoke irritated my lungs and I began coughing and wheezing. Tears streamed from my eyes and I wiped my face furiously. I was pretty sure the dead didn't suffer runny noses, either.

"Oh no," Jang's thready voice said in my ear, accompanied by a freezing blast of wind. "This is all my fault."

A lump rose in my throat. *Mine as much as yours,* I mouthed, trusting that he'd be able to understand me.

"Status," Chul said before he, too, started to cough.

"The *Pale Lightning* beat us here," the pilot said hoarsely. It sounded as though he was speaking through a hand over his nose and mouth. Good idea — it reduced the effects of the smoke. "We must have been stuck in that warped Gate for so long, they got here first by using different Gates. And they seeded the area with EMP mines."

Electromagnetic pulses. The *Pale Lightning* had shielding against EMPs, but this ship didn't, apparently. And I hadn't seen any sign of mines . . . but then I remembered one of Lieutenant Hyosu's lectures on the subject. In space you wouldn't necessarily detect any glow. The first time you'd know was when you ran into one and all your systems fizzled out.

The darkness — both inside and outside the ship — unnerved me. On a planet, even on a clouded night, you still had faint hazy light filtering from the sky, and of course the domes and settlements had artificial lighting. Out here in space, near a dead colony, there was little for us to see by. In this region there wasn't much in the way of starlight.

Also, we had no artificial gravity anymore. I hadn't noticed it at first, because I'd been too busy trying to adjust to the darkness. But my stomach and inner ear complained, and I was overcome by nausea. Good thing I hadn't eaten recently. I was pretty sure puking in nullgee was even more disgusting than doing it was in normal gravity. Just the thought made my gorge rise.

I growled slightly at the clomping sound of magnetic boots, then caught a whiff of mixed smoke and sweat and realized it was the engineer. She tapped the bulkheads as she went so she wouldn't bang into things. I heard her rummaging around and wondered what she was up to. Then something crackled, and a pale green chemical light flooded the cockpit.

"These light sticks might make it easier for any boarders to find us," she said as her shadow loomed against the deck, "but it beats hanging around in the dark unable to get anything done. Let me guess" — she nodded at the pilot —

"mines?"

"We emerged in one of the standard lanes, and they were waiting for us," the pilot said. The green light made a bizarre sickly mask of his face.

We got out of our seats to retreat from the billowing smoke, but we couldn't escape it entirely. The first order of business was to get suited up. The EMP attack meant that our life support system was down, too, and if intruders breached the hull, we'd lose atmosphere. I was grateful for the shielding on the suits' locker, which ensured that the suits' old-fashioned boots hadn't been demagnetized.

According to the engineer, with the four of us on board, we had about twelve hours before the lack of power to the air recyclers would become an issue. I could extend that time a little by taking on an inanimate shape, like a table, but that meant I wouldn't be able to help the others. Once we put the helmets on, the suits themselves would provide us with enough air to last for twenty-four hours, with two backup canisters apiece. The dubious silver lining was that none of us believed the *Pale Lightning* would leave us alone for that long.

"That's it, then," Chul said. His voice sounded calm, but I could smell his bitterness. "We're floating here without power of any kind and Captain Hwan can capture us at his leisure. I doubt he'll be merciful this time around."

I felt a stab of guilt. If it weren't for my plan, the mercs wouldn't be in this position. Then I reminded myself that they'd already been looking for the Dragon Pearl. They would have run into Captain Hwan anyway.

The engineer knelt and popped open a locker I hadn't spotted earlier. She drew out a toolkit. "I can't do much with the tools when we're in this condition, but we might as well arm up."

She also pulled out a blaster, which she holstered in her belt, then a second one, which she gave to the pilot. "Sorry," she said to Chul, who remained empty-handed. "I know how bad your aim is."

Chul gave her a pained smile. "I'm not offended."

The engineer presented the scholar

with a miniature welding torch from the kit and showed him how to use it. "This may come in handy in a fight," she said. Then she added, "If you burn your face off, don't blame me."

"I'll be careful," he said.

It irritated me how, even now, they consciously avoided addressing each other by name around me. *I'm not the enemy,* I wanted to say.

On the other hand, for all they knew, I'd been working with the captain all along and had set them up. No wonder they were paranoid.

I noticed, too, that they hadn't offered me any weapon.

I wasn't the only one who saw that. "Should I surprise them so you can grab one of the guns?" Jang whispered in my ear. "I could spook them good."

I considered it, then gave a tiny head-shake. I didn't want to start a firefight with my so-called allies. If we faced hostiles, the mercenaries were likely to have better aim than I did. Besides, I had fox magic and they didn't, so I wasn't defenseless.

"Are we splitting up or staying to-gether?" I asked. As much as I wanted to be involved in the decision-making, I had to defer to their judgment. I didn't know their ship's layout, so they'd have a better idea of how to defend it. Plus, they were mercenaries. They'd had more experience with boarding actions.

Chul, at least, took me seriously. "Ordinarily I'd say we should stick together and prepare to ambush boarders," he said. "I could be used as bait."

The engineer rolled her eyes at this.

"But this time we have the advantage of a fox on our side," he said, raising his eyebrows at me.

"If you're thinking I can trick them with magic, forget it. They'll be expecting as much. I revealed my heritage the moment I impersonated Hwan."

"Do you have any other suggestions?" Chul asked.

I did have one. "Do we have time to set traps for them? Or at least make it look like we did? If they're led to believe that any random crate or seat could be hiding a vicious attack fox" — the pilot snorted at this — "that might slow them down. . . ."

"Not a bad idea," the engineer said grudgingly. "Let's get started, because we don't know how much time we have before they show up."

We all put on our helmets. Now we would all communicate via headsets that we could switch on or off. I didn't like the way it deadened my fox hearing.

"You still willing to help me?" I whispered to Jang with my headset turned off. "I know the *Pale Lightning* is your former ship, but something's clearly rotten with the captain. And if my mission ends here, so do your hopes of getting more answers."

"I know." Jang sounded torn. "I'll do what I can as long as no one gets killed."

I was about to retort that I didn't want to hurt anyone, either, but then the engineer gestured for me to follow her, so I shut up.

Rearranging crates in the ghastly green light gave me the creeps. I kept expecting ghosts to jump out of the shadows. Which was ridiculous, because I was already accompanied by one. Every time I saw a flicker out of the corner of my eye, I wondered if Jang was about to say something to me.

"Can ghosts see in the dark?" I whispered to him.

"Yes," he answered softly. With cold air he nudged my left shoulder, then my right. "I can warn you which direction they're coming from."

"Thanks," I said. "That might come in handy."

We constructed makeshift forts to hide behind, leaving narrow gaps between the crates through which we could spot any hostiles. The thought of my comrades firing on people I'd served alongside made my gut clench.

A jangling sense of *wrongness* pricked at my nerves. And no wonder. Not only was our ship badly damaged, not only was Jang's presence bringing us ill fortune, but we were making matters worse by rearranging the crates haphazardly. The gi flows throughout the ship had to be going completely haywire. But it couldn't be helped. I just hoped we wouldn't be stung by disaster at the worst moment.

The ship's clocks were down, but the helmet's air gauges gave me a way to estimate how much time had passed. Scarcely an hour, though it seemed like much longer. The combination of shadows and weightlessness and the unwavering green glow of the chemical light made me feel as though I'd become unanchored from the outside world. I couldn't give in to that sensation, though. I had to stay alert.

I felt a faint vibration. I took off my helmet and listened. There was a slight hum in the air. I replaced my helmet, then motioned to Chul to get his attention. "I think they're coming," I said in a low voice.

The others didn't question my sharp hearing. The engineer gave us just enough time to take up our positions behind the floating walls of crates, then snuffed out the chemical lights. Violet afterimages danced and flickered in my vision. I heard myself breathing too fast. My attempts at meditation didn't help, not when the vibrations were getting stronger.

Finally there came the sound of metal screeching, and a *clank* that I was sure even the others could hear. Captain Hwan and his crew must have breached our hull.

Sweat dampened my palms and trickled down my back. Part of me wished the boarding party would hurry up already. But I knew from drills on the *Pale Lightning* that they'd be trained to proceed carefully, checking for ambushes and traps as they went.

Clomp, clomp, clomp. Not just one set of footsteps, but several. I held my breath, trying to figure out how many people were coming. The pilot had crouched down and pressed his helmet to the deck in a vain attempt to hear better, which I only discovered when I bumped into him by mistake. Like all fox spirits, I had good vision in low light, but this was *no* light. In total darkness I had to rely on other senses. And Jang presumably was saving his warnings for real threats so I wouldn't accidentally blast one of the mercs.

At last the hatch to the hold opened, and a piercing, blue-tinted beam sliced through the darkness. I squinted so it wouldn't blind me. The pilot and engineer raised their blasters to the shooting holes we'd made.

I waited for shadows to fall across the threshold, for Jang's warning touch. If we were really lucky, maybe the boarding party would make the mistake of silhouetting themselves against the blue light, making themselves easy targets. It didn't look like they were going to commit such a basic error, however.

A familiar voice hissed from the corridor: Captain Hwan's. I'd been expecting him to shout, or roar, but he spoke so quietly that I had to strain to hear him. The effect caused my skin to prickle.

"Scholar Chul," Captain Hwan said in his deep voice. "And Gumiho." I couldn't help biting my lip when he said that. "In a moment I am going to send in a couple of people to accept your surrender."

My glance went to the engineer, who was shaking her head dubiously, then to the pilot, whose brow was furrowed in concern. None of us trusted the captain. There had to be some kind of trick involved.

Two figures marched through the entrance, their shadows cutting across the floor. A faint, wavering glow in the air told me that they had personal shields. I didn't know how much blaster fire it would take to overwhelm the armor. We might have to find out the hard way.

It took me a moment to identify the soldiers. They were backlit, and the light reflecting off the crates' surfaces didn't do a very good job of revealing their faces, especially through their helmets. But once I got used to the alien-looking combat suits, I knew exactly who they were. The one on the left was Sujin. The one on the right, Haneul.

"No!" Jang cried in anguish, loudly enough to be heard by everyone.

The mercs glanced about wildly, but I had no attention to spare for them.

Neither Sujin nor Haneul was armed. That didn't make sense. Unless . . .

"I have learned," Captain Hwan went on, his voice still soft, "that Cadets Sujin and Haneul failed to recognize the intruder in our midst."

I couldn't help it. I sucked in my breath

and stared wide-eyed at my friends. *Former* friends, I assumed, since they now knew that I wasn't Jang. Was Hwan holding them hostage? He wouldn't. . . .

He would. "Gumiho, if you and your comrades surrender to the cadets," Captain Hwan said, "you will be treated fairly. As long as you cooperate with our operations."

Bile rose in my throat. I had a pretty good idea of what Hwan meant by "cooperation," at least from me. Surely he'd figured out that I was, if not related to Jun, connected to him somehow.

Chul squared his shoulders. I could tell he was tempted by Hwan's offer. I couldn't blame him, to be honest. At the same time, I couldn't imagine this ending well for any of us.

Instead of capitulating, though, Chul signaled to his two comrades, and they raised their blasters. My heart almost plunged to the deck. But they didn't fire, not yet.

"If you don't come with me," Captain Hwan said, "the cadets will be court-martialed for treason. Right here. Possibly even executed."

What? This was insane! "You can't do that!" I shouted.

Sujin's expression was stubbornly impassive. Haneul looked stricken, and lightning crackled around her.

Chul squeezed his eyes shut.

"In deep space, a captain's word is law," Hwan returned. His voice never wavered from its eerie calm. "I have to be able to rely on my crew. Any *real* cadet knows that."

I flinched.

The engineer mouthed, *Should we?* at Chul.

Chul shook his head and mouthed back, *They're unarmed.* It made me think better of him.

"All right," I said in defeat. I couldn't let Captain Hwan kill Sujin and Haneul, who had done nothing wrong.

I heard Jang's sigh of relief.

Chul reached for my shoulder to hold me back, but I slipped past him. "I'm coming out. Don't shoot."

TWENTY-SEVEN

I started to speak to Haneul and Sujin, but the dragon only stared stonily at me. Sujin wouldn't meet my eyes. Hwan didn't bother putting restraints on me, which made sense. Given my shape-shifting abilities, handcuffs wouldn't slow me down. Regardless, I didn't want to get the cadets into even more trouble by slipping out of his grasp.

The march to the breach in the ship's hull and into one of the *Pale Lightning*'s sealed airlocks took only minutes, but it felt much longer. I had to put the helmet back on, which frustrated me, because it dulled my senses. I had a little difficulty walking in the magnetic boots, which had a stronger pull than the ones I'd worn on the *Pale Lightning,* but I wasn't about to admit that.

"All right," Jang's voice said inside my helmet. Although he spoke in a whisper, I jumped. "This is where we part ways. Thank you for leading me to these mercs. I'll have fun haunting them."

"Wait —" I started, but I couldn't feel his cold presence around me anymore. Desolation overcame me. We'd been coconspirators, in a sense, and now he was gone. Since I was no longer borrowing his form, Jang had no reason to stick close to me. While he'd originally been interested in finding out about the specific pirates who'd caused his death, it now appeared that he'd become more generally vengeful toward the whole category. I didn't envy Chul and his comrades.

Behind me, soldiers were escorting Chul and the other two prisoners. *Sorry for siccing a ghost on you,* I thought in their direction.

I craned my head but didn't catch sight of Captain Hwan. I couldn't use my sense of smell to track him, either. At a guess, he was with the other soldiers, too. My shoulder blades tingled unpleasantly.

The *Pale Lightning*'s airlock was vaster than the other ship's. I fought a surge of panic at being surrounded by soldiers. They could easily gun me down. One of the lieutenants gestured sharply at Haneul and Sujin, and they stepped back, leaving me alone in the center.

Captain Hwan strode forward to loom over me. I'd already been sweating, and this didn't help. It took all my courage not to shrink from his ruthless predator's glare. I wished for claws and sharp teeth — but I knew that even if my friends' lives weren't at stake, there was no way I could best Hwan in a physical fight. If I was going to escape this situation, I'd have to do it another way.

"Captain Hwan," I said, bowing courteously. I was glad that my voice didn't quaver — much.

"Your name," Hwan said. I hated the way his voice sounded even more threatening through his helmet.

"Kim Min," I said. I didn't want to be a liar, not right now. Besides, he already knew the most dangerous thing about me — that I was a fox. Best to keep things straightforward.

"Ah," he said. "The lost cadet's sister."

So Jun had mentioned me. For a moment I felt a mixture of outrage, fear, and pride. What had Jun said about me? I doubted the captain would reveal that, though.

"What did you do to my brother?" I said.

"You appear to be misinformed," Hwan said coolly. Once again I wished I could take off my helmet and find out if he smelled of deception.

"I gave myself up like you told me to," I said. "You'll let Haneul and Sujin go?"

"The cadets still have a lot of explaining to do," he said, "but yes. You have my word."

Strangely, I believed him.

"Take Min to solitary confinement," Hwan ordered some soldiers. "Return the mercenaries to their cells in the brig."

Every one of my nerves screamed at me to flee, change into a spiky metal ball, anything to avoid being locked up like an ordinary animal. Hwan had complete power over me, though. I thought of Su-jin refusing to meet my eyes, of Haneul's stiff back. We might not be friends any-more — if we'd ever been friends to begin with, considering how I'd deceived them — but that didn't mean they de-served to suffer.

I didn't think I deserved to be impris-oned, either, but I'd have to deal with that myself.

Four soldiers fell in, two in front of me and two behind. I bowed my head and walked with them. Despite their size, the *Pale Lightning*'s passageways, which I'd started to think of as a second home, felt like they were about to collapse on me.

I recognized the brig's cells, but we walked beyond them to a section I hadn't visited before. We reached a bleak, empty room with a shimmering force shield for a door. That spelled trouble. I could get through bars, but a force shield? No way.

One of my guards punched a code into

the keypad. Unfortunately, she shielded her right hand with the other so I couldn't see the numbers. It figured that they'd stick to security protocol now.

The force shield flickered out. "Take off your suit," the guard said, "and go in. Don't try anything funny or we'll vent air out of this entire section. If you shape-shift, we'll blast anyone — or anything — that looks suspicious."

"I won't," I said. At least, I wouldn't right then. Not when they were alert. Later, though . . . later was another story, especially if I could get Sujin and Haneul to come with me. While deserting was a serious crime, I couldn't imagine that they had much loyalty left for a captain who had threatened to execute them for something they couldn't have known. Or so I told myself.

As much as I hadn't enjoyed suiting up, I discovered that peeling it off made me feel even worse. The suit only provided limited protection from blaster fire, and it wouldn't have been much good against regular bullets, but it was better than nothing. Now, if the guards decided to get rid of me, I wouldn't have any armor at all.

I held my breath for a second. But no one raised a blaster and roasted me. Good to know. The guard cleared her throat, and I obediently trudged into the cell.

The force shield thrummed back into existence, trapping me inside. "I don't recommend ramming into it," the guard said. "It'll knock you out, and we'll be happy to leave you that way."

I almost retorted that she didn't scare me, then thought better of it. I wanted her to think I was defeated, get her to let down her defenses. I'd take any advantage I could scrounge up. So I only responded with a shaky nod.

My act was in vain. She'd already turned her back, leaving me alone in the cell with a harsh light blazing from the ceiling. I curled up on the combination bench/bunk and settled in for a nap. Maybe ideas for how to escape would come to me after I'd gotten some rest.

Dreams plagued my sleep. In one, Jun and I were standing at the edge of a cliff beneath a sky strewn with white stars.

Jun was about to plunge over the edge, and even worse, he wasn't looking where he was going. Instead, he glanced over his shoulder, gesturing for me to follow. I grabbed for him and —

"Min," said a voice I had grown to hate. Captain Hwan's.

I jolted awake and sat up, resisting the urge to rub the grit out of my eyes. Then I clambered to my feet. My knees felt rubbery, and it was difficult not to sway. But Hwan, standing just beyond the force-field door, was already a lot taller than I was. I didn't like having him tower over me.

His shadow fell before him, as sharp as a sword. I had to resist the temptation to tuck in my feet so they wouldn't be cut by its edge. There was something of the tiger in that shadow, and I could smell his confidence.

"Min," he said, "let's talk."

I was suddenly glad I'd never heard any lore about tiger folk using people's names against them. But I eyed the blaster holstered at his belt and shivered. "Talk about what?"

"Show me your true form," Hwan said.

I held my hands out before me and said, "This *is* my true form."

He frowned slightly. "That's the shape you wear when you go among humans, yes," he said. "But you are a fox, not a human."

Well, if he was going to be *that* way about it . . . "Fine," I said. A shiver went down my back. I hadn't taken on fox shape for years, because Mom disapproved of it so much. But I wasn't ashamed of it.

I closed my eyes, telling myself that if Hwan wanted to shoot me, he would have done it by now. Besides, he'd have to turn off the force shield before he could zap me, and he hadn't, because that might give me a chance to escape.

Magic swirled around me as my bones changed and my flesh condensed into a fur-covered shape I immediately felt at home in, even if I rarely used it. Smells became sharper, the cold of the deck beneath my paws more acute. I sat back on my haunches and twitched my whiskers as I looked up at the captain.

As odd as it was being a fox on a starship, it couldn't be any odder than being a dragon or a dokkaebi or, well, a tiger. I refused to grovel on my belly. He might be a predator among predators, but I came from a long line of foxes. He hadn't defeated me yet.

I paced in a circle to show off my fine red pelt and white-tipped tail, then reared up and returned to my human shape. "All right," I said, "now you have proof that I'm a gumiho. What are you going to do about it?"

"I could use your assistance," he said quietly, even though no one else was in sight. "I know where the Dragon Pearl is hidden, but the ghosts of the Fourth Colony guard their treasure ferociously."

Either he didn't realize I'd broken into his quarters, or he was hoping to trick me into thinking he didn't know. I knew better than to give myself away, however. "What does that have to do with me?" I asked, playing along.

"Your Charm could persuade the ghosts to allow us to approach the Dragon Pearl," he said.

"That's probably true," I said, "but what guarantee do you have that I won't turn them against you?"

"Do you trust yourself to pilot a shuttle, or a starship?" he asked coolly. "Your shape-shifting is impressive, but from talking with your brother, I know you can't change yourself into a ship — not one that can go anywhere useful. And it's not just a matter of transportation, either. Do you want to capture the Pearl only to become a target for every bandit and mercenary in the galaxy? You might be able to impersonate me" — his eyes lit up with an unexpected mixture of humor and malice — "but are you going to gamble that you can successfully captain a battle cruiser against mercenary and pirate attacks?"

I scowled at him, but he had a point. Even though I learned fast, there were limits to my knowledge. "One question, then," I said. "What happened to my brother?"

His teeth gleamed in a not-smile. I imagined them lengthening into sharp points, even though they remained eerily human. "I'd originally hoped to work with him," Hwan said. "Unfortunately, your brother proved to be less than cooperative. I trust you won't repeat his error."

Outrage choked me. It took a couple moments before I was able to speak. "Where is he?"

Hwan shrugged. "I've stowed him where you'll never find him. And that's where he'll stay for the rest of his life unless you cooperate with me."

I lunged at the force shield that separated me from him, too angry to care that it was a terrible idea. Sure enough, it sizzled when I hit it. A burning sensation surged through my body, and I was surprised that I didn't smell smoke or the stink of charred flesh. My limbs convulsed. I had just enough presence of mind to tumble sideways rather than continue to batter the shield.

"I see you take after him," Hwan said, very dryly. "You won't reconsider?"

I squeezed my eyes shut so I wouldn't cry from the pain. No way was I going to give Hwan the satisfaction. "If you imprisoned my brother," I gasped out, "how do I know you won't do the same to me?"

A memory nagged at me: Hwan's sword

in his office, the scent of my brother upon the hilt, suggesting a secret they had shared. What kind of game had they played at? But it was too hard to think through the searing pain.

"Little gumiho," Hwan said, and I bristled. "Do you really think you hold a winning hand right now?"

I opened my eyes long enough to shoot a glare at him, although it wasn't very impressive, because I was curled up on the floor.

"You should accept my offer before my patience wears thin," Hwan said, "or your brother suffers any longer."

If he wanted my cooperation, that was exactly the wrong thing for him to say. "Forget it."

"You're going to have to learn to control that temper," Hwan said, as if I was going to listen to him like he was a *teacher.* "Very well. I'll leave you until you come to your senses. The guards have ways of making that happen sooner rather than later."

With that, Hwan turned his back and strode out of the brig.

I listened to his footsteps and cursed myself for not taking the deal, if only to get me out of there. I couldn't bring myself to shout after him, though, not even when the stakes were so high.

I'd just have to escape some other way.

TWENTY-EIGHT

Despite my shaky limbs and the agony running through my body, I dragged myself up onto the bunk. Falling asleep took forever, partly because of the pain, partly because of the bright light. I shielded my eyes with my forearm, but that didn't help as much as I'd hoped. Keeping my arm bent at that angle was its own special form of torment, because hitting the force shield had done something to all my muscles. I kept tossing and turning, hoping for a more comfortable position, until I finally drifted off.

"Jang!"

Why was someone calling for me?

"Jang!"

I groaned and turned on my side to face the wall, then regretted it immediately. I had never realized the muscles between my ribs could hurt that badly.

"Go away," I mumbled, then blinked in confusion. I'd responded to Jang's name in my own clear soprano pitch.

Then the owner of the other voice penetrated. It was Sujin.

I sat up, moving more carefully this time. *Yes?* I mouthed, looking around me, wondering if this was a trap.

I saw nothing in the harsh light, not even a shadow out of place. Then I remembered that dokkaebi had invisibility caps, even if I'd never seen Sujin put theirs on before. I couldn't pinpoint the goblin's location by smell, so they must have been standing on the other side of the force shield.

"How did — ?" I started.

"Shh," Sujin hissed now that they had

my attention. "Can you change into the shape of Lieutenant Hyosu or something?"

I didn't waste time with questions, like where were we going. I was just grateful that Sujin was talking to me at all.

I called to mind Hyosu's smiling face. After all the classes I'd had with her, it was a familiar one. But my first attempt to imitate her went wrong, and Sujin cleared their throat in warning. I glanced at my shoulder tabs — by force of habit I'd magicked up the tabs for a cadet, not a lieutenant. Hastily, I concentrated and fixed the mistake.

While I was sorting that out, I heard clicking on the number pad, then a faint thrum as the force shield went down. I didn't waste any time sprinting out of the cell, pain or no pain. I collided into something that I couldn't see. The breath whooshed out of my lungs.

"Ouch," Sujin said plaintively.

"Sorry," I said. "Why — ?"

"No time," they said. "We'll talk about it later. As a fox, you must have good hearing. Can you follow my footsteps if I stay invisible?"

"Yes," I said.

Sujin didn't speak again while they led me out of the brig. I wondered how they'd gotten into this area — perhaps they'd used their invisibility to slip in during a shift change or something.

I couldn't make myself invisible, and Sujin needed their cap to avoid arousing suspicion, but I had some tricks up my sleeve. As we approached the exit, I put on a frown and used a little Charm to convince the guards that I — Hyosu — had been sent here on an errand. I also persuaded them not to question the fact that there was no record of the lieutenant having entered the brig. They signed me out without a fuss. My attempt to forge Hyosu's signature wasn't very good, but it wouldn't last long on the screen, and I bet that people didn't check handwriting very closely most of the time.

We took an elevator up two levels. Several enlisted crew members waited patiently as Sujin and I got out. I admired Sujin's deftness more and more. Being invisible was handy, of course, but you still had to make sure you didn't bump into people, especially when they crowded close. In one instance, a corporal wrinkled her nose and glanced around, and I hastily used Charm on her. Whether she was a human with an unusually good sense of smell or someone with supernatural heritage, I didn't care. I had to make sure no one caught Sujin helping me.

From the direction we were going, I guessed we were headed for an escape pod. It took an effort to hold my head up high and smile at people as I passed the way that Hyosu did, especially when my nerves screamed that I was going to be unmasked as an imposter any moment now. The continued ache in my muscles didn't help. Fortunately, I wouldn't have to use Charm for much longer, because the dock was close.

Still, I couldn't afford to get overconfident. It was only a matter of time before my escape was discovered. At that point Captain Hwan would turn the entire ship inside out and try his best to recapture me. Worse, he might do something to my brother to force me to turn myself in again. I had to get to the Pearl so I'd have the upper hand.

Sujin's footsteps slowed as we approached an intersection. I cocked my head to make sure I understood where they were going, then followed them around the bend. My pulse raced as we approached the emergency escape pods for this section. Was this actually going to work?

That wasn't all. Standing guard at the doorway to the pods was Haneul. She smelled of fear and dismay, but I could also see determination in her expression.

I slowed to a stop in front of her and said in a hushed voice, "It's me, 'Jang.' "

"We have to hurry," Sujin said, almost in my ear.

I jumped, even though I knew Sujin was there. Haneul didn't bat an eye, but I guessed she was more used to dealing with her invisible friend. I longed to ask why they were helping me. It would have to wait — I didn't want to delay my getaway.

The escape pods had very simple entry codes that everyone in the crew knew, even me. But Haneul was the one who punched it in. As the door to the pod swished open, eerie violet-tinged lights flickered on and cool air whispered past me.

"Get in," Haneul said.

I hesitated for a moment. "I don't know how to pilot this. . . ." And there was more to it. Despite the drills on the *Pale Lightning,* I felt uneasy about escape pods. On the holos, they were always haunted by the ghosts of people who'd died in them. I didn't need to fly with yet another spirit who was feeling vengeful and might bring me bad luck.

"We can handle that," said Haneul. "We're coming with you."

My heart expanded in gratitude, and I flashed them a grin. "I hope you know what you're getting into." I clambered inside, taking the farthest seat, and began strapping myself in. Haneul was next. Then Sujin, who pulled off their invisibility cap and appeared piecemeal, like a jigsaw assembling itself out of the air.

"This is going to buy you a lot of trouble," I said to the other two, seriously this time. "You could face court-martial, maybe even . . ." I couldn't say the word *execution.*

I hadn't thought Haneul's face could get any paler. "Sujin managed to sneak in and listen in on what the captain said to you," she said. "I swore loyalty to the Space Forces and the Thousand Worlds, but what Hwan did, coercing you by threatening your brother, isn't right. We have to get you out of here."

"But you don't have to desert as well," I said, as much as I hated the thought of being alone.

"What, you want to leave us behind to be tiger snack food?" Sujin said.

"Don't joke about it," Haneul said sharply. To me, she said, "We only have one chance to get this right. We're hoping the captain will want you alive and he won't shoot down the pod."

I gulped. "What about the EMP mines?"

"I thought of that," Sujin said smugly. "I downloaded a map of the mine locations on the sly. We'll be able to navigate around them."

"Then we'd better hurry down to the

planet so we can look for the Pearl before the captain reaches it," I said.

I briefly wondered if I should remind them about the probability of our encountering angry ghosts there, but I decided against it. I needed my friends' help if I wanted to save Jun. I just hoped my Charm would be enough to get us by.

"I was thinking of just hiding there until we could signal another ship to come rescue us," Sujin said. "Are you saying you know where the Pearl is?"

I nodded without going into detail. I still remembered the landing coordinates and site's location from the captain's private log.

"Then there's *really* no reason to stay here," Haneul said. "Er, Jang" — she faltered, then nodded at me — "Min, whatever you call yourself, you'd better program in the landing coordinates and then we'll launch."

Luckily, there was a control panel within reach. Sujin input the map they'd smuggled out. Then it was my turn. The pod's system plotted an arcing trajectory that would skirt the mines and take us down to the Fourth Colony's surface, near one of the ancient settlements, a city named Jeonbok. The communities had been spread out over the planet's largest continent, but the location I wanted was near a forest. I hoped the trees wouldn't prove too much of an obstacle when it came to landing.

I double-checked the coordinates, wishing I had the captain's logbook in front of me. Using the wrong numbers could send us into an expanse of ocean, or half a continent away from where the Dragon Pearl was supposedly hidden.

"Everyone strapped in?" Haneul asked.

"It's now or never," I said, and hit the commands to start the launch sequence. The doors to the escape pod's launch chute slid closed. Then the lights blinked red three times and a bell-like tone sounded.

Meanwhile, gel cushions came out of the walls. As the cushions inflated, surrounding every part of us except our faces, I fought the panicky desire to claw at them. I knew that in a few moments I'd be grateful for the padding.

The lights flashed again, and the launch

indicator lit up. For a second I thought there had been a malfunction, and my heart sank. Then the escape pod rocketed out the chute and I was slammed back against the couch.

Something nagged at me. Didn't we need to get clearance from the ship before launching? Or had Haneul and Sujin somehow overridden the system before springing me? As tears streamed from my eyes, due to the sudden acceleration, it was difficult to think clearly. I couldn't reach up to wipe my face because of the cushions, but that didn't matter. At this speed, I wouldn't have been able to move my arms anyway. I closed my eyes against the unpleasant pressure and lost consciousness.

"Min! Min, wake up!"

I groaned and started to thrash, but I was trapped. There was something important I had to figure out, but I resisted opening my eyes and facing it. *Just give me a few more moments of rest. . . .*

"Come on, Min, you need to be awake for this."

Eventually I recognized Sujin's voice. I

peeled my eyes open. The goblin was unstrapped from the crash couch and their hair floated around their face like they'd been zapped by Haneul's lightning. Belatedly, I realized this meant we weren't accelerating anymore — we were back in free fall.

"What's going on?" I asked, hating how weak my voice sounded. "How's Haneul?"

"I'm right here," she called from the next couch.

"If we're alive," I said, "that means Captain Hwan hasn't shot us down yet. So what's the bad news?"

"The bad news is down there," Sujin said. "Haneul, show her."

Haneul brought up the scan display. Or rather, failed to. The scanner was blank, refusing to tell us anything about the Fourth Colony. We couldn't even determine whether we were headed toward the correct coordinates.

If we landed planetside, I could probably find some way to survive. The Fourth Colony had been settled at one point, so it should have a breathable atmosphere and, with any luck, edible plants and/or wildlife. If we missed the planet entirely and floated out into space, however, we would be at the mercy of whoever found us — if anyone came to rescue us at all.

"How long was I out?" I said.

"A couple of hours, I think," Haneul said. The air around her was moist, and it crackled with suppressed lightning, a sign of how miserable she was. "I didn't think the ghosts would be able to influence our systems this far out."

So the spirits were already making their presence known. "Well, if the ghosts *are* affecting us, maybe they're affecting the *Pale Lightning* as well," I said. "I thought it would have caught up to us by now."

"I might have done a little extra sabotage on the way out," Haneul said. The air around her grew even more crackly. "It was you who blasted the wires on Deck Three, wasn't it, just before you escaped with the mercenaries? That's where I got the idea."

Clearly, I hadn't been a very good influence on these two. "Help me get out of this couch," I said.

"What are you going to do?" Sujin said.

"See if I can fix the system," I said, "before we swing past the planet and into outer space" — Sujin turned green — "or crash-land in some ocean." I was pretty sure I could deal with the problem, given my knack for repairing machines, but I had to get free of those cushions first.

"Well, ocean wouldn't be horrible," Haneul said, "although I'm not sure how much control I would have over waters on a planet ruled by ghosts." As she spoke, she came over to unstrap me. I suppressed a yelp when she touched my shoulder and static electricity sparked at the contact. I knew she hadn't meant to hurt me.

The acceleration hadn't helped my battered body recover, but I had no choice but to get moving. I clomped over to the interface and began digging through the menus. It became clear pretty quickly that the problem wasn't in the scan software, though, but somewhere in the hardware.

Sujin wordlessly handed me the repair kit. I unscrewed a panel and took a look.

A little quick testing confirmed my worst fears. Some of the computer systems had shorted out.

Still, not everything was lost. The computer contained survey data for the Fourth Colony, which it would have been updated with when the *Pale Lightning* Gated nearby. I hastily looked over the maps for what remained of the city of Jeonbok and committed them to memory.

"There's a slate with local scan capability in the supply kit," Sujin said. "Won't help us out in space, but once we get on the surface, maybe we can use it to gather some information."

"You don't think this pod somehow got sabotaged, too, do you?" I asked.

"Well," Haneul said slowly, "when I sabotaged the *Pale Lightning,* the escape pods *were* technically part of the ship . . ." Her voice trailed off unhappily. "Given the way luck works, it might have backfired on us."

I continued poking at the systems. I might not be able to repair it entirely, but I could restore the most basic navigation functions and guide us toward our original destination. "Since we have time before we land," I said as I worked, frowning at the delicate wires, "tell me why you turned coat."

Haneul winced, but Sujin said steadily, "Because some things are right and some things are wrong. We had to do what was right."

"The captain has lost it," Haneul said. Her voice was subdued. "I know Jun — he's a loyal cadet — and what happened to him is horrible. Hwan is holding him hostage who knows where. When the captain threatened us as well, I figured all bets were off."

"You have some explaining to do, too," Sujin said to me. "You went around pretending to be Jang. After you left, the captain told us that he'd died. Is that . . . is that true?"

"Yes," I said with a sigh. "It happened right after the boarding mission on the *Red Azalea.* His injuries were too severe. I . . . His ghost allowed me to use his body." I hoped that Jang was having better luck back on the *Pale Lightning* than I was here.

The others looked shocked.

"I guess you can never tell who to trust," Sujin said. I wondered if the goblin was making a dig at me.

I flinched. "I'm sorry I couldn't tell you the truth," I said to them. "I was trying to find out what happened to my brother, Jun. I didn't mean for you two to get dragged into this mess. I really do consider you my friends."

"Yeah, nothing creates a bond like a common enemy," Haneul said with a grimace. Still, the air around her stopped crackling. "Besides," she added, "I'm worried about Jun and the other 'deserters.' If there's any chance that we can help rescue them, we have to take it."

The navigational system came back online. "One moment," I said. I bent to the task of correcting our course.

Sujin and Haneul fell quiet, not wanting to distract me. I was grateful for a respite from the conversation.

"It's done," I said after I'd triple-checked the coordinates, only to be embarrassed when my stomach growled loudly.

Haneul smiled at the sound. "We

should eat while we have a chance," she said. "Sujin?"

The goblin nodded and produced their spork. They waved it around, conjuring packets of shrimp crackers. I could almost hear my mom scolding me for eating junk food. A wave of homesickness washed over me. Would I ever see her again? I wanted nothing more than to bring Jun home to her.

Sujin passed the crackers around, and we ate in glum silence, trying not to think about the vastness of space and how tiny the escape pod was. Then we returned to our couches and harnessed ourselves back in to prepare for landing. I stared out the viewport at the planet and prayed to every ancestor I knew to watch over us. Soon enough we'd find out whether we'd land near the Dragon Pearl — if we made it at all.

TWENTY-NINE

The planet loomed below, with great tumbling whirls of lightning-lit clouds set in a deep azure sky. I had a difficult time catching sight of the surface with its violet-green haze. The colors were deceptive and the ground might look quite different once we got up close, without all the mist and dust in the way.

I'd learned a long time ago that a planet's atmosphere didn't start or stop abruptly like a boundary wall. Rather, it faded gradually, extending into space like an ever-thinner blanket the farther you got from the ground. But when you were making a landing, there was a moment when you knew you'd entered an atmosphere.

The temperature inside the pod rose uncomfortably as the friction of entry took its toll. The tiny ship was supposedly shielded so the excess heat wouldn't cook us, but it grew hot enough that sweat was pouring off me. My fear didn't help, either.

Haneul and Sujin didn't say anything about it, but I could smell their perspiration as well. The entire capsule had a rank stink that only grew worse by the minute. It was almost a welcome distraction from the knowledge that soon we'd be crash-landing on the surface.

I dozed fretfully, then woke to Haneul and Sujin conversing in low tones. "Anything happen?" I asked.

"No, we're just waiting for the inevitable," Haneul said. "I was talking about ways I might be able to use weather magic to soften the landing, but my control over air is not as strong as I'd like. I don't suppose you could change into an airbag big enough to protect all of us?"

"I could," I said dubiously, "but I wouldn't be a very good airbag, and I couldn't keep myself from smothering you if we landed wrong and I got knocked out. How much longer until we land?"

"Another ten minutes," Sujin said. Despite the forced cheer of their tone, their voice wavered. "At least we haven't seen any ghosts yet."

"They're waiting to greet us as equals," Haneul said. Her attempt at a joke was followed by a dismal silence, and she sighed. "Sorry. That came out wrong."

I twisted and turned in the harness, trying to find a more comfortable position. All my limbs ached, and my back was sore from being stuck like this for the past several hours. I wondered if whoever had designed the straps had ever been forced to put them to the test. The heat kept rising. By now I was soaked with sweat, and thirsty, too.

"I should have had more to drink while I was unharnessed," I said. I couldn't get anything now, when we were so close to landing.

"Maybe after we walk away from this I'll conjure you some plum soda," Sujin said, and we both laughed uneasily.

The capsule began to brake, and it became hotter than ever.

"I see trees," Haneul said abruptly. "This might not have been the best place to land."

All thoughts of thirst vanished. A forest was a sign we might be near Jeonbok. But I didn't want to crash into it. . . . Unless the branches would soften our landing?

I strained for a glimpse of any signs of past civilization, hoping that Captain Hwan's maps were up-to-date. "If even the most recent survey maps aren't reliable," I said, suddenly full of dread, "who knows what we'll find on the surface when we get out. . . ."

"Ghosts," Sujin said. "Navigating is going to be interesting, that's for sure."

We lapsed into an unhappy silence.

"Five minutes to landing," Sujin announced. "See you all on the other side."

"To survival," I said.

To my surprise, Haneul laughed, although not without some bitterness. "To survival."

The pod's emergency-landing parachute deployed. One moment we were slowing, slowing, almost to the point where I imagined us as a feather burning up as it floated down. The next moment, we collided into something — a great overgrown copse of trees, from the crazed impression of branches and leaves and broken twigs that I glimpsed through the viewport as we turned topsy-turvy.

We rolled and tumbled. I yipped in spite of myself, digging my fingers into the harness as if it could keep me from swinging from side to side. The safety straps helped, although not as much as I would have liked. I heard the others shouting as well. At last the ship settled into a less alarming back-and-forth rocking.

"Everyone okay?" Sujin called out.

I shook my head to get rid of a crick in my neck, staring cross-eyed at the hatch. I was almost upside down and all the blood had rushed to my head. The second time Sujin asked, I was able to answer, in a shaky voice. "Still here. Do you think it's safe to get out?"

"*Safe* is relative," Haneul said.

It was good to hear her voice. "We can't stay in here forever," I said. "We need to grab whatever supplies we can from the pod and go out and retrieve the Pearl. Then we can figure out what to do next."

"At least food and drink won't be a problem as long as I'm around," Sujin quipped.

"First things first," Haneul said. "Be careful getting out of your harness. We don't know how stable the pod is, and we don't want it to tumble down from the trees."

I unhooked myself as carefully as I could and still managed to land hard on my shoulder. It was pure luck that I didn't dislocate it. Haneul and Sujin had an easier time. Still, every time one of us moved, the pod swayed alarmingly, and we could hear the creaking and groaning of the branches that cradled it.

The other thing I noticed was the gravity, significantly lighter than what I was used to on Jinju or what was standard on starships. It gave a bouncy feeling to all my movements, which would have been fun under less harrowing circumstances. Given our precarious position, I didn't dare experiment with it yet.

Sujin rummaged quickly through the supplies. Cautiously, so we didn't over-balance the ship, we divided up the slate, medical kit, and survival gear. I got the slate and quickly loaded it up with the survey data so we'd have something to work with.

"Assuming we landed where we wanted to," I said, "once Captain Hwan gets down here, this will be his first guess for where we've gone. So we have to move fast."

Haneul's shoulders hunched. "I wish things hadn't turned out like this."

"Me too," Sujin said. "But the situation is what it is."

"Let's all take a look at the map," Haneul said, recovering her poise, "just in case something happens and we end up getting separated." This took more fina-gling, since we couldn't cluster together without risking the pod tumbling down.

If we could trust my repair of the

navigation system, we'd landed at the southern edge of Jeonbok. The maps had indicated that the woods had been cleared at one point, but they must have grown back over the years. A nearby river wound past Jeonbok toward a lake. If we got really lost, we could navigate by the river.

Eventually we were ready.

I'm coming for you, Jun, I thought fiercely. I had to hold on to that, had to believe I could rescue him easily once I got this business with the Dragon Pearl sorted.

"Now what?" Haneul said.

I took a deep breath and immediately regretted it. The air inside the pod was still unpleasantly damp and smelly. I checked the gauges. "We have barely enough fuel to launch back into orbit. There won't be any margin for error. So if Captain Hwan catches up to us while we're in flight, we won't be able to evade."

"I don't think it's going to make a difference," Haneul said. "How would we get the pod out of these trees? And anyway, Captain Hwan has a lot of ways to track us."

I had to concede that. Everything was going wrong with this plan. We'd have to figure out a solution later, once we'd secured the Pearl.

"Check to see if the atmosphere out there is breathable, would you, Min?" Sujin said. "I'd hate to crack the hatch open only to suffocate."

"I can do that," I said, glowering at the pod's computer display. It took me some time to bring the sensor suite online. It wouldn't be accurate enough for real survey work, but we only needed to know if there was sufficient oxygen and no poisonous gases. Fortunately, the display lit up blue. We were in the clear.

We all looked at each other and exhaled in relief at the same time.

"Okay," Sujin said, "let's open this tin can."

Things could have been worse. Sure, we were marooned on a plague-infected planet where we'd probably be murdered by ghosts, but at least we had breathable air. Some planets had a toxic atmosphere or none at all, or were too cold or hot for even supernatural creatures to survive without serious gear.

"Here goes nothing," Haneul muttered, and slid open the hatch.

I coughed immediately at the thick, pollen-scented breeze that swirled through the pod. At least, it started as a breeze. It quickly became more forceful, almost as if it were responding to our presence. "Let's hurry," I said.

Haneul didn't need to be told twice. "Let me ask the winds to calm down," she said, although she sounded dubious. She shut her eyes and began to meditate. After a few moments, she opened her eyes, and though I didn't notice much change in the air current, she began clambering down. Her voice wafted to us from outside the capsule: "Be careful out here. Some of these branches have thorns."

Wonderful. "I'll go next," I said. If necessary, I could shape-shift into something that would take less damage in a fall, or offer cushioning for anyone landing on me. Being a mattress might not be dignified, but it beat Sujin ending up with broken bones or a concussion, or worse.

The trees grew thick and tall. Their limbs were bent or snapped around the capsule, and the remains of the parachute were draped over the treetops. A few of the trees had needlelike leaves that glistened with a pale sap. I got some of it on my hands and found that it improved my grip on the branches.

The thorns were another matter. Haneul hadn't been kidding about them. Some of them were almost the length of my forearm. If I fell on one, I might join the ghosts before reaching the ground.

I momentarily wished I'd changed into my nimbler true shape for the job of climbing down, but my longer human arms had better reach. I swallowed a cry when a smaller thorn jabbed my arm as I leaped unsteadily toward one of the larger branches beneath me. The unfamiliar lighter gravity was interfering with my reflexes. When I flinched, I inadvertently moved my foot and took another thorn to the back of my knee.

"Not that way!" Haneul shouted up from the ground now that she could see me clearly. "Take a couple steps to the side, and — you see that branch with the weird knot? Move to that one instead. It's safer."

With her guidance, I made it the rest of the way down. "Thanks," I said.

"It's nothing," she said. "Sujin, you ready?"

"I watched you both," they said, some of their cheer restored. "I can manage it. To free up my hands, I'm going to have to wear my hat, so here goes nothing!"

I could only follow Sujin's progress by the rustling of the branches and leaves. At one point a twig pelted me from above, and I jumped. "Stop that!"

Sujin sounded puzzled. "That wasn't me!"

"I have to agree," Haneul said. "This isn't the time, Sujin."

"No, it really wasn't —"

More twigs began to bombard us.

Haneul and I exchanged glances. "The ghosts," she said thinly.

"You'd better hurry," I said to Sujin.

"You're telling me." The branches

rustled more vigorously.

At last the three of us had made it safely to the ground. Sujin pulled off their hat and reappeared right next to Haneul, who didn't bat an eyelash.

Hardly any light filtered down this low, and I shivered as the wind picked up again. The smell of pollen almost overwhelmed me, even though I couldn't see any flowers in bloom, either in the trees or among the mosses and underbrush.

At least the wind was carrying away the stink of our sweat. I would have given a lot for a bath right then, or the opportunity to wash my face.

"Here," Sujin said, pulling out their spork. "A few quick snacks, we can eat and drink on the way. It won't do us any good if we faint from hunger, and we need hydration after all the sweating we've done." With a few passes of their spork, they produced orange sodas and honey cookies.

Silently, we each took our share. From Haneul's dour expression, I knew she thought the snacks were too sugary. I normally liked sweets, though, and I wasn't about to complain. Any calories were good, especially considering our situation.

"It's hard to tell which way is north," Sujin said, subdued, as they looked around. There was only forest in every direction. "How are we going to . . . ?" Their words trailed off as hopelessness set in.

I dug in the survival kit and found a compass. I pointed out what it claimed was north. "I don't know how reliable this is, though," I added when the needle began to spin. Ghosts again.

"We'll have to do our best," Haneul said. She raised her chin and turned until she was facing into the wind. As she did so, it grew even stronger, buffeting us with fallen leaves and snapped twigs. "If the ghosts don't want us to go in that direction, chances are something valuable is there."

I couldn't argue with the logic. I just hoped we weren't making a terrible mistake.

THIRTY

For the first hour, the shadows deepened as we made our way through the forest. The trees rose around us like stern sentinels, veiling the sky with their leaves. Haneul showed no sign that the increasingly chilly wind affected her, but Sujin hugged themself miserably and huddled close to her. For my part, I conjured myself a warmer coat. I wished I could do the same for Sujin, but my magic didn't work that way.

"Are you sure we're going in the right

direction?" Sujin asked Haneul. I was starting to wonder the same thing.

"Do you have a better idea?" Haneul snapped.

Sujin didn't ask again after that.

In the meantime, I marveled at the forest. At first I'd been overwhelmed by the masses of trees in every direction. We had no wild forests like this on Jinju due to the inadequate water. The longer we walked, the more I began to appreciate nuances. I spotted elaborately woven bird's nests in the branches, like ornaments in the trees' hair. The mosses that grew on the trees' bark looked rich and soft. I trailed my fingers through some as I passed and marveled at the cool, furry texture. I caught sight of a clearing where boulders glittered faintly with fantastic outcroppings of crystal and curling ferns grew shyly at their sides.

The winds seemed less cruel whenever I paused to admire the forest's wonders. It was almost as if the spirits who were stirring up the air were mollified by my flattering gaze. I guessed it appealed to their vanity. Ghosts were people, too, after all — they just happened to be people who hadn't yet fully crossed over to the realm of the dead.

The Fourth Colony was supposedly a dead world, yet in the space of a few hours, I had encountered so much more life than Jinju had ever supported — except in enclosed, pampered gardens reserved for the richest families. I knew the entire planet couldn't be like this. It would have its deserts and its glaciers, different climate zones. But as I walked through the solemn forest, I could dream that Jinju would someday look like this, too, at least in the parts where people lived. That could only happen, though, if I found the Dragon Pearl and rescued my brother.

If I succeeded in doing those two things, maybe — just maybe — my family would forgive me for everything I'd done.

The density of the woods dwindled little by little, until we finally reached the edge. Dusk light broke through the trees, tinting their trunks and the forest floor a ruddy color that contrasted with the cooler violets of the shadows.

"It's going to be night soon," Haneul

said. Her breath puffed white in the cold. Alone of the three of us, she traveled in a bubble of calm, and I envied her. "Should we keep going, or look for a campsite?"

"Let's take a brief break at least," Sujin said. "I don't know about you two, but I'm hungry again."

As the sun's reddening light faded, we sat on the ground, where Haneul used a twig to scratch out a map in a patch of dirt. I compared her diagram to the survey data on the slate. Together we did some calculations.

"This" — Haneul pointed with the twig — "is where we started, and that's our destination. We're most of the way there. Should we carry on?"

"Yes, let's," I said. "I don't want to be caught out in the open if ghosts show up at night." I didn't know if spirits were more dangerous in the dark, but I didn't want to take any chances. I cast a nervous eye toward the sun, which had almost sunk below the horizon. Being able to see the sky also told us that clouds had been gathering steadily.

"It smells like rain," Sujin said, pulling a face as we got up. "We're going to get soaked soon."

"Don't borrow trouble," I said.

"I'm afraid Sujin's right," Haneul said.

We started off again, huddling together against the gusts. This time, in the moaning of the wind, I thought I detected voices like whispers out of the shadows. I slowed from time to time in an instinctive effort to hear the voices more clearly.

"What's the matter with you, Min?" Haneul demanded after the fifth time I'd lagged behind. "You're holding us up."

I bit back a retort. "You don't hear them?"

"Hear what?"

The voices rose, then ebbed. If I unfocused my mind, I could almost understand what they were saying. "I feel like the ghosts' voices are trying to talk to me." After all, Jang had spoken to me to make a bargain; maybe the Fourth Colony's ghosts wanted something, too.

Haneul's expression became troubled. "Are you sure they're not trying to lure you into a trap? I've never heard that the Fourth Colony's ghosts were *friendly.*"

It was a good point. "I don't suppose

either of you have shaman ancestry?" I asked, only half joking.

The others shook their heads. "It's too bad," Haneul said. "The ability to banish the dead would be useful right now."

"Well," I said, "I'll try to keep up." Haneul was right to chastise me: We couldn't delay. We needed to find the Pearl — and shelter.

Too late. Rain started falling, slowly at first, then pelting us with freezing drops. Water poured down from above and splashed up from the ground. Haneul tried to persuade the weather spirits to shield us from the worst of it. Apparently they were in an uncooperative mood, because we still got drenched. It grew difficult to see more than a pace or two ahead, especially in the dim light, which came from a break in distant clouds through which beams of moonlight slanted, and the occasional jagged flash of lightning.

I stumbled often, not helped by the distracting voices. One of them started to distinguish itself from the others, fitfully growing louder. Despite my inability to figure out what it was saying, it sounded familiar, as though I'd heard it in another lifetime. I tried my best to concentrate on Haneul's shoulders ahead of me and listen only to the miserable sloshing of our boots in the mud. But the voices wouldn't go away.

I eventually slipped into a trance. It seemed like we had always been walking with the rain in our faces, and always would be. I was glad enough to drift away and leave the cold water and squelching wetness of my clothes behind for a different reality. For a while the voices quieted. Then the loudest one started up again. This time, however, perhaps because of my half-dreaming state, I could understand it.

"Min," the voice said. It sounded male. "Min, you have to hurry."

"Jang?" I asked blearily. Had he left the *Pale Lightning* to accompany us after all? Or was this an illusion?

"Min," he said, "I may have all the time in the world, but you're in danger. You've drifted off course. I can show you the way to shelter."

I jolted back to wakefulness. "Which way are we supposed to be going?" I wasn't sure whom I was addressing.

Sujin grabbed my arm and shook it, peering into my face as though they could diagnose what was wrong with me even in the dark. "Min? Min, snap out of it!"

"It's those ghosts," Haneul said. She stopped, too, and grabbed my chin painfully. "Min! Wake up. You're dreaming about ghosts while standing up. Don't listen to them." The wind rose and howled, obliterating her words.

We'd reached the bank of a creek. The waters rushed past, and while it didn't look impassable under drier conditions, I wouldn't have wanted to risk it right now. "No, you're right," I said.

"Min," said the voice again.

This time the wind quieted a little, and Haneul heard it, too. She whirled around, her eyes narrowed into slits. "Show yourself!" she called out.

A pale form coalesced before us. At first it took on the indistinct shape of some four-legged animal, crouching low to the ground. I blinked, and the animal's outline blurred and shifted, gradually becoming human. Through the disheveled locks I recognized the face — what remained of it, anyway. Half of it flickered with ghostly flames, as though he were on fire. Between that and the hair, I could barely see his surviving eye.

It wasn't Jang. It was someone else I knew.

THIRTY-ONE

Sujin figured it out before I did. "Cadet Jun!"

My brain finally caught up. "No," I whispered. My heart sputtered in my chest, and for a moment I was afraid it would stop beating entirely. "Jun, you can't be . . . can't be . . ." I couldn't bring myself to say the word, as if doing so would make it real.

The captain had told me that he'd stowed Jun away somewhere. Did he not know Jun was . . . ? Or had Hwan lied to me?

Tears pricked my eyes. How long had Jun been like this? Silently I berated myself for all the time I'd wasted getting to the Fourth Colony, all the hours I'd spent doing silly chores on the *Pale Lightning* while impersonating Jang. If I'd acted sooner, could I have saved my brother from this fate? My stomach clenched with guilt.

I fleetingly thought of the stupid bet I'd made with my cousin Bora about Jun coming home. I'd lost. We'd all lost.

How would I ever tell my mother?

The tears started rolling down my cheeks, and I reached up to scrub them away. Haneul awkwardly patted my shoulder. She opened her mouth as if to speak, then closed it again. Sujin made soft comforting noises. I didn't know how to thank either of them, but I was glad for their presence, warm and solid and alive.

My brother half smiled at me. I forced myself to study him closely. His long hair, the spectral flames, the way his body faded out from the waist down so I couldn't see his legs . . . I couldn't deny the truth, no matter how much I wanted to.

"Yes," Jun said. "I'm sorry, little sister. I no longer dwell in the world of the living."

I closed my eyes and clenched my teeth against a howl. To come this far only to discover that I was too late, that it had probably been too late before I'd even set out. All my dreams — his dreams, *our* dreams — were over. We would not serve together in the Space Forces. We would not save our planet or travel the Thousand Worlds. Who would I look up to now?

"What happened?" I asked at last. It was difficult to breathe.

"I agreed to work with Captain Hwan to get the Dragon Pearl away from the ghosts and bring it back," Jun said. His tone was eerily matter-of-fact. "I came down here with a landing party from the *Pale Lightning.* We didn't survive the experience."

"So it wasn't desertion," Sujin said.

"I knew it," said Haneul. "Captain

Hwan misled us all."

None of this was a surprise to me. I'd read about the captain's plan in his logbook. But something Jun had said bothered me. I made myself think, despite the stabbing feeling in my heart. He'd said *agreed to work with.* Captain Hwan had claimed Jun *proved to be less than cooperative.* Those two things didn't add up.

Jun's next words interrupted my train of thought. "Come on," he said. "The rain doesn't bother *me* anymore" — his simple acceptance of being dead made me feel even worse — "but we've got to get the three of you to shelter. I can take you to our landing site. Staying in the shuttle will be better than using the few survival items you've got, and we have extra supplies as well. If you need to, you can use the shuttle's comm gear to signal for rescue."

I glanced nervously at Haneul and Sujin. With Hwan looking for us, signaling for help was the last thing I wanted to do. I was about to say so, when Sujin said, "Show us the way."

I didn't argue. Why bother? We could

discuss the situation once we got there. Details like this felt insignificant when I'd made it to the Ghost Colony only to discover that my brother was one of the ghosts.

Jun floated ahead of us, his phantom flames lighting the way. I couldn't help wincing at every flicker. They couldn't hurt him anymore, but they indicated how he'd died.

Died. As we sloshed after Jun, my eyes stung. How had it happened? *If the shuttle was still intact enough to provide shelter and supplies, then he couldn't have been killed in a crash landing . . .* I thought, trying to console myself.

"The rocks are going to be slippery," Jun warned as we approached a faint trail zigzagging up a hill. Water ran down it in glistening rivulets. We splashed onward. I was pretty sure my toes resembled wrinkled prunes from being soaked for so long, and the rest of my skin wasn't much better.

Haneul only nodded. If she and Sujin were having any dire thoughts about being lured to their deaths by a fox spirit, as in all the stories the humans told about my ancestors, they were keeping them under wraps.

As we crested the top of the hill, my question was answered. We saw the ruins of a shuttle, half-crumpled, part of it buried beneath layers of upflung earth. A sob of anguish tore its way out of my throat and I stopped in my tracks. I couldn't stay there, the site of my brother's death.

Lights emerged from the crash site. Six spirits, including my brother, floated up and surrounded us. All of them had long, tangled hair and were outlined by unnatural fire.

Spooked, Sujin jammed their cap on their head and disappeared. Haneul and I stood back-to-back. My legs trembled with exhaustion, but I knew I couldn't give in to weakness, not now.

Jun turned to face a taller woman — did height mean anything when you didn't have legs and hovered in the air? — and saluted. It was the first time I'd ever seen him do so, and it underscored how little I knew about his life after he'd left home.

"Here they are, ma'am," he said. "As

you requested."

Oh no. I'd followed Jun because I trusted him — and now we were at the mercy of these ghosts.

Haneul had a different reaction altogether. "Lieutenant Seo-Hyeon?" she asked. "Is that you?"

"Yes," the tall spirit said in a voice that echoed oddly.

"So none of you survived?" Haneul asked, peering around at all the ghostly faces.

"Not a one," the lieutenant confirmed. "But surely that's no surprise."

"I'm so sorry," said Haneul. "We were told you had deserted. Of course I never believed it. . . ." She trailed off. What did it matter now?

Seo-Hyeon's mouth twisted. "Come in and rest. The rain may not affect us, but the three of you aren't dead — not yet, anyway."

I wavered. Haneul, however, was already striding toward the shuttle. Sujin must've taken that as a good sign, because they removed their cap, reappeared, and followed her. Wondering what we'd let ourselves in for, I headed after them both.

When we got to the wreckage, I turned and asked the lieutenant, "What do you want from us?"

"Oh, for heaven's sake . . ." Haneul grabbed my hand and dragged me inside the shuttle, which offered some refuge even though one end of it was completely crumpled and its hatch was permanently smashed open. The interior's metal walls were scorched black, and the deck was littered with dead leaves and gravel. Sujin was already huddled in one of the passenger seats, shivering.

I hesitated, looking around for signs of dead bodies. If they existed, they must have been somewhere in the wrecked end of the shuttle. I shuddered.

"No need to be paranoid, Min," Haneul said. She set down her gear on one of the empty seats.

Reluctantly, I did the same. What did Haneul know about ghosts? I, on the other hand, had firsthand experience. Spirits walked among the living — or haunted starships sometimes, like Jang — for one reason: They had unfinished business from their lifetimes. These ghosts needed something, I was sure of it.

Once we were settled, Jun received a *go ahead* nod from Lieutenant Seo-Hyeon's ghost. "Captain Hwan charged us with finding the Dragon Pearl," he said to us. "I assume that's why you're here, too."

"I came here for *you,*" I said, hugging myself. "I never thought I — I . . ." I stuttered to a halt. What could I say to him? It had been so long since I'd last seen my brother, and now he was . . . like this.

The intact half of Jun's face twisted up in a smile. "We'll catch up later, Min."

I doubted that. Now that I knew I couldn't rescue him, everything had changed. I didn't need to linger here any longer. I . . .

Linger . . . What was keeping *him* on the Fourth Colony? Was it because he hadn't been able to complete his mission?

Suddenly, any thought I'd had of giving up my quest vanished. In fact, finding the Dragon Pearl had become that much more urgent — that much more personal now. If Jun couldn't fulfill his goal to save Jinju, then it was up to me to do it and make sure he could go on to his final rest.

I choked up at the thought. I didn't really want to say good-bye to my brother. At the same time, I knew from the old stories that ghosts didn't stay in the living world because they wanted to. I doubted Jun was any different.

Haneul bit her lip, and I caught a whiff of unease from her direction. Then she said to the lieutenant, "Unlike you, we weren't sent here by the captain. We're fleeing from him. He has been behaving oddly, and some of it's related to your mission. His obsession with the Dragon Pearl has sent him over the edge. He threatened all of us."

Sujin shook their head and groaned slightly.

Haneul turned to Sujin. "What? It's not like we can keep it a secret," she said stiffly.

"So he is pursuing you?" Seo-Hyeon said. When she spoke in her soft voice, ice trickled down my spine, colder even

433

than the enduring chill of the rain and the wind. "The captain did not come for us."

I looked uneasily at Haneul, mouthing, *Why not?* She shrugged.

"Or if he did send a rescue team," Jun said, "it never reached us."

The wind outside howled louder, and Jun saw me grimace at the sound. "The Fourth Colony's ghosts are still holding a grudge against the people of the Thousand Worlds for leaving them to their fate," he explained. "We can hear their anger in the wind."

It made sense that ghosts could understand other ghosts. I could pick up the suggestion of muttering voices, the background noise that had put me in a trance earlier, but no actual words. "What do they want after all this time?" I asked.

"You'd have to ask them," Lieutenant Seo-Hyeon cut in. "What *we* want is to talk to the captain. The ghosts may have been the ones who influenced the weather spirits to crash our shuttle, but Hwan owes us for abandoning us afterward."

I felt the blood drain from my face. So

that was it. Jun had led us to this spot to be bait for Captain Hwan. I glanced at Haneul and Sujin, and from their expressions I knew they'd come to the same realization.

I stared accusingly at Jun, who wouldn't meet my eyes. Then I signaled Haneul and Sujin. *We have to get out of here.*

But just then Sujin pulled out a comm device that I didn't remember from the escape capsule. They punched a code into it. "Not going to happen," Sujin said to the ghosts. "I've warned the captain to stay away from this wreck."

I blurted, "You *what?*" Why was Sujin talking to the captain? We could have bluffed our way out of the ghosts' trap without giving away our position to Hwan.

A more chilling thought occurred to me. Had Sujin secretly been in communication with the captain this entire time? And if so, had our escape from him been staged, as a trap for me?

Before I could confront Sujin, the lieutenant exploded into a silhouette of fire. Even her eyes blazed. I had to squint to avoid being blinded. "That won't stop

435

him," she said. "Captain Hwan already knew he'd have to reckon with us if he came back down here. And he will, sooner or later, because he wants the Dragon Pearl more than he's ever wanted anything. He won't risk leaving it in your hands."

That was all I needed to hear. According to the old stories, wrongful death warped people's souls and made them vengeful toward the living. Jang hadn't seemed too bad, but he hadn't been dead for as long as these six ghosts, and he hadn't been left behind by the captain. A shaman might have known how to pacify Lieutenant Seo-Hyeon and her team, but I was no shaman.

Instead, I did the only thing I could think of.

I unleashed Charm in the ghosts' direction. "Nature's calling," I said.

THIRTY-TWO

I was too panicked to come up with a more elaborate ruse. Which was just as well, since complicated lies are harder to pull off.

The lieutenant scowled at me. "Out in the rain?"

"I'm not going to do it in here," I said. I gestured at the crumpled end of the shuttle, at the seats jutting at odd angles from their fixtures. "But I don't want to be out there alone with ghosts of plague victims, either. Right, Haneul? Come with me."

Haneul caught on to my plan right away and nodded once. Not wanting to be too obvious, she stared hard at the cap that Sujin was holding, clearly willing her friend to follow us.

I scowled. Haneul might be all right, but I didn't trust Sujin anymore. Still, I didn't dare get into an argument with the goblin in front of the ghosts.

"I suppose that would be okay," the lieutenant said as Charm took hold. The fires around her form banked, and I was able to see her more clearly.

I held her gaze and smiled weakly, willing her to believe me. Surely she hadn't been dead long enough to forget the inconveniences of dealing with a body. Meanwhile, Haneul kept trying to signal Sujin. She fussed conspicuously with her dripping hair, which was so unlike her that Sujin frowned in her direction.

Finally, the goblin's eyes widened in understanding. They quickly slipped on their hat and vanished from sight.

"We'll be back soon," I said to the ghosts, trying not to sound breathless. I all but knocked Haneul over in my rush to leave the not-shelter of the shuttle.

As soon as we stepped outside, Haneul pressed her palms together and chanted prayers to the spirits of wind and water. As before, her magic didn't have much effect, but even slight protection from the rain was better than nothing. We started sprinting away, and I heard footsteps splashing behind us. It had to be Sujin, trying to keep up.

"Good thinking back there," Haneul said to me.

"Nice to know my Charm magic *does* work on ghosts," I said. "Even my brother." That thought made me so sad I tripped and almost crumpled to the ground. Haneul grabbed my arm and pulled me up.

The night swallowed us, and I couldn't help missing the spectral flames that had lit our way previously. Before Jun had led us astray, we'd been headed in the approximate direction of the Dragon Pearl, but who knew how far off course we were now?

"Too bad we don't have a flashlight," I muttered to no one in particular.

"You're in luck," Sujin said. Their voice sounded hoarse. "I grabbed this on the way out." A case was pressed into my hands, becoming visible as it left Sujin's grip.

I froze in my tracks and blinked. It was a survival kit. Only one, but that was better than nothing. "Thank you," I said stiffly, glad I didn't have to look into the goblin's eyes when I did. I didn't want to have to rely on Sujin for anything.

"That kit will be good to have," Haneul said, her tone ragged from running. "We're going to have to stop for rest eventually."

"How long before they catch up to us, do you think?" I asked her. I didn't have any idea how fast ghosts moved when they went all out. Jang just popped up whenever and wherever he wanted — maybe these guys could, too.

"Doesn't matter," she said. "We need to rest regardless."

I agreed, not least because, as miserable as it would be sleeping out in the open, my eyelids wanted to crash closed.

We created a campsite in the lee of a

craggy boulder near a copse of young trees. Haneul resumed her chants in an attempt to persuade the wind and water spirits to leave us in peace for the next few hours.

Sujin took off their hat. "We can set up a tent using the thermal blanket," they said. "It'll go faster if we work together."

I gave way with ill grace. We worked in silence for a time, neither of us looking directly at the other.

"We'll have to take shifts," Haneul said. No one argued. "I'll go first. You two get some rest."

The last thing I wanted to do was huddle under the one remaining blanket with Sujin. I was still angry that they had contacted the captain. But even more, I wanted to be alone with my thoughts.

I was plagued with guilt for dragging the three of us into danger and arriving too late to save my brother. Now I had no one to bring home, and no way to *get* home. There was still a chance we could find the Dragon Pearl, if we could orient ourselves, but what good would that do when we were marooned here? And how would we keep it out of Captain Hwan's clutches?

"Hey," Sujin said after a while. It was clear from our tossing and turning that neither of us was having any luck falling asleep. "Can we talk?"

"If we have to," I said ungraciously. "How long have you been working with Captain Hwan, anyway?"

"It's not like that," Sujin said.

Was their hurt tone real, or was it an act? I wondered.

"Lieutenant Hyosu was always telling us to carry a means of contacting the ship in case of emergency," Sujin went on. "I brought the comm device as a backup plan. The captain might be our only ticket out of here now."

I did remember Hyosu drilling that into us during her lessons. And it was true that we needed some way to get off-planet, but . . . "Didn't you warn Hwan to stay away?" I asked.

"I said that for the ghosts' benefit."

I couldn't help being impressed. "Tricky," I said. "You're starting to think like a fox."

Sujin gave a light laugh. "Guess I've

been spending too much time around you," they said. Then, "It didn't matter what I told the captain. Like the lieutenant's ghost said, Hwan is going to come down regardless."

"But how will he get past the ghosts?" I asked. "He's lost his two secret weapons: Jun and me."

Sujin shrugged. "There are other supernaturals in the crew, and a couple of shamans," they said. "I'm sure he'll find a way. He's too desperate not to."

I nodded, remembering what Hwan had written about the Pearl in his logbook: *it would be the ultimate threat, able to devastate an entire world . . .* The idea of the artifact in his paws made me shudder.

"Are you cold?" Sujin asked. "Here, take more of the blanket."

"No, no, I'm fine," I said. After a moment, I added, "I'm sorry about getting mad. You just took me by surprise. We were on the run from him, after all."

Sujin exhaled in relief. "I'm sorry, too. We're in a no-win situation, but maybe we'll figure out something. Let's try to

get some rest before it's our shift."
Shortly after that I heard their breathing
slow as they fell asleep.

Just before I nodded off myself, I
thought I heard muttering, but whether
it was ghosts or my imagination I
couldn't tell. I slept deeply and dream-
lessly.

Eventually, Haneul shook me awake for
watch duty. I moaned and mumbled but
got up. We allowed Sujin to continue
sleeping. We were both in silent agreement that the goblin looked pale and
should get as much unbroken rest as possible.

"Wake me if anything seems odd out
there," Haneul said, then yawned hugely.

"Will do," I said, although I had promised myself that I wouldn't disturb her or
Sujin for anything short of an emergency.

"Good," Haneul said. She stretched
with a popping of joints, then crawled
into the tent to take my place.

I sat cross-legged and squinted. My
eyes had adjusted to the dark as much as
they were going to. The rain had dwindled, and the clouds had thinned enough

that more moonlight could filter through, cloaking the world in a haze of blue and silver. Everything smelled simultaneously of earth and leaves and the threatening wildness of water. It was seductive, in its way.

Then my nose tickled, and I sneezed. Was I coming down with something? The thought was especially concerning on a planet once cursed by disease spirits.

"Min," my brother's voice said out of the darkness. His pale shape, half outlined in fire, emerged little by little, like the inverse of a shadow.

I jumped up in alarm.

"Wait," he said. "I got away from the other ghosts. Hear me out."

"Why?" My voice shook. I could have said a lot of things, like *You betrayed me to them!* for one. Before, when Jun and I were growing up together, I would have spat out words carelessly. But now I didn't want to say anything I wouldn't be able to take back. I'd changed since I set out from Jinju, even if I couldn't pinpoint how exactly.

"When the crew realized that you'd run

off, I talked them out of chasing you. I convinced them to go after Captain Hwan instead," he said. Was his voice trembling, too? "We spotted one of the larger shuttles descending. They've gone to try to jinx it."

I hesitated, biting my lip as I studied Jun's wrecked face. I'd already paid a price for trusting him once before. He might be telling the truth this time — but then again, he might not. And my friends' lives depended on my ability to read him.

"Sujin warned Captain Hwan to stay away," I said carefully, "but he's going to come down here anyway, with some heavy-duty protection magic." I was half bluffing, but I assumed that the captain would bring some kind of defense. "That can't be good for ghosts, no matter which side you're on."

"The only side I'm on is yours, Min."

I wanted to believe him. I loved my brother, and things would be so much better if I could trust him.

"Then why did you lead us into a trap?"

"I wanted the crew to think I was still

one of them, rather than abandoning them for my sister," Jun said. "I thought it would give me more control of the situation so I could protect you."

Protect you. That sounded like the Jun I knew.

"Thank you," I said softly.

"Besides, you did need shelter. Cadet Sujin isn't looking so great. You don't want them to come down sick, not on this planet."

I winced, hoping we'd all avoid the plague like, well, the plague.

"I was going to help you escape eventually," Jun went on, "but you did it before I could."

"I didn't want to stick around to be meat for the captain's quest," I retorted.

Jun's rueful smile flickered so quickly I almost wasn't sure I'd glimpsed it. "If I'd really wanted to hand you over to him," he said, "I wouldn't have let you slip off like that. The other crew members might not recognize when they're being Charmed, but I certainly do."

I couldn't argue that point. "Good to know," I said. "I'm still learning about . . .

er, you know . . ."

"Ghosts?" he finished. "It's okay, you can say it. I know what I am."

There were a hundred things I wanted to tell him, but I couldn't think where to start. So I just said, "Someone came to our home on Jinju and said you deserted. I knew you hadn't, though."

His smile returned, lasting longer this time. "I appreciate that," he said. He didn't sound like a bitter, vindictive ghost at all. "That means a lot. So does your coming here. I thought I'd never see you again."

My throat closed up. When I was able to speak, I said, "I wanted to find you and the Dragon Pearl, to bring you both home. I failed. . . ." Tears pricked my eyes.

"We'll figure it out, Min. I promise," he said in that reassuring older-brother way he had. "Right now, we have to deal with the fact that Captain Hwan is on the way."

Once Jun and I were done talking, I woke Haneul and Sujin. When Haneul saw Jun, she started, and her eyes clouded.

"My brother came to help us," I explained.

"Why should we trust him?' Haneul asked suspiciously.

"Lots of reasons," said Jun. "First, I can Charm the other ghosts. They are bent on getting revenge on Captain Hwan by driving him mad. But that isn't going to bring rest to anyone."

Sujin wore a thoughtful expression. "So you're going to help the captain?" they asked. "After all, you were willing to work with him once before. . . ."

"That was a lifetime ago," Jun said with macabre humor. "Now he's threatened my sister and her friends" — he made a sweeping gesture to indicate Sujin and Haneul — "and he wants to use the Pearl as a weapon. If it comes to that, I'll do everything I can against him. I haven't been a ghost for very long, but I might be able to bring him bad luck."

"Useful to know," Haneul said in an undertone. She was frowning. I wondered if she was worried about facing court-martial.

"Second, I can lead you to the Pearl," Jun said. "I know where it is — the exact location."

"Well, what are we waiting for?" I asked. "Let's get going before Hwan beats us to it. If we reach it first, we'll have a bargaining chip."

And with that, we broke camp and headed into the moon-silvered night.

THIRTY-THREE

When the rain returned, trudging through the mud and sodden underbrush felt worse than before, maybe because we'd had a chance to rest and dry off a little. Every time I accidentally splashed into a puddle, I was reminded of the threadbare comfort I'd found not long ago in the emergency tent. But the others didn't complain, so neither did I.

Jun floated ahead of us. I envied his lack of legs and the fact that he didn't have to care about getting wet. Almost as soon as I had that thought I realized how stupid it was. It couldn't have been fun to be a ghost on a deserted planet. My face burned with shame.

The winds rose around us again. "They're coming," Jun said quietly.

Haneul turned toward me. I had mistaken the beaded moisture on her brow and nose for rain, but some of it had to be perspiration, considering the smell that was rolling off her. Was she getting sick, or struggling to keep the storm in check, or both? "I can only do so much with my weather magic," she said, her voice quavering just slightly. "Here the ghosts rule. I think —"

She never got to finish, because the darkness lit up in a cascade of white fire. At first I thought we were under attack, some kind of bombardment. But the fire brought no heat, only waves of chill that sliced to the bone. Then I remembered: White was the color of the dead.

Soon we were surrounded by the glow of thousands, perhaps tens of thousands of ghosts, unnaturally bright in the last hours of the night.

Jun stopped. Haneul, Sujin, and I

banded together behind him, as if he could shield us from the spirits' anger. As they stared accusingly at us with their blank, dark eyes, I felt the weight of their judgment.

Voices rose and ebbed in the wind. I quelled a surge of despair. How were we going to get past all those ghosts? They might not have any physical presence, but they could confuse us with hallucinations. I'd heard stories of ghost-crazed people running off cliffs or jumping into rivers. As long as the spirits could reach into our minds, we were in danger, especially on unfamiliar terrain.

Swallowing, I stepped up until I was standing side by side with my brother. Haneul warned me against it, but I had no attention to spare for her.

What I had at first mistaken for a mass of identical spirits, all with ragged long hair and no legs, resolved into unique individuals as I got closer. In the front ranks I saw a woman wearing a robe. Its embroidery would once have displayed lucky colors, but now all I saw were traceries of black upon gray. Another was an elderly man holding hands with a child who carried a stuffed bear. I saw Space Forces officers in full uniform, and figures wearing clothes in styles I'd only seen in historical holos, fashions from two centuries ago.

Once upon a time these ghosts had been people as distinctive as Haneul or Sujin or me, as unforgettable as power-hungry Captain Hwan or greedy Nari. They might be united in their anger, but that didn't mean they all wanted the same thing . . . or did it?

They had something besides anger in common. All of them had emaciated faces, the bones of their skulls showing prominently, as if ready to erupt through the skin. They didn't have the gruesome lesions of smallpox, the disease that gods had once wielded to teach humankind respect, but the ravages of their illness looked grotesque enough.

One of the ghosts, the robed woman, stepped forward. "Fox," she said. "Dragon. Dokkaebi."

"Honored ancestor," I said with a bow, but my voice sounded hollow even to myself. I threw some Charm her way, hoping to keep any ghostly bad luck or mind control at bay.

"Tiger," the woman added.

I gasped. As one, Haneul, Sujin, and I turned to look back the way we'd come.

A shuttle painted with the white tiger emblem of the *Pale Lightning* was streaking down from the sky. We couldn't see who was inside, but I had no doubt the ghost was correct. Captain Hwan had tracked us down, and the ghosts had allowed him through.

"What are we going to do? We can't outrun ghosts," Sujin said through gritted teeth.

We were trapped.

I looked to Jun for answers, but he remained silent, his gaze locked on the ship as it landed. The ghosts parted for it, but I imagined the captain wasn't under any illusions that he was safe. Angry spirits weren't the kind of threat he was used to confronting as a military officer.

I cast my eyes frantically among the ghosts, searching for any clue as to the Pearl's whereabouts. This was my last chance — I had to reach it before Hwan did. If I succeeded in finding it, maybe I could bargain with him. My friends and I could get a ride to safety, and he could promise not to persecute us. In exchange, I could give him the Pearl and . . .

. . . steal it back before he had a chance to exploit it.

Or he could simply use his superior firepower to take it from me. But I preferred the first plan.

I scanned the landscape. In one direction, small hills furry with grass rippled away from the forest. In the other, boulders stippled the ground up until what looked like a steep drop-off. I thought back to Captain Hwan's map, and my heart sank. From what I remembered, the Dragon Pearl lay beyond that cliff.

If I broke away from Haneul and Sujin, they would think I was abandoning them to Captain Hwan. They might never forgive me. Still, I knew what I had to do.

"Jun," I whispered, "show me where the Pearl is." I needed to reach it as quickly as possible. The less time I had to spend searching for it, the better.

Jun smiled at me, and for the first time

the wrecked asymmetry of his face didn't gnaw at my insides. "How fast can you run, little sister?"

"Run?" I said to him with a grin, despite the desperate situation. "I can do better than *run.*" Certainly a fellow fox should know that. I wish I'd thought of shifting into a faster shape earlier, when we were trudging through the mud. Then again, I wouldn't have wanted to leave Haneul and Sujin behind.

I turned to my friends. "I'll be back shortly. In the meantime, keep the ghosts distracted."

"Min, wait! There's something you should —" Haneul shouted after me, but Sujin had elbowed her, and I was already shifting.

I shed my human shape for that of an enormous hawk. On a planet with stronger gravity, I wouldn't have been able to fly. But the Fourth Colony's lower gravity worked to my advantage. Here I could soar.

It was a risk — the ghosts could have flown after me. But they didn't. They were too focused on Captain Hwan.

I caught an updraft and wheeled higher.

The wind buffeted me, and it took several moments to steady myself. As a hawk I had keener eyesight, and I surveyed the valley beyond the cliff. Surely an artifact as powerful as the Dragon Pearl couldn't be concealed easily?

"Let me guide you," Jun whispered in my ear. I was grateful for his help. Following him would be a lot easier than trying to remember the coordinates from Hwan's map. We banked and arrowed downward.

Another group of ghosts swirling below us made it easy to spot the Pearl. In the center of the throng, my hawk's vision picked out a glow coming from a shining sphere. Unlike the death-white spirits, the orb was a tumult of colors, like a living ocean — from jade-green to turquoise, from aquamarine to deep blue, with foam-pale flickers in all the colors of the rainbow. It looked to be about the size of my fist when I was in human form.

I circled, frantically considering my options. No way did I want to swoop down among the ghosts. But I didn't have a choice, not if I wanted to retrieve the Dragon Pearl.

"You can do it," Jun urged me. "You've got me — I can protect you from the ghosts."

Anxiety seized me once more. Would Jun betray me again? It might be safer to trust my own defenses.

But the fact remained that he was my brother. Sujin and Haneul couldn't help me now. It was Jun or no one.

I dove for the Pearl. The ghosts shrieked in fury. I could feel them battering against the boundaries of my mind. But they could find no purchase. As the ghosts tried to assault me with images of pox-ridden humans and corpses piled high, Jun created a spiritual shield around me, countering with memories of our life together on Jinju, from watching for falling stars late at night to playing tag around the house.

Cold wind swooshed against my wings. I kept my eyes focused on the orb and my talons outstretched. When they closed around the Pearl, it exuded a swelling warmth that I felt to my core, all the way to my wing tips. The ghosts howled as I snatched it up. I let out a hawk scream of triumph and beat my way back into the sky. I was literally holding on to hope.

Then, with my hawk vision, I spied the captain's shuttle on the ground. I could see every detail clearly. The shuttle's hatch opened and several soldiers poured out, followed by a familiar tall figure. Captain Hwan stood silhouetted by the lights within. In his hand was a blaster. And it was aimed upward — at me.

THIRTY-FOUR

I flapped my wings frantically to gain altitude, then folded them and dove again, this time right for his hand. The one wielding the gun.

I had to give the captain credit for remaining calm. He didn't blink as I arrowed straight toward him. He had time to shoot once. Fire pierced my right wing — what would have been my shoulder if I'd still been in human form. I plummeted, struggling to keep my grasp on the Pearl.

The pain made me light-headed. It was so tempting to retreat into the shape of some inanimate object, even if it would only be a temporary respite. But if I did that, I'd lose hold of the Pearl.

I landed badly, breaking my fall with my injured wing. The impact jolted me. This time when the cry broke from my beak, it wasn't one of triumph but of shock.

The captain's shadow fell over me as he advanced down the shuttle's landing ramp. In a panic, I shifted back into human form. My right shoulder ached abominably, and I hugged the Dragon Pearl to my chest with my left arm as I tried to shield it from him. Its sweet, changing glow seemed to soothe my pain.

I looked around for Haneul and Sujin. They were now surrounded by the captain's soldiers. I stood up and attempted to make a dash for them, only to be stopped cold by the voice of a ghost. I recognized it as belonging to the robed woman who had spoken to us earlier. She reared up before me, her hair blowing wildly about her face.

"Not the wisest decision, bringing more

of the living down here," she said. Considering everything that had happened, her tone was distressingly friendly. "Four supernatural creatures, even."

"The captain brought himself." I was shaking, sensing that I was missing something important. Maybe more than one thing. But the pain made it so hard to think clearly. "At least tell me your name, honored ancestor." I figured a little buttering up couldn't hurt.

"I am Eui," she said. Her smile thinned. "But your flattery won't save you, fox."

More ghosts swarmed toward us, and their presence became suffocating, even though I knew they couldn't physically smother me. I heard a growl erupt from Captain Hwan.

Together the ghosts spun a vision in the air before us.

An old starship touched down on the promontory formed by the cliff. From it emerged a woman in old-fashioned clothes bearing a small translucent casket that glowed in familiar changing sea colors. I recognized the woman. Anyone from Jinju would have. Hae had been the greatest shaman of her day, and she'd come here to the Fourth Colony instead of going to my homeworld to finish terraforming it. No one knew why.

In the vision, ghosts gathered around Hae. There was no sound, but they were clearly beseeching her. What wasn't clear was what they wanted.

I was just about to ask, but the captain got there first. "Why didn't you come to an understanding with the shaman?" he questioned Eui. "Surely she could have assisted you."

Eui looked down her nose at him. Hwan was tall, but Eui had the advantage of being able to hover in the air above him. "Hae's only concern was the glory of the Thousand Worlds. The glory of the Dragon Society. Glory for *herself*. It was all politics to her." With a bitter chuckle, she added, "She, a shaman, didn't care about matters of the spirit."

I frowned. "What matters of the spirit? Why did she come here?"

"She was going to rid the Fourth Colony of its ghosts by singing us into the underworld. Then she would return in triumph with the Pearl. She would take control of the Dragon Society, and after that, who knows? She might have declared herself empress of the Thousand Worlds . . . if it weren't for us."

In the vision, the ghosts crowded around Hae turned from plaintive to enraged. But the shaman had strength of will. She eventually broke free of their influence . . . dropping the Pearl in the process. Frantically, she searched the ground for it, but the ghosts obscured her vision. She let out a wail of defeat, and I watched in horror as she flung herself off the cliff.

"Imagine how that must have felt," Jun whispered in my ear. "Losing the Pearl, along with all her dreams. Cling tightly to it, sister."

I bent over, practically wrapping myself around the Pearl, and shut my eyes, fearing that the ghosts would turn on me next. "Stay close, Jun. I need you to protect me."

"You don't need me, Min," Jun said. "You know what to do. You've always been the cleverest one in our family."

I opened my eyes. The ghosts were swirling around me, but they hadn't called down any lightning strikes, or driven me off a precipice, or frozen the blood in my veins. They gazed at the Dragon Pearl, but not in anger. In expectation.

I didn't know exactly what they wanted, but I was beginning to get an idea.

"Long ago, you were wronged," I called out, my voice shaking. "Let me make it right."

"Don't believe her!" said the captain. "She's a fox. All foxes are liars. She only wants the Pearl for herself, like that shaman did."

I opened my mouth to protest, but then I spotted Haneul and Sujin, still ringed by Hwan's soldiers, and the words died in my throat. I'd lied to them from the beginning. There was no reason they should believe me, either.

The wind picked up again and Eui floated toward me ominously, interpreting my lack of response as an admission of guilt. "On the day you come to the gate between the world above and the world below," she said, her voice rising, "no one will guide you to the welcoming dark, and no one will say the rites over your grave. No one will —"

"Honored ancestors," I shouted, standing my ground, although what I really wanted to do was run and hide like a small child. "You shouldn't have been abandoned by the rest of the Thousand Worlds. You need us to help you. You can't wield the Pearl yourselves, because you're dead, right? But we can do it for you and give you what you're looking for."

From behind me I heard bitter laughter. "Pretty words, Min," Captain Hwan said. "But what makes you think you can control the power of the Pearl?"

"Let Haneul and Sujin go," I said, clutching the Pearl, "or I'll use it against you." I wasn't sure how I'd do that, exactly, but if I had to, I'd figure out a way.

Then I noticed Haneul's and Sujin's expressions. Haneul wouldn't meet my eyes, and her cheeks were flushed. Sujin, on the other hand, stared defiantly at me.

My heart sank. I waited for an explanation. But I'd already started to figure it out — why Sujin had called the captain, why Haneul had tried to warn me before I flew off in hawk shape . . .

"The two cadets were never in any danger," Captain Hwan said, confirming my guess. "It was a ploy to win your confidence so you'd lead them — and me — to the Dragon Pearl."

The truth stung, even though I knew I didn't have any right to feel hurt. After all, I'd tried to dupe them, too, and I hadn't admitted my true identity until the captain unmasked me.

"Why?" I asked them. Over the howling wind I heard the ghosts' mocking laughter, and I flushed hotly.

"Jang was a friend," Sujin shot back, even as Haneul shook her head. "Did you ever think about how the people who knew him would feel about the way you pretended to be him for weeks? You didn't let us give him a proper funeral."

A proper funeral . . .

The ghosts crowded closer and closer as Sujin spoke, drawn to an anger that echoed their own. We could be in big trouble if Sujin went on like this. I had to calm the goblin down.

"I talked to Jang's ghost," I said, keeping my voice level even though I was tempted to shout back in my defense. "He wanted me to continue his training cruise and help him find out who hired the mercenaries who killed him. I promised to do it. I even swore it on the bones of my ancestors."

"Words are cheap," Sujin said. "How — ?"

Whatever Sujin had been about to say died in their throat.

Slowly, another ghost materialized next to me. I was buffeted by a familiar cold breeze. "Jang? I thought you —"

"Min is telling the truth," he said to his friends. Then he addressed the other spirits. "She helped me, and she will help you."

I wasn't sure if it was my imagination, but the roaring of the wind seemed to die down a little.

The captain narrowed his eyes at Jang. *"You,"* he spat. "If you'd gone properly to your rest, instead of plaguing us with ghost luck —"

Jang glowered at Hwan. "I served you loyally," he hissed. "And what did I get for it? You knowingly sacrificed me!" It looked like he wanted to lunge at the captain.

"Not now, Jang!" I said through gritted teeth. I clutched the Dragon Pearl more tightly. It hummed at my touch, and gradually I felt a sense of serenity wash over me. I shut my eyes. *Help me,* I asked whatever spirits dwelled inside it.

In answer, I saw a momentary vision of a calm ocean, its waters the same changing colors of the Pearl itself. In the pale sand along the shore, I saw the shadow of a fox. My shadow.

I opened my eyes and gazed into the Pearl. Its glow brightened. Whether it was an answer from the artifact I didn't know, but a thought sprung to my mind. In the old stories, the number four signified death — the Fourth Colony had turned its own name into a prophecy. I might not be a shaman, but I knew magic responded to suggestions, just like people responded to Charm. And between Haneul, Sujin, Captain Hwan, and me, there were now four living supernatural creatures on the Fourth Colony. Perhaps this was all meant to be. . . .

"You are coming perilously close to

promising something you can't give," Captain Hwan said to me over the ghosts' rising hisses. "There's still another way for us to get out of this. Your brother may no longer be . . . available, but —" He raised his eyebrows at me.

The captain was referring to Charm. He didn't want to say the word out loud, in case the ghosts caught on.

I remembered Nari's parlor and how she'd used her Charm to manipulate whole crowds of people. Over the past few weeks I'd learned that my power with Charm was even stronger than hers. I wasn't confident that it was persuasive enough to sway the thousands upon thousands of ghosts who had gathered around us, though, and I only had one chance to get it right.

No, my idea was safer. Maybe, for once, I could help *without* using Charm.

The ghosts' angry glares had settled on Captain Hwan. As glad as I was that the force of their hatred and misery wasn't directed at me for a change, I had to get their attention again.

I lifted the Dragon Pearl into the sky with my good arm. The ghosts were drawn to its pulsing colors. "You have gone too long without a proper burial," I shouted.

The wind subsided into murmurs of assent.

"With the Pearl, I can turn this land into a tomb for you," I said, enunciating each word as clearly as possible. "I can give you your peace at last."

"How do we know we can trust you?" Eui said.

I brought my arm down and held the Pearl close to my heart, as if swearing an oath. "Jang trusted me. He is one of you now, and so is" — I gulped — "my brother. They deserve funeral rites, too." I looked at Jun, but he was gazing at the horizon. The lump in my throat was never going to go away. "I'll do it for their sake, if no one else's."

Captain Hwan regarded me with furious eyes. I started to sweat. What if he tried to snatch the Pearl away? With my injured shoulder, I wasn't sure I'd be able to resist him. If I couldn't sell him on this plan, we were doomed.

THIRTY-FIVE

The captain leaned forward ever so slightly and hissed, "You'd trust the Pearl? When taking it doomed a shaman at the height of her powers?" Then he grabbed my upper arm before I could dart away.

I stifled a gasp as his fingers dug into my flesh and he yanked me toward him, wrenching my injured shoulder. I could shift and try to escape with the Pearl, but where would I go? And I couldn't Charm him into releasing me — the ghosts were watching, and that would only renew their distrust. I had to find another way.

I stared at Haneul and Sujin, willing them to look at me. "Think of Jang," I pleaded with them. He stirred next to me and I held still, refusing to flinch from his wintry touch. "Don't you want to lay him to rest?"

Sujin's brow furrowed. "Is that what you want, Jang?"

The Fourth Colony's ghosts muttered and clamored. The wind was whipping up again. Jang hugged himself, looking more vulnerable than I'd ever seen him before. I was forcibly reminded that he'd only been a couple years older than me, the same age as my brother.

"You kept your end of the bargain," Jang said to me. "Now it's my turn to help you."

Turning to Hwan, he said, "Let her go." He didn't speak in a deferential tone, as a cadet to a captain, but in a hollow, detached voice, as one of the dead to one of the living. He rested his insubstantial hand atop the captain's, which was still wrapped around my arm. The chill bit my skin. Surely the captain felt it, too.

"Captain, sir," Haneul said unexpectedly, her voice shaking, "we've already been cursed by enough bad luck. Don't you think it would be better for us to do what the ghosts want?"

Sujin hesitated, then nodded. "Haneul's right, sir," they said. They were carefully avoiding my eyes.

"But it would be such a waste," Hwan said almost under his breath. "When I think of what the Pearl could do . . ."

His grip on me tightened, and I thought his next act would be to strangle me then and there. In anticipation, the breath stopped in my throat.

Jun said, "This is your chance to bring honor to the Space Forces, Captain. And some measure of peace. If nothing else, do it for your lost comrade, Myung."

Hwan went still at the sound of her name. Then, suddenly, he exhaled explosively and let me go. I almost dropped the Pearl out of sheer surprise.

I whispered to the orb before Hwan could change his mind. "Let's do this together," I said. Its soft, swirling light enveloped me, and warmth spread through my body. Even the pain in my injured shoulder felt distant. "Let's make a proper grave for the dead."

The ghosts' spokeswoman floated up to the four of us. "Swear on the bones of your brother," she said to me. To Captain Hwan: "Swear on the bones of your comrade." And at last, Eui said to Haneul and Sujin, "Swear on the bones of Jang, who was your friend."

I shuddered as her words reverberated through me. If I broke such an oath, I could expect my own ghost to wander until I found some way to redeem myself.

"I swear," I said. "I swear on my brother Jun's bones" — I heard him sigh quietly — "and on the bones of all my ancestors, and on the bones of everyone who has died for the Pearl."

The others murmured their oaths as well.

For a few moments, nothing happened. I held my breath in dread. What if we'd been doomed by my overconfidence, and Captain Hwan had been right after all? Would the ghosts swarm us?

Then the Pearl hummed as if in approval, its iridescent surface glowing so brightly I was dazzled. Its colors swirled in a maelstrom of glimmering blues, greens, and grays lit by starry gleams of silver. I stared at it, enthralled by its beauty. A questing presence moved inside my mind, and in response I held out the Pearl. My living companions formed a ring around it, moving slowly as though hypnotized. Haneul's eyes had gone soft with wonder, and even Sujin looked less angry. As for Captain Hwan, something like peace touched his face.

The Dragon Pearl's radiance reflected in everyone's eyes. I almost closed mine, but I wanted to see what would happen next. Haneul started a chant to the spirits of wind and water, wood and earth and metal.

The ghosts took up Haneul's song. Their voices wove together in an intricate harmony. The wind rose as well, and in its howl I heard phantom drums. Captain Hwan's human soldiers clustered near us, seeking protection from the terraforming magic.

A false dawn started to brighten the horizon. As the rainy mist eased, I could see a couple of the Fourth Colony's moons floating. Then all the clouds scudded away until the sky was clear in every direction.

Next the ground began to shake. I crouched instinctively, not wanting to be bowled over. The tremors didn't get too bad where we were standing, but all around us gravel and soil geysered up where the old settlement had stood, where the ghosts had once lived and breathed and died. If not for the clear sweet billows of wind that buffered us, we would have been suffocated by the stinging dust and loose dirt.

My heart threatened to pound its way out of my rib cage. Light from the sky now took on a red-orange tint thanks to all the dirt in the air. I wondered if the ghosts intended for us to be buried with them.

"Steady, little sister," Jun said.

I glanced sideways, and there he was just outside the circle, the pale flames of his face flickering and unaffected by the windstorm. He was smiling. My heart ached, thinking of having to say goodbye to him soon. But for now he stood with me, and I had to treasure whatever time we had left.

Just beyond Jun, Jang smiled at me as well. We exchanged solemn nods. He was also facing the end. I'd miss him, too.

The Dragon Pearl blazed even brighter, which I hadn't thought possible. Within the light I saw a vision. Rather, I saw it in the afterimages that danced behind my eyelids after I shut my eyes to avoid being blinded.

Volcanoes vomited forth fire, and ash clouded the air. Streams of lava rolled over the old cities with their decaying spires and domes, then hardened into shapes just as beautiful and eerie. Lakes flashed up in lethal gouts of steam, while rivers ribboned in new directions. I could see how the Dragon Pearl, in the wrong hands, could be used to destroy whole worlds and their populations.

But we were the only living people on the Fourth Colony, and the Pearl was keeping us safe. All the ghosts wanted was rest, a proper burial. The entire world would be their tomb.

And it wasn't only destruction we witnessed. Slowly the land stopped churning, and I dared to open my eyes. Trees of all sorts, from pines to sycamores and maples, grew from the mountainsides, and speared toward the sky. Flowers blanketed the hills and plains, and fringed the rivers like necklaces. Grasses swayed in the winds. For their part, the winds grew gentler, caressing the landscape rather than buffeting it.

The ghosts shimmered, and I could sense their joy. Eui didn't smile, exactly, but she made a point of meeting my eyes, and she bowed slowly and solemnly to me. Then she and the others began to fade.

Jang looked longingly at the others, then turned to me. "It's time for me to go," he said softly. "I stayed too long. I realize that now. But I want you to do one final thing for me."

I nodded, a lump in my throat.

"I want a proper military funeral," he said. "I died in the line of duty, after all."

"I'll make sure you get one," I said. If we got off this planet safely, I would find a way.

"We all will," Haneul said. A damp

cloud hovered over her head, reflecting her mood. Sujin nodded, their eyes sad.

Jang smiled back at them, then reached out for my hand. His ghost-wind brushed against my fingers one last time. Then he was gone, and the cold breeze with him.

Tears streamed down my face. The Dragon Pearl had finished its work. "It's over," I said.

"Not yet," said my brother's voice.

I yelped.

Jun stood — floated — next to me. The other five ghosts from Captain Hwan's mission had also materialized. I'd forgotten all about them.

Hwan, who'd been mesmerized by the Pearl's terraforming, now snapped back to reality. He took a few steps back as his former crew members bore down on him menacingly.

"*You*," Lieutenant Seo-Hyeon said to Hwan. No *sir,* no *Captain.* Her smile split her face grotesquely, as though it was on the verge of cracking open. "It's time for you to pay for leaving us here."

Haneul summoned a bolt of lightning, but it had no effect on the ghosts.

"Stay back, little sister," Jun said in my ear. "This is going to get ugly."

I almost laughed. After I'd just faced down thousands of angry ghosts, he was warning me about this pitiful group? Still, I moved closer to him.

Seo-Hyeon and the four other ghosts — all except Jun — now surrounded Captain Hwan. Their hair blew wildly about their faces, and their mouths stretched in ghastly, impossible grimaces.

Hwan drew his gun and fired wildly, even though he must have known it would do him no good.

"No, Captain, don't!" Sujin warned. "You'll just make it worse!"

Sujin, Haneul, and I scattered, not wanting to be hit by stray blaster fire. In a shaking hand I held out the Dragon Pearl, hoping it could help in some way, perhaps send these ghosts to their final rest, too. But it was spent. Its swirling had ceased, and it was now just a dull metal-gray color.

I watched in horror as the ghosts snatched at Hwan's eyes and hands. Even though their fingers passed through him, his face contorted, and I wondered what visions were tormenting him. He bellowed in rage, then flung the blaster aside as if its grip had burned him.

Hwan swung his fists in vain at the ghosts. I winced at his wordless shouts. He careened several steps before regaining his balance, only to lose it again.

Or had he? Hwan's form shimmered as it lengthened and expanded. Automatically, I froze as his scent reached me. He'd always been a predator, but now he was shifting into his true form, that of an immense white tiger. I stood transfixed by the sharp fangs revealed when he roared. He almost seemed to flow as he circled, swiping at the ghosts with his paws.

Hwan's amber eyes met mine for a single moment. No trace of the man remained in them. A tiger looked at me, cunning only in the way that an ordinary animal predator — rather than a supernatural one — is cunning. Haneul tried to approach, to calm him down, but he roared and lunged at her, swiping the air with a huge paw. The ghosts kept him at bay, hissing and howling. He shrank back, snarling, and in this way they herded him away from us and toward the woods in the distance.

It was the last I would ever see of them.

Only one ghost still lingered. Jun. I opened my mouth to ask why.

He anticipated my question. Of course he did. "Every ghost is a different person," Jun said quietly. "Sometimes we want different things, too."

He was going to make me ask. "What is it *you* want, Jun?"

"I still want to visit every one of the Thousand Worlds."

I hadn't expected that answer. A traveling ghost — was that even possible?

I wasn't sure how to talk about this. "Um, don't you have, uh . . . limitations? Like only being able to linger near where you . . . ?" I hoped he'd catch on without my having to say it.

"I could haunt you instead of the shuttle," he said with a shrug. "If you don't mind, that is."

"I don't mind," I said quickly. I'd gotten used to having Jang around; this would be even better. "But won't you, um, affect our fortunes wherever we go?"

"Bring bad luck, you mean?" he asked with a gleam in his eye. "Seems to me, Min, you make your own luck."

That would have to be enough. He was family, after all.

"Works for me," I said with a curt nod. "We can see the Worlds together." I caressed the orb that was still warm in my hands and whispered, "I swear it on the Dragon Pearl."

It pulsed a glow in response, and I knew that it approved.

THIRTY-SIX

Now that the ghosts were gone — either to their final rest or to exact their revenge on the captain — I had hoped for a brief respite, perhaps even a nap under a tree. But my work wasn't over.

The soldiers who had accompanied Hwan looked dazed and disorganized, as if unsure what to do next. The most senior of them, a lieutenant, finally pulled herself together and focused her attention on *me*. She drew her gun as she advanced.

I held the Pearl out before me, and she flinched from the way it flared, splashing the entire area with multicolored light.

"You need to hand that over to the proper authorities," the lieutenant said. She tried to sound authoritative, but her voice shook.

The Pearl emitted a piercing silver glare. Ominous thunder crackled above, even though the sky was completely clear. She cowered.

"The Pearl stays with me," I said.

She didn't argue the point after that. "You'll still have to come with us," she said. "Unless you want us to leave you here. Your fate will be determined once we get back to the *Pale Lightning*."

Haneul mouthed to me, *Just play along.*

Had she and Sujin forgiven me? I was too tired to care at that point. Or so I told myself.

I could have used Charm on the lieutenant to make her think I was an ally, but why bother? Instead, I hefted the Pearl and said, "Fine. But don't try anything stupid. I'm not your enemy. I just want to go home."

■ ■ ■ ■

When the shuttle docked in its bay, the head physician, two medics, and a pair of shamans, all wearing hazmat suits, cordoned off the entire area in case of disease. They eyed the Dragon Pearl warily when we told them what had happened on the Fourth Colony. I refused to let it out of my hands, even when they disinfected us with a spray so acrid that it burned my nostrils. Then they examined us and declared us clean. Haneul and Sujin were taken to Medical for rest and rehydration. A medic gave me first aid for the blaster shot I'd taken in the shoulder.

I thought I'd be ushered to the brig next, but instead Captain Hwan's XO, Lieutenant Commander Ji-Eun, requested that I report to her quarters. Jun directed me there, then flickered out of sight.

Ji-Eun paled when she learned what had become of the captain. "I suppose there's no helping it," she said slowly. Her voice sounded strained, and I sensed that she mourned his loss. I couldn't help but feel a little sorry for her, even if *I* didn't miss him. "I'll have to assume his duties until we're assigned a new captain." Her expression softened slightly when she said, "And I'll see to it that Cadet Jang gets his military funeral."

"What will happen to me?" I asked. "And the Pearl?" I gulped hard.

"From what I've been told," the XO said, "the Pearl has declared you its new guardian."

The orb pulsed and glowed a little brighter.

"That appears to be true," she added.

I couldn't help grinning. I stroked the Pearl affectionately.

"Given this awesome responsibility," Ji-Eun went on, "and the fact that you are not a member of the Space Forces, we need to get you back home. Where is that again?"

"Jinju," I replied. "But I can just catch a ride from the next station. I don't want to be any trouble. . . ."

Ji-Eun burst into laughter. "No, not you, a stowaway who impersonated a cadet, sabotaged the ship, stole an escape pod, and cleared the Fourth Colony of all of its ghosts. You're no trouble at all."

I laughed then, too, more out of exhaustion and relief than anything else.

The XO pulled herself together and said, "Once we're fully shipshape again, we'll take you to Black Locust Station. We'll arrange transportation for you from there."

"Thank you, Lieutenant Commander."

She raised her eyebrow at that. "While I'm at it, it would no longer be appropriate for you to bunk with the other cadets."

"I understand," I said, though I was a little disappointed. "I'm not a member of the Space Forces, after all." I'd completely blown any chance of getting in for real, something I'd been trying not to think about.

Ji-Eun nodded. "We do have guest cabins. I'll have someone bring you meals. That will be the easiest way to keep the Pearl safe."

Ji-Eun herself escorted me to the cabin and gave me the security code. I suspected she wanted to limit my movement around the ship as much as she wanted to restrict others' access to the Pearl. I thanked her, then fled inside, expecting to be miserable for the rest of the ride to wherever we were going.

I set the Pearl gently in the bed and tucked the blanket around it. After I'd finished taking a shower and changing into a clean set of clothes that had been left for me, Jun reappeared in a corner of the room, shedding ghost-light.

"It'll be okay," he said.

I clamped down on the desire to throw something at him, partly because it wouldn't do any good, partly because I wasn't sure how I really felt anymore. *How could you go and get yourself killed like that?* I wanted to ask.

"Nothing turned out as we expected, did it?"

I wished he hadn't come right out and said it like that. It was going to be impossible to keep secrets from him now that he was haunting me.

"I don't know how I'm going to explain this to Mom," I said, blinking away a prickling sensation behind my eyes. "And

I'm going to lose that bet with Bora."

"What bet?"

"I said you'd be home within the year. She said no way."

"Well, we can't have you losing a bet to *Bora,*" Jun said, with a hint of the old humor I remembered. "You didn't say I'd come back *alive,* did you?"

I choked down completely inappropriate laughter.

"Let me tell Mom," Jun said. His smile was wry. "I got myself into trouble. The least I can do is break the news."

"We'll do it together," I said.

He didn't argue with that.

We spent the next few hours talking. Some of it wasn't very important. Jun laughed as I recounted the number of hours I had spent scrubbing toilets because I'd used the wrong salute when an officer showed up. He told me about his first weeks on the training cruise, and the buddies he'd made in the Space Academy. He described the pranks he pulled, like changing up the seasonings with Sujin in the galley. His stories made me even more sorry we'd both lost the goblin as a friend.

We discussed the endless chores we'd had to do back on Jinju, and how we'd taken turns putting the younger cousins to bed — and trying to make them stay there. We recalled the festival days in Hongok, when we'd bought taffy from the street vendors who clacked their scissors to advertise their candy. We reminisced about staying up late at night to tell each other about the constellations and the legends they represented.

None of it had changed, and everything had changed. It wasn't just that Jun had died. We had traveled into a world of stars and magic and were bringing some of both back with us, just not in the way we'd hoped.

Toward dinnertime, a chime sounded. "Let them in," I told the ship's computer.

The door swished open. Haneul and Sujin stood there, their expressions anxious. Sujin held a tray with a cup of green tea, a bowl of rice, and some dismal-looking vegetables.

"The captain thought you'd like to see some familiar faces," Haneul said as she slipped in. I had to remind myself that she meant the acting captain — Ji-Eun, not Hwan.

I smiled, happy and relieved to see the two of them. Best of all, Sujin no longer appeared sickly.

Sujin followed Haneul and set the tray down on a table. "This is officially what's available to eat," they said, nodding very properly at me. "But since you're a guest now and not a cadet, you could get away with eating something less awful. If you wanted."

Even the cold rice and overcooked vegetables were welcome after the ordeal we'd undergone on the Fourth Colony. I wasn't about to turn down this overture. Sujin didn't exactly sound friendly, but the offer counted for something. "Yes, please," I said.

Sujin conjured me some green tea cookies. Then they turned to Jun. "I'd make some dried squid for you, but under the circumstances . . ."

"You like dried squid?" I asked Jun, my nose wrinkling. I'd only tried it once, a long time ago, and hadn't enjoyed the tough, chewy texture. Mom and the aunties, who considered it a delicacy, had been happy to claim my share.

"Nobody's perfect," Jun said, and the two of us chuckled.

Sujin fidgeted, then looked at me. "I've had a chance to think things over," they said. "I shouldn't have given you such a hard time."

"No," I said, "I deserved it. I was a troublemaker. You two were being good cadets, following your captain's orders. You just didn't know him like I did."

I proceeded to tell them what I'd read in his logbook. They both looked shocked, and I wasn't sure what surprised them more, the captain's determination to use the Pearl for destruction, or my snooping.

Haneul was eager to change the subject. She eyed the empty tray and said, "We'd better take that back to the collection point."

I must have looked crestfallen at the thought of losing their company so quickly.

"We can stay for a few minutes," Haneul said. "We'll say we were entertaining an official guest." She winked.

"Let's play baduk," I said, inspired. "There's a set in the closet."

"I'm not giving you a handicap this time," Haneul said, and we laughed.

The two of us played a full game, which didn't last long, because Haneul surrounded and isolated my stones no matter where I placed them. Sujin and Jun took turns giving me blatantly terrible strategy advice. I was having difficulty concentrating on the match. All I could think was that this would probably be the last time we'd play together.

At last we counted up the score. Haneul won by so much it would have been embarrassing under other circumstances. "I didn't throw the game, honest," I blurted.

Her eyes danced. "No one throws a game by *that* much, Min!"

Even Sujin smiled. They said to Jun, "Keep your sister out of trouble. She's dangerous! Well, at anything that isn't a board game."

"Hey, I'm just an older brother," Jun said. "You think she listens to *me*?"

My protests were drowned out by the

others' good-natured laughter. When it had died down, I said, "You'd better head back to your duties. Maybe I'll see you again tomorrow?"

"Maybe." As Sujin picked up my tray, they patted my back awkwardly.

Haneul pulled me into a sudden embrace. "Take care of yourself and your brother," she said fiercely into my ear.

I hugged her back tightly. "I will," I said. "Cadet's honor."

THIRTY-SEVEN

At last the day came when we docked at Black Locust Station. When it was time to depart the ship, I stood at the hatch fretfully, awaiting instructions from the local authorities. Even the warmth of the Pearl, which I now carried in a specially made pouch slung across my chest, brought me small comfort.

Several nervous soldiers filled out slate forms, looking like they couldn't find the ones for "captain turned into tiger and went AWOL" or "passenger is escorting a magical artifact" and resented it terribly. Before they would let me leave, one of them called for a shaman.

The shaman had definite opinions about what to do. "You're haunted," she said, frowning. "I don't think this is going to be an easy exorcism, either."

Jun shot me an alarmed look.

I was already bristling. "Jun is my brother," I said. "I don't want him exorcised."

The shaman shook her head. "Are you sure? Ghosts can't be trusted, that's what I always say."

"I'm sure," I said. "I'd take him over most people any day."

The station authorities put me up in a luxurious hotel suite. I cooled my heels for two days, wondering what the holdup was now. On the third morning, a visitor arrived.

"Min," said a voice I had heard a long time ago, one I'd never expected to encounter again. "We need to talk."

I grabbed the Pearl from its place next to my pillow, then opened the door.

The man on the threshold was the investigator who had come to my house so long ago. Only this time he wasn't wearing an investigator's badge, but the formal gray uniform of the Thousand Worlds' Domestic Security Ministry. He must have been undercover before. He gripped a briefcase in his left hand and nodded at me with a thin smile. "I'm Security Officer Seok," he said. "You know why I'm here. You've led me on quite the merry chase."

I lifted my chin. "You can't have it."

Seok showed no sign of intimidation as he stepped past me into the room. He calmly sat down at the desk, opened his briefcase, and pulled out a slate, as if we were in his office. He invited me to sit down across from him, but I chose to remain standing.

"By all rights it belongs to the Thousand Worlds as a whole," he said. "And not as a weapon, as the unfortunate Captain Hwan planned. Yes, I've read the reports." He held up the slate.

I didn't relish the prospect of bargaining with someone I'd once knocked out with a saucepan. Served me right for panicking. But I was a different person now. I lifted my chin and said, "Considering I helped bring the Pearl back, I want the Dragon Society to offer their terraforming services to my homeworld — to all the worlds — at a price that our governments can afford."

Seok shook his head. "The Dragon Society is unlikely to agree to that." He grabbed at the Pearl with his free hand, so quickly that I was caught off guard.

I instinctively snatched up the orb, grazing the top of his head as I pulled it away from him. It flared with a piercing bluish glare, like lightning. Then it went completely dark.

For a horrible moment, I thought I had destroyed the Dragon Pearl forever. But it still felt warm in my hands.

Seok groaned and backed away. Smoke rose from his hair where the Pearl had singed it all the way down to the scalp. It made him resemble a badly shorn sheep. "I take it," he said, breathing raggedly, "that the Pearl has opinions of its own."

Trying not to laugh, I pressed the advantage while I could. "That's right," I said. "Don't mess with me again or I'll do more than ruin your haircut." I stroked the orb, and its colors began to glow.

"You may hold the Pearl — for now," Seok acquiesced. "At least until we've consulted with the Dragon Society." He looked down his nose at me. "But then there's the matter of what we're going to do with you."

I braced myself, gritting my teeth.

"You impersonated a Space Forces cadet. That offense carries a serious penalty."

I knew all about it from reading the code of conduct. I stood up straighter and puffed out my chest in a military posture. "I don't care what you do with me," I said. "The only thing that matters is using the Dragon Pearl for good. Agree to my proposal, and then I'll take my punishment."

I felt a chill as Jun manifested next to Seok. He gave me a smile and a thumbs-up.

When Seok spotted Jun, he drew back in alarm and muttered some impolite words under his breath. He took a moment to collect himself, then said, "Maybe I can offer you an alternative."

"Yes?" I asked warily.

"You've been very busy, Min," Seok said. "Over the last two months or so, you've run away from home, deceived spaceport security, gotten involved with a gambling den, been in a shoot-out with mercenaries, impersonated a dead cadet *and* an active captain, released prisoners without authorization, stolen an escape pod, and broken the Fourth Colony's quarantine."

It was a good thing I couldn't see my own face.

"But you have also showed a remarkable combination of abilities and resourcefulness. And you're still only thirteen. The Domestic Security Ministry could use someone of your talents — if you learned some self-control, that is."

I had never imagined myself in such a role.

I gestured at Jun. "Could my brother come, too?"

Seok raised his eyebrows. "You're asking me to hire a ghost? What good would he be to us?"

Jun vanished for a couple moments, then reappeared. "You might want to get a new stylus," he said. "It looks like someone chewed on the one in your briefcase. I can read the documents you have in there, too, even though it's dark. . . ."

Seok huffed in exasperation. "The two of you might make a good team," he conceded. "And, Min, I should point out that the Domestic Security Ministry is one of the branches of the Thousand Worlds government that can shield you from the wrath of the Dragon Society and the Space Forces."

"You mean I wouldn't get punished after all?"

"Yes, that's what I mean."

Put that way, I had to agree.

"This way we can visit the stars, Min," Jun said.

"Yes," I said softly. "But first, Mom."

THIRTY-EIGHT

Seok and I reached Jinju by civilian transport. It was dizzying to see that familiar reddish sky beneath me, and to imagine it becoming less dust-choked, more vibrant. I patted the Pearl, snug in its pouch, which by that time I had embroidered (not particularly well) with a fox. Eventually I planned to add a goblin, a dragon, and maybe even a white tiger. Seok had assured me that the Dragon Council would take my petition seriously. But even if they agreed to it, nothing was going to happen overnight. Jinju wasn't like the Fourth Colony. It was a fully inhabited planet, and I couldn't terraform the whole place willy-nilly without first figuring out how to keep people out of harm's way.

My scooter was long gone. Seok rented us a hover-car. I was disappointed but not exactly surprised that he wouldn't let me drive it, considering all the illegal things I'd already gotten away with. At least I didn't have to give him directions to the house, because he'd been there once before.

I spent the ride contemplating the red dust and chafing at the straps of my face mask. While the hover-car had its own filtering system, everyone wore masks anyway as a precaution. The rule I'd taken for granted my entire life felt stifling now that I had breathed freely on the Fourth Colony. I looked forward to the day when I could travel down this same road without worrying about dust-sickness.

At last the house came into view. Mom was waiting in front of the dome, wearing her own mask. The plumes of dust kicked up by the hover-car would have been visible from a long distance, and it wasn't as though many travelers came this way.

The hover-car stopped. "I'll wait here," Seok said.

"You're going to listen in anyway," I said. I'd made a cursory check of my clothes and shoes, but I still hadn't located the bug that I knew he'd planted on me. Was it revenge for my knocking him out, or simple pragmatism? Jun could find it easily — he probably already knew where it was — but I'd made a bet with him that I could locate it myself by the end of the day. "Did you call ahead?"

"I told her you were coming, but no more," he said, unsmiling. "Some news needs to be delivered in person. You should be the one to tell her. Go."

I opened the door, then hesitated. But I couldn't put this off any longer — it would be unfair to Mom. I exited the hovercar, cradling the Pearl.

"You're home," Mom said, embracing me. Then she stepped back to look me over. Were those tears in her eyes, or were they just irritated by dust?

"Yes, and I brought the Dragon Pearl. Everything's going to change now, Mom."

Her eyes grew wide when I showed her what was in the sling.

"But there's something else you need to know," I said.

Just then Jun appeared, glowing white with phantom flames. He floated toward her, then stopped. "Mom?"

Her expression clouded for just a moment, and then, in typical Mom fashion, she collected herself. Her family was together once again, and that was all that mattered. "Come inside," she said quietly. "Come inside and tell me everything."

I glanced back at the hover-car. From within, Seok nodded. Then I took Mom's hand and followed her into the dome.

Seok was going to have to wait quite a while, because we had a long story to tell. I knew he would give us the time we needed. Then Jun and I would begin our personal mission to visit all the Thousand Worlds together.

PRONUNCIATION GUIDE

(Pronounce all syllables with equal stress)

Areum: ah-room
baduk: bah-dook
Bae: beh
banchan: bahn-chahn
Bora: boh-rah
Byung-Ho: byuhng-hoh
Chae-Won: cheh-wuhn
cheongju: chuhng-joo
Cheongok: chuhng-ohk
Chul: chool
dokkaebi: do-geh-bee
Eui: oo-ee
Eunhee: yoon-hee
geomdo: guhm-doh
gi: ghee
gimchi: geem-chee
gukhwaju: gook-hwah-joo
gumiho: goo-mee-hoh
Gyeong-Ja: gyuhng-jah
Hae: heh
haetae: heh-teh
Haneul: hah-nool
Hongok: hohng-ohk

Hwan: hwahn
Hye: hyeh
Hyosu: hyoh-soo
Hyun-Joo: hyuhn-joo
Jaebi: jeh-bee
Jaebo: jeh-boh
Jang: jahng
janggi: jahng-ghee
Jeonbok: juhn-bohk
Ji-Eun: jee-yoon
Jinju: jeen-joo
Jun: joon
Ju-Won: joo-wuhn
Kim: geem
Madang: mah-dahng
Manshik: mahn-sheek
Min: meen
Myung: myuhng
Nari: nah-ree
Seo-Hyeon: suh-hyuhn
Seok: suhk
Seonmi: suhn-mee
Sujin: soo-jeen
Woo-Jin: ooh-jeen
Yong: yohng

ACKNOWLEDGMENTS

Thanks to my wonderful editor, Stephanie Lurie, and Rick Riordan, both of whom made this a much better book; and to my agent, Jennifer Jackson, and her assistant, Michael Curry. I am also incredibly grateful to my beta readers: Joseph Betzwieser, Dhampyresa, David Gillon, Helen Keeble, and Yune Kyung Lee.

.

ABOUT THE AUTHOR

Yoon Ha Lee (yoonhalee.com) is the author of several critically acclaimed short stories and the Machineries of Empire trilogy for adults: *Ninefox Gambit, Raven Stratagem,* and *Revenant Gun.* Yoon draws inspiration from a variety of sources, including Korean history and mythology, fairy tales, higher mathematics, classic moral dilemmas, and genre fiction. Yoon's Twitter handle is @motomaratai.